D1118807

ROBERT'S

RULES

ROBERT'S

RULES

A Novel

J.F. RIORDAN

For Eileen and Bob
with love

✤ Author's Note

Washington Island is a real place, and many of the places that appear in the book are real, too. But this is a work of fiction, and sometimes what appears in my mind's eye does not conform precisely to reality.

It is also the case that some of the events in this series may have some relationship to public controversies or circumstances on the Island. In the books, however, the ideas that come from reality have been transformed to meet the requirements of the plot and the characters. Once they are in the book, they are subject to the needs of fiction only, with fictional people making fictional decisions, and should be considered only in that context. This is also true for Wisconsin statutes, which have been altered to suit the whim of the author. (Although coin-flipping to determine the outcome of tied elections is an actual scenario prescribed by law. See Book Two.)

Robert's rules are not original, but have been borrowed from many sources. If they are not properly attributed, it was unintentional, and I apologize in advance.

For assistance in some of the technical details of this book I am indebted to my friend Susan Ulm, to Lindsay Obermeier, Raptor Program Manager at the Schlitz Audubon Nature Center, and to my patient and affectionate brother-in-law,

Robert Kalinoski, for his clarification and insights on Physics, which are always highly necessary for an English major.

My thanks also go to my publisher, Eric Kampmann, my delightful editor, Megan Trank, interior designers Jane Perini and Mark Karis, and cover designer Michael Short for their great work, patience, and unfailing moral support.

I thank, too, my unerringly kind, generous, and welcoming hosts on the Island, Susan and George Ulm, and Bo, who offer both companionship and solitude as required, and who embrace the watchful presence of two zealous German Shepherds with equanimity.

I owe a particular debt of gratitude to my good friend and copy editor, Alicia Manning, for her relentless precision, discerning advice, and witty marginalia. She makes criticism fun. Any remaining errors are most definitively of my own choosing.

The work of writing a book of necessity takes time from many other things. I am grateful to my neglected friends, and especially to my family, who endured my early morning risings and enforced silences throughout our family vacation. But I am most especially grateful to my brilliant, erudite, and insightful husband for his patience, his love, and his thoughtful criticism.

Finally, in response to many questions, with the possible exception of Pali's muse, there is not one character in my books who is based on any real person who lives on the Island. These characters have lived only in my mind, then on these pages, and now, I can only hope, in the minds of my readers.

J. F. RIORDAN
WASHINGTON ISLAND
JANUARY 9, 2018

If you have no trouble, buy a goat.

—*Persian proverb*

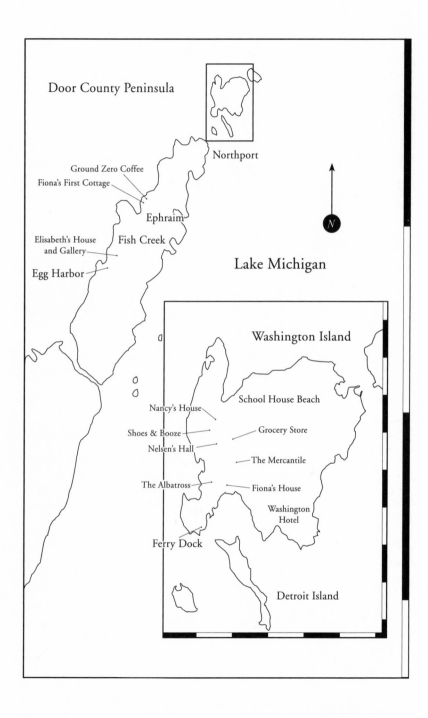

Prologue

My earliest memories are of fire.

I was lying in my crib in the dark, and my father woke me, wrapped me in my blankets, and carried me from the house. There were sirens coming closer. I remember the scratchy wool of his jacket on my cheek, its dusty smell in my nostrils, and the feel of the cool night air. Then the smoke was everywhere.

My mother and father and sister and brother were all there, with jackets over their night clothes. My father carried me in his arms as we all moved toward the fire down the street.

"The pig farm," my mother said.

I knew the pig farm. I knew the comfortable smell of well-kept animals; the sight of the red barn on the hill, the pleasures of catching a glimpse of a tractor, or better yet, a family of piglets, on an afternoon ride.

Instead, I could see the silhouettes of men against flames that reached into the sky, the yellow and orange fire that flickered and shot up; the black shadows of men in big coats, and boots, and helmets, carrying hoses and axes.

There was a low rumbling sound from the diesel engines of the fire trucks; the crackling static voices of the radios and walkie talkies.

My father hoisted me up on his shoulders, and I could look down at the tangle of hoses, the gleaming puddles everywhere, with the circling red lights. I could hear more sirens in the distance, more fire companies arriving, the undulating shift of their sound changing as they moved.

"The poor animals," murmured my mother, watching the flames. There was another smell in the air that was not wood burning.

I was afraid, but I did not cry.

Maybe I slept on my father's head.

At last, the men's voices changed from shouts to words. The brilliant, intoxicating light in the night was gone, leaving a gray dawn. The red lights of the trucks still turned, reflecting in the puddles of water as the firemen coiled the hoses. The voices on the radios still crackled, but with less frequency, as the firemen, weary, diminished their conversation.

I do not remember being tucked back into bed. But, I remember the flames.

I always remember the flames.

Chapter One ✺

It was after school on a warm June afternoon, and Ben Palsson was on his way to School House Beach. The public entrance to the beach cut through the Island cemetery, and graves from other centuries along with those from the recent past were on either side. It was a pretty cemetery, carefully maintained, surrounded by trees, and within the sound of the waves of Lake Michigan. The place held no fear for eleven-year- old Ben, who, if he had thought about death much at all, had the comfortable assurance that it was a very long way off, if ever.

Ben almost always went for a ramble before heading home from school. These days his pattern had shifted a bit, in order to go first to visit the rescued goat living in Nancy Iverssen's barn. It was Ben who had found the animal while it was living in the wild, befriended it, and saved it from drowning when it had fallen through the ice. These experiences had formed a deep bond of affection in Ben's young heart.

But, now that spring had finally come to the Island, the warm weather was so enticing that even his love of animals in general—and of this animal in particular—could not keep him from his walk. The visit today had been brief.

Ben's habit of rambling in the woods and fields of the

Island was also the way he coped with problems. Like his father, his mother, and many of his Island neighbors, he took solace in nature, and although he might not have been able to express his feelings with any precision, he knew that he always felt better out on the trails he knew so well. There had been an unpleasant encounter with a classmate at school that day, and Ben needed to sort through the tangle of anger and embarrassment he felt, or at least, to forget that it had happened. It was difficult to have problems with another student when the school was so excruciatingly small.

It didn't take long for the sounds of the waves, of the birds, and the scent of June air to cleanse his spirit. Ben was a keen observer of animals, and he stopped to look for the woodpecker he heard somewhere nearby. He liked to challenge himself to see how many different kinds of birds he could hear, and as he listened, he counted five, including one he did not recognize. He made a mental note to remember it and to ask his friend, Jim, the ranger.

Starting along the driveway again, heading toward the beach, Ben was looking forward eagerly to the vast expanse of summer vacation stretching before him, when he would have all the time in the world. Only one more day. Then he would be free.

He leaped to try to touch the low-hanging branches of a hundred-year-old beech tree along the way. It was getting closer, but he still couldn't quite make it. Maybe in that far away time at the end of summer.

One balmy, early summer evening, the Town Board of Washington Island was having its usual monthly meeting.

"I ran on a promise not to raise taxes! I cannot go along with this plan."

"But we really need new parking spaces at the beach. Last time I was there in season, cars were parked all along the road. It's a hazard."

"Three cars along the road do not constitute a hazard."

"Well, you know," added someone else, "when Mel Karnen had his stroke, those cars he hit along the side of the road saved his life."

"That was a fluke. You can't sit there and tell me that people's lives will be saved by not paving the beach parking lot."

"Why do you always have to twist my words? I never said that."

As the arguments went on, a small childlike tune was playing over and over in Fiona's head: "*totally meaningless drivel, totally meaningless drivel.*" She instinctively liked the rhythm of it, with the two three-syllable words at the beginning, and the smoother-sounding two-syllable word at the end. Its rhythm reminded her of a cart rolling along a bumpy sidewalk. It played in her head in minor thirds, like a child's taunt.

"This is ridiculous. Adding three more spaces won't break the budget."

"Have you looked at the cost of paving these days? And it's

not as if there's any extra money lying around..."

Fiona was unaware that a vague drifting smile had come over her face as she sat fiddling mindlessly with her pen. Her yellow legal pad was covered with doodles: storm clouds, lightning bolts, flying cattle, and a rather loopy and bedraggled daisy. Fiona hated meetings.

Unfortunately, as the newly-elected town chairman of Washington Island, meetings were the one thing she had in abundance these days.

"Fiona? What do you think?"

This question, which she had dreaded, now burst through her awareness. She took a moment to look at the faces around the table, all watching her with varying degrees of patience and condescension. By and large, her fellow members of the town board did not expect much from this newcomer—from Chicago, of all places—and even though most of them had voted for her, it had been more a case of voting against her opponent—the almost universally detested Stella DesRosiers—than an endorsement of Fiona's knowledge or experience. They were united, at least, in their conviction that she had neither. Lately, Fiona herself was increasingly convinced that they were right.

She took a deep breath and changed her smile to one of rueful deference. Her chin was down as she raised her eyes and looked directly at each individual around the table, reading them one by one.

No matter what her fellow Islanders might think, Fiona was no fool. She was fully aware that the triviality of the issue was inversely proportional to the rancor it could stir in the hearts of Islanders. Though she had discovered this insight into human behavior on the Island, it is a universal truth of small town life.

She smiled again to assuage them. "Of course, we will need to consider it in the context of our budget cuts, but these are the kinds of decisions that our constituents like to be part of." She saw a few heads nodding thoughtfully. "I think we should handle this exactly as it has been handled in the past. We will invite public comment and allow the voters to have their say. No one appreciates changes in tradition, and there's no good reason to upset everyone about this by being high-handed." She did not add that she found the entire topic utterly trivial. She paused, watching as her words sank in, and then finished with a fillip:

"As Lars Olufsen likes to say, 'if it ain't broke, don't fix it.'"

This folksy allusion to Fiona's beloved predecessor was greeted with solemn nods around the table. During his decades of leadership, Lars had used a steady hand and good sense to herd this particular group of the Island's notoriously unruly cats.

"I agree," said Mary Woldt, who was prone to agreeing with whatever had been said last. There were murmurs of assent as heads nodded around the table.

Fiona sighed inwardly. Another example of committee work in action. One decisive voice could almost always determine the matter, but only after hours of wandering conversation. *Totally meaningless drivel,* sang the child's voice in her head.

"Well, that's enough for today, then," she said briskly. She started to rise. "Thank you, everyone."

"But what about the fire department question?" asked Tom Sumner. Fiona stopped, as did everyone else around the table.

The fire chief had been raising serious concerns about their cuts to his budget, but, ears to ground, the elected officials were determined not to raise taxes. Nevertheless, they were all well aware that trouble loomed, and no one more so than Fiona herself.

Fiona knew, too, that she could not discuss this without first having some kind of solution to propose, and although she had been studying the budget nightly, she still hadn't found anything she could cut to make up for much needed new equipment. The matter was urgent, but its urgency made it all the more imperative for her to be prepared.

"This is too important to take up as a secondary matter," said Fiona, firmly. "And we need to give notice for it to be on the agenda. Let's address it first thing next time when we're all fresh." And with a grace and swiftness that would have made Lars Olufsen proud, Fiona gathered her doodle-filled notes and glided smoothly and smilingly from the room.

A small voice from her inner self observed disapprovingly. "You are starting to sound like a politician," it said. Fiona shoved this unpleasant thought aside and replaced it with anticipation of a well-earned glass of scotch.

Chapter Two ❖

Fire Chief Gil Einarsson hung up the phone, set it unseeingly on the kitchen counter, and ran a hand through what was left of his blond hair. The call had been a notice of resignation from Jonah, one of his young firefighters. This was the third such resignation in as many months, and Gil was getting worried.

Gil had been the chief of the Washington Island Fire Department for fifteen years, and a firefighter before that. His father had been a firefighter on the Island, too, and both his uncles. Their family code, born of generations of Island life, demanded community participation, service, and a fierce Island loyalty that expressed itself in a hearty distrust of outsiders.

Chief Gil, as he was known, took his job seriously, knowing that the Islanders depended upon him. They, in turn, knew that their trust in him was well-founded. The number of calls on the Island's department were few, but that made the department no less necessary. Fires were mercifully rare, the most recent being that barn fire at Fiona Campbell's place last year. Medical calls, when needed, were particularly vital, since there was no doctor, no hospital, and in serious cases, it was an eighty-mile helicopter ride to the hospital in Green Bay. There was no neighboring community to come in to assist. There was no one to call for a second alarm. Everything came down to the Washington Island Fire Department. When the need arose—as inevitably it must—the fire chief's responsibilities were heavy, indeed.

But this year, things were more worrisome than usual. The slow economy had taken a toll on the Island, and the Town Board wanted to cut the budget rather than raise taxes. The state and the feds had new requirements that would force the purchase of ruinously expensive new equipment, and the old fire house was in such disrepair that renovation made less sense than demolition.

Gil stared at the numbers on the paper before him and shook his head. He needed more money in his budget, not less. The part-time fire fighters—like Jonah—on whom the Island depended were taking other jobs that paid better and had fewer hazards. You couldn't blame them; they had families to support and bills to pay. But, firefighters needed training and the proper equipment. It was a dangerous situation. Somehow, Chief Gil needed to make his case. As he was thinking these things the phone rang again.

"Hello?"

"Chief Gil?" came a woman's voice. Without waiting for his acknowledgment, she continued speaking rapidly.

"This is Emily Martin. I suppose you know that the town board tabled the discussion on the fire department budget?" Chief Gil had opened his mouth to reply—the meeting could only have just ended, he thought, how on earth did she know that already?—but Emily moved on without waiting for an answer.

"Apropos of which, I've been thinking about the fire department, and you know, with all my experience in civic affairs, I have to say that I think I am just the right person to figure this out. I've come up with a little plan, and I want to tell you about it. It's perfect. Absolutely perfect."

On her way home from the meeting, Fiona stopped by, as always, at Nancy Iverssen's farm to make a visit. Having fully recovered from his near-drowning and broken leg, the Goat Formerly Known as Robert was there in the field along the drive, industriously demolishing some small scrubby bushes along the fence.

Since Fiona's own barn had been destroyed in the fire that had supposedly also caused the demise of the original Robert, Fiona's friend, Nancy, had kindly offered to shelter the animal for the time being.

Fiona was still unsure whether this goat was hers, or some other goat. He did not appear to recognize her, despite her regular visits, nor had he demonstrated any of Robert's uncanny vocal abilities. This goat, it appeared, merely made blood-curdling screams at unpredictable intervals. The first Robert's peculiar speaking abilities had been preferable, Fiona felt.

Nancy's truck was gone, and Fiona recalled something about a trip to Green Bay for supplies. Unencumbered by the need for social niceties, she leaned over the fence and spoke to the animal with a mixture of acerbity and reluctant affection.

If, in fact, he were Robert, he had been practically her sole companion during her first year on the Island. She had come to realize rather belatedly that the responsibility of his care had given her early days here a focus and purpose that had kept her going through a particularly bitter winter. It had not been an unmitigated good time, however, and their relationship—if that's what you'd call it, she thought drily to herself—had been a rocky one.

Robert was not a creature whose personality inspired devotion, and yet he seemed to fit well with Fiona's unacknowledged affinity for eccentric characters.

Leaning on the fence, Fiona mused over the dramatic and unpredictable shifts in her life during the past two years. It had started when she had quit her highly stressful job as a newspaper reporter in Chicago and moved to Ephraim, Wisconsin in hope of finding some tranquility. So far, tranquility had proven elusive.

Within a few months after her arrival in Door County, she had accepted a dare that she couldn't survive the winter on Washington Island; bought a house; acquired a goat as a gift; held on through a difficult winter which had included a campaign to publicly humiliate her and drive her from the Island; endured a barn fire in which Robert seemed to have perished—until he didn't, or possibly did—decided to run for chairman of the town board; mounted a campaign against her vicious neighbor, Stella; won; and now was keeping body and soul together through a grim series of particularly mind-numbing meetings.

There was, of course, one adventure that had more than

made up for the various trials of her Island life. Smiling to herself, she said goodbye to the indifferent animal and headed home, where, undoubtedly, Peter Landry was waiting. Even more undoubtedly, he had a scotch already poured.

Chapter Three

Having made her phone call to the chief, Emily Martin of Windsome Farm Goats was preparing to finish her final visit of the day to the barn. Looking around, she noted with satisfaction that everything was in order: stalls were clean; food troughs full; fresh water available; tools put away. She gave a small sigh of self-congratulation.

Emily's satisfaction did not come merely from the order of her little empire. The conversation with Chief Gil had gone extremely well, she thought. "I will take this little matter in hand, and bypass all of those bumpkins on the town board," she thought to herself. Fiona Campbell, of course, was no bumpkin. She was a city girl, like Emily herself. *But,* thought Emily, *she needed the guidance of someone with wisdom and experience: someone,* thought Emily, *like Emily.*

There were few topics about which Emily was not convinced that she knew best, and in the case of the Island's budget problem, she found the dithering of the town board particularly frustrating. She had supported Fiona Campbell in her bid to be town chairman, but only because she herself had not been on the Island long enough to launch a campaign. She had assumed that Fiona would be easily influenced, but this was turning out not to be the case.

As she left, she carefully latched the barn door and made her way to the house, barely noticing the beauties of the early summer evening.

Emily's care in locking the barn had come hard won, since the winter's errant goat escapade had resulted in the feral animal—now known tentatively as Robert and residing in Nancy Iverssen's barn—impregnating more than a dozen of her does. Emily's profound irritation over this turn of events had been mitigated by the tidy profit she had made selling the offspring, and she now chose to laugh merrily about it whenever someone might happen to mention it.

"Goodness!" she would say, laying a hand on her chest to quell her hearty, mirthless laughter. "What a to-do! Well, we certainly made out well on that little episode, didn't we, Jason?"

And her husband, his eyes darting in confusion as he tried to pick up the thread of a conversation from which he had mercifully drifted away, would just as heartily agree. "Oh yes!" he would say. "We certainly did!"

Islanders would exchange secret glances over these conversations, fully aware of the Martins' real feelings about the incident. Emily Martin had been mortified when young Ben Palsson had innocently divulged his discovery of the coming flock of baby goats at a community Boy Scout event. She had immediately contradicted him just as heartily as she now laughed. Loss of face in this community of people whom Emily considered her inferiors was something she could never accept with good grace, and although the Islanders were too polite to show it, there was not one person on the Island who was not aware of her feelings toward her new home and its inhabitants. The contempt was wholly mutual, but on the islanders' side, it was mixed with an equal portion of amusement.

As she drove up to the house, Fiona looked eagerly to see if any work had been done on her new barn. Fiona had gotten a deal from the builder in exchange for allowing his men to work on her barn between other jobs, so the progress was slow, but it was beginning to take shape. The last remnants of the burned-out structure had been cleared away, and the rough skeleton of the new one was just beginning. It was being rebuilt on the original stone foundation, well over a century old, and would replicate, as nearly as possible, the one that had been lost. There would be no aluminum pole buildings for Fiona.

The wooden bones of the new building had a sculptural quality, and Fiona rather regretted that it would all be covered up. She loved the feeling of a new beginning, when there was only promise and fresh hope. There was the smell of raw lumber in the air, mixing with the scent of peonies that were blooming nearby.

When she bought the property, and was still innocent of goats, Fiona had had no reason for wanting a barn, but she had fallen in love with it from the first moment she had climbed the ladder to the loft. She remembered the late afternoon sunlight slanting through the diamond window at the western end of the building, the smell of hay, of animals long gone, and the childlike sense of belonging that had come over her. It had been the barn that had led her to make the dubious decision to come to the Island, and now it was the re-building of it that absorbed her. The little house seemed incomplete without it, and although she knew that finishing the barn would mean the repatriation of the errant goat who may or may not be Robert, she found herself filled with pleasurable anticipation.

It was a feeling, she suspected, that would not be reinforced by reality.

As she walked up the path to the house, her thoughts shifted to what was to come. Pete's months-long leave of absence was nearly over, and Fiona was trying not to think about his departure. She loved coming home to find him there.

Pete was waiting for her when she opened the door, sprawled on the couch with his feet up, listening to music at high volume. The house smelled deliciously of dinner.

"So, are you providing Adequate Bland Service to the taxpayers?" asked Pete, looking up at her with a teasing smile.

"Well, adequate, anyway," said Fiona, as she put her things away in the hall closet. "Bland may be a bit beyond my reach."

"I've always thought so."

She smiled indulgently.

The music was so loud it vibrated the glass vase on the table.

"That sounds familiar. What is it?"

He answered without moving. "Elgar's *Enigma Variations, Number IX.* It always reminds me of my father."

"What are you thinking about your father?"

Feeling that she was shouting, Fiona came and sat next to him on the couch, pushing his feet aside. He sat up to make room, handed her the glass of scotch that had been sitting on the table nearby, and leaned over to kiss her neck. If his thoughts had been dark, he did not show it.

Pete turned down the music so they could talk. "I was missing him, I suppose. He always played this music when he was in a particular mood." He frowned, picking through his thoughts. "I was too young to confide in, but I always knew he was unhappy about something when I heard Elgar."

"Are you unhappy about something?"

Pete frowned again. "Not unhappy, no." He looked at her with a quizzical, half-smile that she knew well. "Enigmatic, perhaps." He grinned. "And hungry. Want to eat?"

"Yes," said Fiona, "and you're always enigmatic. I seem to recall, by the way, your telling me that you were only known for omelets, but that smells suspiciously like a roast."

"I prefer to undersell and over-deliver."

"I'm starving. Let's see how much underselling you did."

They went together into the kitchen.

Captain Ver Palsson had one more ferry trip before his day was over, and he was more than usually tired. Tourist season was still in its early days, but the more frequent trips on the schedule and the buzz and rush of the summer traffic required some mental and spiritual adjustment after the long quiet days of winter.

Pali, as he was known, had the calm, almost stoic demeanor

of his Scandinavian forbears, but he had a deep and rich emotional life, which manifested itself in a growing body of poetry. His work was building a reputation for him among the small, incestuous world of the literati, a reputation of which he was only partly aware. His life on remote Washington Island protected him from the internecine politics and jealousies of academia, and his blissful ignorance of the mixture of jealousy, disdain, and respect with which he and his work were held was most certainly for the best.

Pali lived in a state of innocent joy and gratitude for his success that was untinged by any sense of entitlement. He felt, instead, a sense of wonder that anyone could like his work, and that it could be received with acclaim from people he admired. Had he known of the disdain, it would not have surprised or upset him. It was, rather, what he would have expected, had he thought about it at all.

For Pali, his poetry had come to feel as organically of himself as his hand or arm. It had not always been this way. His early forays into poetry had filled him with torment and self-doubt because he had been so unsure of its source. Now, however, the form of his inspiration had become also a source of mystery and personal strength. He felt, in some way, chosen.

As he guided the placement of vehicles on the ferry for its last trip home that night, however, what occupied his mind was something of an entirely different nature. Tonight, he was thinking about his son, Ben.

Pali had left the Island as a young man, but its siren call had lured him back. He was more than merely happy there. It was where he belonged, and the sight of the Island looming up on the horizon as he crossed Death's Door filled his heart with a profound and resonant joy. The roots of his family history on the Island went deep into the generations, and of his wife's ancestors, too. The beauty, the mystery, and the fierce loyalties of the place were in their blood.

Life in the world outside was so unutterably different, not just from life on the Island, but from what it had been when he and Nika had tried out a life away. Ben would be ready for high school in a few years. Given the realities of contemporary life, its fast pace and quicksand culture, would it really be best for him to continue at the tiny Island school with so few classmates, and such limited opportunities? Ben was so trusting: utterly innocent of betrayal, or cynicism, or vice. Without some experience of the world as it was, how would he be able cope with adulthood? How would he able to survive in a bigger place? Shouldn't he have the opportunity to practice navigating the shoals of The World before he was on his own? How could he find happiness in life when the possibilities on the Island were so few and so narrow?

Pali and his wife, Nika, had spoken together many times of the restlessness and frustrations of their own adolescent years on the Island, and of the shocks they had felt at their first encounters on the mainland with dishonesty and treachery. Was this lack of preparation what they wanted for their son?

Pali checked his watch and signaled a crewman to finish the loading. Taking the metal steps two at a time with his hands on the rails for balance, he headed up to the pilot house to start the engines. The ferry had to be kept on schedule. There would be plenty of time for thinking later.

Chapter Four ❖

Nika was putting dinner on the table when Pali came in from the ferry. He put his jacket on the peg by the door, and kissed her on the cheek. "You're just in time," said Nika. "Go call Ben, would you please?"

Dinner at the Palssons' was normally a pleasant coming together. Just as his own father had done with him, Pali liked to use the conversation to instruct and examine, and the meal had become an opportunity to stay close to his son.

Ben was usually a cheerful boy, and he looked forward to these conversations as much as his father did. Tonight, however, Ben seemed withdrawn and preoccupied, answering in monosyllables. His parents exchanged glances over his head. They had long been dreading this transition from delightful child to sullen adolescent, and they interpreted Ben's behavior at the table as an early warning. Nika made a mental note to nip any incipient rudeness in the bud. Pali decided that a father-son fishing trip was in order.

The truth, however, was that Ben had something on his mind. Caleb Martin, a newcomer to the school this past year, had been causing trouble for Ben: teasing at first, then taunting, now shoving when no one was looking.

This morning he had deliberately tripped Ben in the hall, and Ben had gone sprawling, his books flying, his chin hitting the ground hard, and his pride severely wounded. The unspoken code did not permit tattling to adults, and Ben was nothing if not a keeper of honor. Seething and humiliated, he had picked up his things and marched steadily to his classroom.

His chin and neck were still throbbing at dinner, but his injuries—particularly those to his morale—were not visible, and he was not in the mood to listen to his mother's anxious inquiries, or, God forbid, a phone call to the other boy's mother. No. Ben would handle this himself.

It was almost ten o'clock at night, but the sky still carried a dull glow of salmon pink and deep blue. The moon was almost full. A heavy breeze blew away the mosquitoes. Fiona and Pete lay carelessly on the grass watching the dull movement of the water in the dark.

The silhouettes of the trees against the paler sky resembled a Maxfield Parrish painting, or an N.C. Wyeth, and although the Island teemed with life and the breeze, all was tranquil.

In this moment of dreamy calm, Fiona's mind drifted to one of the many murder scenes she had witnessed when she had been a reporter in Chicago. It had been a summer night like this—beautiful, tranquil, moonlit—and she had seen the body of a young man surrounded by police and forensics people on the beach of Lake Michigan. His dead eyes had been open and catching the light, like a fish in the marketplace. She shook the mood away, trying to push the sight out of her head. She knew it would be with her forever. She only hoped she would have better images to crowd it out from her own dying vision. It had been the same lake, the same waters. But, everything here was so different. "Let me remember this night, instead," she prayed silently.

Fiona breathed in the summer night air. This place was not a talisman against death or ugliness. Those things roamed the whole earth, and the Island had its share. But here, at least, death was untinged by evil. That was a greater comfort than anything she had been able to find in the city, and it kept her here. Fiona was always in need of comfort. She felt too deeply; saw too keenly. Her life as a reporter in the city had cut deeply into her soul and made scars on her heart.

The wildness of her surroundings on this night made her think of the Island's history. She thought of the hard lives and fierce battles of the Indians, who may have lain just where she was, on just such a night, centuries before. She thought of the Frenchmen, four hundred years ago, who had left safety and civilization to venture into this dangerous wilderness. They built ships and sailed them. They endured almost unimaginable trials of the flesh: the cold, the hunger, the bugs, the disease, the eating of dogs, the eating of men, the fearsome weather and the lake's invisible dangers, the often hostile local people. Fiona thought she could feel the spirits of them all in the air and ground around her, as if their centuries of restlessness had been left behind in the breeze.

She thought of the shipwrecks on the infamous passage

between the Island and the mainland, where Indians in their canoes, Frenchmen in their sailing ships, and Americans in their freighters had all gone down to the depths. She had heard it called the most dangerous stretch of fresh water in the world. *Portes des Morts*, the French had called it, Death's Door, but the name may have originated with the Ho-Chunk or Winnebago tribe centuries before. And Door County, the peninsula that reached out toward the Island six miles away, had taken its name from those ancient disasters.

The great French explorer who had claimed the Mississippi River for France, Robert de LaSalle, had been on the Island. His ship, *The Griffon*, mysteriously lost, had last sailed from Washington Harbor in 1679, near what was now known as School House Beach. Jean Nicolet had surely been there, too, when the archipelago that included Washington Island had been known as the Potawatomi Islands. No doubt there were others. Pere Marquette, perhaps. Fiona was drifting now, comforted by the wind, and by Pete's presence nearby. She was not asleep, but nearly so.

The lake was oddly quiet, unlike in winter when it strummed and sang, and battered and broke the ice. Tonight, it lay silent and tranquil with a slow, steady movement. It was, instead, the air that sang with the many breezes. The distant sound of private fireworks floated amidst the wind.

"Want to go in?" Pete's voice drifted lazily from the grass where he had been lying beside her. He, too, had been allowing his thoughts to wander, even though he had long ago trained himself to live in this moment rather than in memories past. "We're beginning to get damp."

"I do. But I feel as if it's a waste of my hours on earth to go inside to sleep."

Pete was silent again, and they lay for a while longer, listening to the breezes. After a while he stirred. "I'll be right back."

He returned a few minutes later, his arms filled with blankets, and spread them on the grass.

The night really was too beautiful to waste indoors. They stayed entwined in one another's arms in the open air, sleeping in the breezes, until morning.

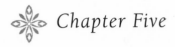 *Chapter Five*

Mike and Terry were seated at their customary places at Ground Zero, Ephraim's eccentric coffee shop. The shop itself was, perhaps, less eccentric than its owner, but its atmosphere had changed dramatically over the course of the past few months.

The morning yoga practice that now materialized there every morning had been more crowded than usual, and a good many would-be practitioners had been turned away. Many of them having come a long distance to participate, the men were a determined and highly-motivated group, who tended to linger in the parking lot, waiting for an opening. Even if they missed the yoga session itself, most were eager to experience the atmosphere of the little shop that they had read about in national yoga and travel magazines, where a group of local men had a daily practice.

Most of the crowd had thinned out by this time of the morning, but the fame of the place—or, more accurately, of the men's yoga practice—had brought the drastic change in Ground Zero. There were strangers all the time—lots of them—asking questions, talking loudly, and generally disturbing the formerly quiet ambiance.

Amid this new and unwelcome hubbub, Terry and Mike

sat at the counter eating egg sandwiches and drinking their third and second cups of coffee, respectively.

The changes had been good for the finances of the place, but they were not good for the regulars. Terry missed the morning peace of the shop before he headed off to work, and he already longed fervently for the end of tourist season. Mike, calm and easy-going as always, observed the bustle around him with a keen eye, smiling the beneficent smile that reflected his inner nature. Terry, less sanguine about life in general, had to remind himself occasionally not to glower at the newcomers. "That," he would think to himself, "is Roger's job." Glowering, after all, was something Roger did extremely well.

Terry's and Mike's friendship was one of long standing, and they had been coming to this shop to begin their mornings literally from the first day it opened. Terry's carpentry business and Mike's work as a highly-regarded—indeed, internationally known—painter, though they might at first seem dissimilar, were in fact a source of deep common interest. Both men felt called to their work. The passion, integrity, and creativity of what they did for a living was a bond between them, and since their days were generally solitary, the quiet insignificance of their morning conversations was highly valued by them both. Neither flinched at expressing their love for one another. Mike had been heard to refer to Terry as the brother he'd never had. Occasionally, they would meet at some local event or at someone's house, but the primary venue for their friendship was their morning coffee at Ground Zero.

The burgeoning yoga practice, as even kindly Mike had to admit, had become a bit of a nuisance. There were too many people; there was too much noise and, occasionally, difficulty finding a place to sit. Terry threatened regularly to block off two stools at the counter with a sign "Reserved for Locals."

He glanced around as he finished his sandwich.

"Got room for your elbows, there?" he asked dryly.

Mike looked resigned. "Just." He wiped his mouth and took a drink of coffee.

Terry shook his head. "Seems like it just keeps getting worse."

"Well, you only have yourself to blame. If it weren't for you, nobody would be here doing yoga but Roger."

Terry looked chagrined. "I keep trying to forget that." He looked over at Roger, who was busy behind the counter. "You know what's funny about it all is that Roger doesn't seem to mind. You would think he would be the last person to want a crowd."

Mike, too, looked at Roger, and smiled his benevolent smile. "How would you tell?"

Terry rubbed the back of his head thoughtfully, silently acknowledging the point.

Roger's consistency of temperament was the one bright spot for the regulars in this new regime, and watching the newcomers' first encounters with the shop's proprietor provided daily entertainment. Unchanged by fortune, Roger greeted his new customers just as he greeted his old ones: with a scowl and some kind of noise that could not be recognized as words. That is, of course, if he greeted them at all. A cold stare would do just as well.

The reactions of new customers to Roger ranged from

deflation, to outrage, to confusion. But to the locals, these encounters were a reason to get up in the morning. They would watch as surreptitiously as possible, trying hard to keep their amusement from their faces. Some of the kinder observers felt pangs of sympathy.

No one who came to Ground Zero could evade an experience with Roger. Each time one of these interactions occurred, the regulars would watch as the newcomer left the shop in some state of indignation or humiliation. "Success sure hasn't changed Roger," had become the comment they all made quietly and repeatedly to one another.

It may have been fortunate, then, that Roger's sole employee had an entirely different nature. Joshua was a man so beautiful, and with such an aura of peace and inner grace, that, upon his arrival almost two years ago, Terry had begun referring to him behind his back as "The Angel Joshua." The name had stuck. Although none of them called him that to his face, if anyone had, Joshua would merely have turned his beatific gaze upon the speaker and gently poured his coffee.

Joshua's face was so perfect that at first glance it was as if a light were shining on it. Whether it was his beauty that created his inner nature, or the other way around was the subject of many earnest debates outside of Ground Zero. These conversations had become the local equivalent of medieval philosophers' disputes over the numbers of angels on the head of a pin, having the same capacity for infinite variation without any resolution.

It was Joshua who managed the yoga-loving crowds who swarmed to the shop, and it was he who made certain that the shop was not so overrun that there was no room to actually do yoga. Roger, apparently indifferent, merely strode in every morning at five and began his practice. Whether he was even aware of his following was the subject of yet another debate among the locals.

These cheerful arguments added rich dimension to daily life.

Chapter Six

Ben awoke in a cloud of nameless dread, and he lay in bed for a while trying to remember the reason. When it struck him, he found it more difficult than usual to get up. His mother had to call him three times before he found the will to throw off the covers.

His anxiety about Caleb was lessened by the realization of one dazzling and irrevocable fact: today was the last day of school. The summer stretched before him: long days of solitary rambling; swimming at School House Beach; bike rides; baseball; ice cream; and visiting Ms. Campbell's goat. Ben's courage was renewed, and he set off for school filled with joy.

"Morning, Fiona. Any news today?"

Fiona looked up at the post office clerk from the stack of mail she had been looking through and shook her head.

"Nothing today."

"Ah, well," he said. "There's always tomorrow."

"True enough," said Fiona, preparing to leave. "Well, have a good day."

"You, too. See you tomorrow."

With a wave, she went out into the sunshine.

This conversation had become a daily ritual since Fiona had been elected, and was repeated nearly everywhere she went. True to her campaign promise, Fiona's first priority had been to research and write proposals for grants to dredge the harbor, and now, the paperwork submitted, the Islanders waited impatiently to hear the results.

Merely receiving the funding, however, would not be sufficient. It would only be the first step in a long process. Nature, however, had no respect for bureaucracy. With or without the funding, the water level was continuing to drop, and in order for life to carry on as usual, there needed to be some kind of short-term solution.

Detroit Harbor was the place where the ferries docked, and the ferries were the lifeline of the Island. Aside from the wildlife, nearly everything on the Island had come there by ferry, and the ferry was the primary means of connection with the mainland. There were private boats, of course, and private planes that landed on the tiny airport's grass field. But, since the airport was little more than a windsock and some paths, the ferry line was the prime essential.

In a not-so-subtle undercurrent of popular opinion, the wealth of the ferry owners was a source of some resentment among the Islanders, who viewed the line's monopoly as an evil, if a necessary one. But for the owners, running the line was an expensive proposition, particularly in keeping up with federal regulations that usually bore only a distant relationship to the Island's reality. The costs that might have sunk the ferry were supported by not being undercut by competitors. And if the line were to falter, the grocery supplies, the fuel, the mail, the packages from Amazon, the building materials, the hardware—not to mention the travel to doctors and veterinarians, and all the other niceties of modern life necessary to maintain the community—would all be stopped cold. There was no other way. The ferry line had to be kept running.

So, when the lake levels sank year after year to an historic low, threatening to make the harbor too shallow for ferry traffic, the peril for Island life was real. The harbor must be dredged, but the cost was too high for the small number of taxpayers to support. Confident that their need would be self-evident, the Island appealed to the State for assistance, but after years of deficits, there was no money in the budget for such an expense, and the Islanders were too small a constituency to sway the politicians. The official refusal came as a shock, and it was this state of affairs that had led to the fearsome prospect of Stella DesRosiers becoming chairman of the town board.

As a candidate, Stella had had no personal appeal whatsoever, but her nephew's seat in the legislature seemed at first to be the key factor in reversing Wisconsin's decision not to pay for the dredging.

Fiona, reluctantly roused by an instinct of pure self-preservation, had run against Stella as a newcomer. In part because of her promise to find outside funding, in part because of the Islanders' experience of Stella's tendency toward ruthlessness and bullying, and in large part because of sheer luck, Fiona had won the election. Now, she was faced with two looming existential crises: the rapidly accelerating problem of the water levels and the fire department's budget.

Chapter Seven

It was a perfect June day. Acutely aware that their time together was drawing to a close, Fiona and Pete decided to make the most of it with a day at the beach. Public notice had been given for the fire department meeting, and Fiona had done her homework, so her conscience was clear.

They stopped for a bottle of wine for their picnic at the little store which, because of the idiosyncratic diversity of its merchandise, was known locally as "Shoes and Booze." As they stood studying the shelves, they heard the electronic bell that announced the entrance of another customer.

"Good morning!" said Emily Martin with her usual tone of aggressive gaiety. Fiona wanted to sigh, but observing Pete's impeccably polite and deferential greeting, she felt shamed into putting on a brighter face.

"I am so glad to find you here," began Emily, before Fiona could utter a word. "Although," she glanced at her watch, "it does seem as if a public servant ought to be on the job by now." She laughed to make it seem as if she were joking.

Although it often seemed so to Fiona, the job of town chairman was not a full-time position—in fact it barely paid anything at all—and no one expected nine-to-five hours of their public officials. Everyone on the Island board had real jobs—sometimes more than one—and their public work was regarded as a service to the community rather than a career.

Fiona smiled grimly. "What did you need, Emily?"

"I just wanted to talk to you about an idea I had. About the fire station. You know, that building is just about falling down, and I think we should start planning to build a new one. I've spoken to the chief, and he agrees."

Fiona took a deep breath. She found it highly unlikely that Chief Gil, knowing as he did about the shortfall in the budget, was now in favor of even larger expenditures. Emily had a way of hearing what she wanted to hear. "Well, the building is in bad shape," she began.

"Bad shape?" exclaimed Emily. "Bad shape? It ought to be condemned. No, I think it's very clear that there needs to be some tax money spent on this problem."

Fiona kept her voice low. Even in apparent solitude, the rules of small town life meant that a conversation held in a public place would be repeated all over the Island, and probably incorrectly. Fiona had no doubt that it would become a story that she was going to spend money on a new fire hall. She sighed and looked on the bright side. At least this kind of talk might scotch any chances of re-election.

"The budget is pretty tight right now," she said, with, what she privately noted, was massive understatement.

Emily shook her head and made a dismissive gesture with her hand. "Raise taxes. It's really just that simple. That's what we would have done in Winnetka."

Over Emily's shoulder Fiona could see Pete's expression as he continued to peruse the wine selection with an air of absorption. She suddenly wanted to laugh.

"Times are hard, Emily. Almost everyone is already struggling to make ends meet. We can't ask them to pay more taxes."

Emily made a noise between a snort and a laugh. "I know it seems that way to you," she said, smiling. "But believe me, it's the only way. I know you feel in over your head, my dear, but you just wait and see." She patted Fiona's arm. "You and I will sit down later this week and have a nice little chat. I'll show you exactly what to do. You'll see, it will be the perfect solution."

Still smiling, and without waiting for Fiona's response, she picked up the bottle of vodka she had come for, and after a brief exchange of pleasantries with the clerk, sailed off.

The little shop rang with silence after she left.

Pete gazed after Emily with a look of faint curiosity, but said nothing until they left the shop.

"Why do you suppose that woman tries so hard?" he asked as they got into the car. "I never understand the point in pretending to know things you don't, or to be things you're not."

Fiona smiled as she started the engine, backed the car out of the parking space, and headed toward the beach. "I remember a character in a Cather novel being described—and I'm paraphrasing— as 'pushing her personality before her like a cart'. Emily always makes me think of that."

"But," said Pete, "it doesn't actually fool anyone, and it merely reveals a sad, private sense of inferiority."

He was silent for a while, reflecting. "She always makes me think of that anecdote about Professor Strunk—of Strunk and White fame—who said, 'if you mispronounce a word, say it loud,' his theory being that if you say something confidently, then others will ponder whether it is their own pronunciation that is wrong. Please don't misunderstand me—I am a great admirer of Strunk and White—but there's something about that philosophy that says, 'Emily Martin.'"

"Well," said Fiona, "Emily certainly does say it loud." She stopped. "Shouldn't it be 'loudly'?" She looked over at him with arched eyebrows.

Pete just shook his head, but he was smiling.

"I think we should," she continued, "as a matter of public policy, endeavor to keep all copies of *The Elements of Style* away from Emily. I really don't think I'd want to encourage her in developing her own guide to English pronunciation."

"An important point," said Pete, wryly.

"The thing is," said Fiona, now fully engaged in this discussion, "people seem to value other people's opinions of their own worth, rather than their own, so they push themselves into pretending to be a certain way, or to value things they don't actually care about just to impress other people."

Pete looked pensive, as Fiona warmed to her theme. "It's like people with matching books," she said.

"Matching books?" he was puzzled.

"Yes, you see it in decorating magazines, and in the houses of certain self-proclaimed sophisticates. The books are chosen for the color of their spines. Or wrapped in paper to match the room. I've actually seen decorating websites selling things like 'Linear foot of Faux Ostrich Books, Beige.' You can tell that these are for the homes of unserious people, but who want to pretend to be serious. They obviously don't read the books."

Pete looked over at Fiona. "That stop sign...I'm sure it was only a suggestion."

"Never mind," said Fiona blithely. "There was no one around."

"I'm here," said Pete.

She glanced at him briefly and returned her eyes to the road.

Pete sighed pointedly, but continued the conversation. "It's never occurred to me that books should match," he said.

"That's because you read. Well, also probably because you're male," Fiona conceded. "But serious people. I mean, people who care about ideas, and about actually reading, don't have matching books. If anything, their books are a haphazard reflection of the search for knowledge, reflecting the wanderings of a person's curiosity. There's nothing matching about that."

"I don't think I've ever been to a house with matching books."

"How about a house with just one set of encyclopedias and not one other book? Have you been to one of those?"

"Encyclopedias? Who has encyclopedias anymore?"

"Well, you know what I mean."

"You have thought a great deal about this."

Fiona looked sheepish. "Yes. Because it's a form of pretention, and I detest pretention." She pulled into a parking space that had been more or less invented between the cedar trees and pulled on the brake, continuing the conversation without turning off the engine.

"It's showing off that you have books, even while it's clear that the books are only props. And, also," she confessed, "it bothers me because their houses are so beautiful, and mine is full of haphazardly unmatching books."

"And stacked everywhere, by the way. We need to get you some more bookcases. But if it's clear that the books are props," he said, returning to the main point, "isn't it also clear that the person doesn't actually read them? In which case, I would argue that it's not pretension, it's actually the opposite: no pretense whatsoever, just, perhaps, shallowness. Now, if an unserious person were to have lots of unmatching books that he had never read and were trying to make people believe that he's read them, *that* would be pretentious. So, you should shift the focus of your wrath to owners of never-read, unmatching books. Leave the poor matching people alone. They don't know what they're missing."

Laughing, Fiona looked at him and shook her head. "Stop looking so pleased with yourself."

"I am pleased, though. I have unmatching books, and I read them. Q.E.D. I feel smug."

"If you were the kind of person who felt smug, I wouldn't like you."

Pete smiled. "I feel smug about that, too."

Laughing and shaking her head, Fiona turned off the engine. They gathered their things from the trunk of the car and headed off toward the water and its rocky beach.

"How would you even find the book you wanted if they were all wrapped in matching paper?" asked Pete, slinging the straps of the beach chair bags over his shoulder.

"Exactly," said Fiona.

Ben arrived at school that morning filled with hope for the summer to come, but as soon as he walked up the drive to the main door, all his joy slipped away. There stood Caleb Martin.

At thirteen, Caleb was just enough older than Ben to have an advantage, and he was endowed with a certain amount of extra weight that was the result of his mother's indulgence, and which, not incidentally, was the same reason for his arrogance and sense of entitlement.

Caleb sauntered over and blocked Ben's path. "What's up, little buttercup?" he asked in an infuriating singsong. "What's the secret password?"

"Jerk?" asked Ben, refusing to be intimidated.

Caleb leaned menacingly into Ben's face. "Oh, I don't think you should be talking to me like that. It isn't nice."

A teacher appeared at just that moment. She eyed the two boys suspiciously.

"What's going on here?" she asked.

Caleb, whose face was suddenly a study in outraged innocence, answered quickly. "I was just telling Ben, here, that he shouldn't use bad language at school."

The teacher looked at Ben's reddened face and shook her head. "Nor anywhere else, Ben Palsson. I am going to have to call your mother."

Caleb gave Ben a superior little smile and walked away. "Bye, Benny," he said in a low voice. "See you at lunch."

Chapter Eight ❖

Emily and Jason Martin had three children. The youngest was seven-year-old Noah. Noah, a sweet-natured child, had found many friends among the other children on the Island. This was not the case, however, for his elder brothers, who were generally avoided. Noah, was, in fact, so different from his siblings that people jokingly pondered whether he might be a foundling.

It might have been their early years that had made the difference between Noah and his brothers, or, perhaps, there was simply no more room for petulance in the family. But Noah's kind nature seemed to have been born in him, and his mother frequently wondered how she had managed to have such different children.

The two older boys had grown up in a Chicago suburb, where they were accustomed to bigger schools with more classmates, more activities, and more anonymity. For them, the move to the Island was disruptive, depressing, and a punishment served upon them by their parents. For Noah, who had spent only two years in school before the move, coming to the Island was an adventure.

The eldest brother was Jeremy. He was fifteen and perpetually sullen. His sneering view of Island life had made

him unpopular with his high school classmates, and while he
dreamed of escape, he managed to make himself and everyone
around him miserable. His parents were trying to decide
whether to send him off the Island for the remainder of his
secondary education. They, too, found the small school limited and stultifying, and their guilt prompted an inclination
toward the extravagance of boarding school.

Caleb, the middle child, was thirteen. Caleb had had a
group of friends in his old school. They were sophisticated
boys, the sons of highly educated professionals, and there was
an assumption of entitlement that colored their perceptions
of the world. They were all the careless possessors of smart
phones and video games, imported bicycles, and private tennis
lessons. They were probably not much worse than most other
children of their age and class, but they lived in a world of
privilege and material comfort that would have astonished the
Island children.

It shouldn't be surprising, then, that Caleb was having
some difficulty adapting to life on the Island. After being in a
school of fifteen hundred students, he was now in a school of
seventy. Like his parents, he was convinced of his superiority
to the Islanders, but somehow, in spite of that, when he was
around them, he always felt that he, himself, was missing some
vital component. He was homesick. He was lonely. He didn't
fit in. And he was very, very, angry.

Chapter Nine ✤

Fiona appeared to be dozing in her chair, but behind her sunglasses, she was watching Pete. He was a strong swimmer, and she enjoyed seeing him dive into the deep water from the raft. The water in June was still quite cold, and Fiona was unable to stay in for more than a few minutes at a time, but Pete didn't seem to mind the temperature.

When he returned, he pulled on a shirt, a baseball cap, and sunglasses, and began rummaging in the cooler for the wineglasses. He opened the wine, poured two glasses and, handing one to Fiona, sat down beside her.

"I have to admit, I rather like screw top wine bottles."

Fiona smiled. "Me, too."

She took a sip. In the sun, the wine went straight to her head. She could feel it coursing through her body in a way that wasn't altogether pleasant. Fiona preferred the effects of scotch.

She had been gazing out at the water when she felt Pete looking at her, and she turned to look back. She smiled at him over the tops of her sunglasses. He looked more serious than usual, but his eyes still held a glint of humor that revealed his nature.

"I'm going to be in London for a month or two this fall.

I'm rather hoping you can get away from your political responsibilities and come visit me. My mother wants to meet you."
He grinned. "That should give you the time you will need to
memorize some Byron and Wordsworth. She has a horror of
people who don't know poetry."

Fiona responded instantly:

> *It was an April morning: fresh and clear*
>
> *The Rivulet, delighting in its strength,*
>
> *Ran with a young man's speed; and yet the voice*
>
> *Of waters which the winter had supplied*
>
> *Was softened down into a vernal tone.*

"She will like you. Probably."

"That doesn't sound promising. Is she hard on people?"

Pete made a non-committal gesture. "Only people who
have anything to do with me." He paused, reflecting. "Actually,
I think she will like you. Very much. She admires smart people,
and smart women in particular, and at this point in my life, I
suspect she will be happy if I just bring anybody."

"That's not particularly flattering."

"Actually, if you think about it, it is."

Fiona thought about it, and decided this was true. "Anyway,"
she continued, "I'm afraid I'm not very good with Byron. Is that
an actual requirement? I find his stuff kind of creepy."

"That's because a lot of it is creepy. I can't imagine how my
mother—who is normally a woman of good sense—developed
such a passion for it. But you can forget Byron so long as you

can manage to convince her that Byron is the only omission in your literary education. I've never liked him much, either, but I'm afraid his poetry has been more or less a family requirement my whole life."

"Ugh," said Fiona, "You poor child."

"Could have been worse. Could have been Longfellow."

"Very true," said Fiona, holding out her glass for more wine.

Pete reached for the bottle to pour it for her.

Nancy Iverssen paused in her chores for the moment, and leaned over the fence to look at the animals in her pasture. There were the big brown beef cattle, two horses, and the goat who belonged—probably—to Fiona Campbell.

Nancy, whose energetic approach to life was an Island byword, was a little bit surprised to find herself slowing down. A vigorous seventy, she had never acknowledged the passage of time, and had, so far, simply worked her way through any of the minor ailments that accompany hard physical work. She had had a birthday recently, however, and the prospect of not being able to continue running the farm on her own suddenly seemed an inevitable part of the not-too-distant future.

The farm had been part of her family for generations, and Nancy was the end of the line. Her older brother was gone, having been declared missing in action in Vietnam when she was still a child. Her sister lived in San Francisco, and her grown nieces and nephews had no interest in rural life. Nancy believed in facing things head on, and she had realized some time ago that when she was gone, the farm would have to be sold, and this chapter of the long family history would end. It was sad, she thought, but it couldn't be helped.

One of the horses approached, and Nancy reached out absently to stroke his nose. There was still plenty of time. She knew any number of older people who stayed on in their own places to the end. But the animals, of course, would have to be looked after. She knew them all, with their little quirks and foibles, and she loved them. She held her role in their well-being as a sacred trust, and dreaded to think of having to sell them should she become unable to care for them. It would be hard to be sure that someone else would hold the animals' interests to her own standards.

She enjoyed the soft feel of the horse's nose, and she petted him gently and affectionately. To show his appreciation, he reached over the fence to nuzzle her ear. Nancy chuckled and brushed him away, but not without first rubbing her cheek against his. There was still so much to enjoy in every day, she thought. No sense in looking too far ahead. She reached into her pocket where she always kept a sugar cube or two, and held them out to him.

In the hallway after school, Caleb Martin fell in step with Ben on his way to his locker.

"Hey, Benno. Hope you don't get in too much trouble with your mommy."

Ben was silent, but Caleb wasn't finished. As Ben reached his locker, Caleb grabbed his arm and lowered his voice.

"If you say one word against me, little man, I am going to make sure your father loses his job. My parents have a lot of influence in this town, and I'll make sure of it. So, you just keep your little mouth shut." He gave Ben's arm an ugly twist and pushed him into the locker.

No one saw it happen.

Chapter Ten

Nika studied her son's face. It wasn't like him to be rude or surly, much less use bad language, and yet she had gotten the call from school, and she couldn't ignore it. She had waited until she found the right moment to discuss it, but this wasn't going well.

"Ms. Siefert says you were swearing. Is this true, Ben?" she asked, calmly.

Ben just looked at her.

His mother took a deep breath. "I don't think I've ever heard you say a bad word. What do you have to say for yourself?"

Ben shrugged. "Nothing."

"Well, is it true?"

Ben shrugged again.

Nika raised her eyebrows. "I am more concerned about your silence than about the phone call, Ben. I need you to tell me what happened."

Ben looked out the window. There was a red-bellied woodpecker on the birdfeeder. Ben had a soft spot for woodpeckers.

"Ben," his mother's voice had a note of warning. "I am speaking to you."

Ben stirred and stood up.

"Whatever," he said, and started toward the refrigerator.

For a moment Nika was speechless. "Ben, you will go upstairs and wait until I come for you."

Ben sighed a deep sigh of adolescent contempt.

Nika stood up from the table. "Go."

Nika watched him leave the room feeling slightly shocked. This was behavior that she would not tolerate. She would have to think carefully about a strategy to address it, but meanwhile, she worried about how she was going to get him to talk. Something more than mere adolescence was going on with Ben, and she needed to know what it was.

Roger generally closed down Ground Zero at around four o'clock, when the last of the afternoon coffee drinkers had slipped away. Today, he waited with some impatience for a pair of yoga tourists to finish and leave. They were a man and woman, dressed in casual clothing, and emanating a certain yogic aura.

Roger could always tell which of his customers had been reading a yoga magazine in which a review of his shop had appeared. For one thing, they almost always smelled of lavender or sandalwood or some other botanical aroma, and they always—male or female—wore some kind of wrist band, most often made of leather. For another, there was a quality of personality which Roger found particular to them. It was as if the rough edges had been rubbed away, and what remained was smooth and featureless, like a worn stone on the beach.

This pair had a naiveté that some might have found charming. Their fond smiles and genial conversation with one another showed they were a couple, and they behaved as if they were working themselves up to an encounter with celebrity. All of this was lost on Roger.

"Are you…Roger Mason? The Yoga Master?" asked the man.

Roger preferred not to socialize with his customers, and he considered any conversation beyond what was necessary for the purchase of coffee to be excessive. He looked at the man in silence. He arranged his face in what he considered a neutral expression, but which conveyed instead an impression of loathing.

"We're up from Chicago. To take the class." They smiled warmly.

Roger bestirred himself to reply.

"There is no class."

The two looked at one another in some confusion.

"But," said the young woman, who was continually brushing her long brown hair from her face, "we saw the piece. In the *Tribune*. About the morning practice."

"We came all the way from Chicago for it. Thought we'd scope it out before tomorrow morning. Get the lay of the land, you know." The young man looked hopefully at Roger, expecting some response.

Roger found himself staring at the beaded bracelet on his customer's right wrist. He wondered why this kind of thing was considered of use. Roger, whose only adornment was his plain gold wedding band, found jewelry to be a nuisance. He wore a wedding ring to make Elisabeth happy, which, in Roger's view, was his primary reason for many otherwise inexplicable things.

"There is no class," said Roger again. "There is practice. Private practice."

The pair exchanged another glance, but now appeared relieved. They had the right place.

"Oh, we know that," said the man, waving his hand dismissively.

"We just want to practice, too," added the woman in her earnest way. She leaned in and became even more serious. "We feel we need to challenge ourselves. You know, to break through to a new space." She smiled encouragingly at Roger.

Smiles had no effect on Roger.

"The shop is closing," he said.

The two looked startled at first, and then exchanged another mutually comprehensive glance.

"Ohhhh," said the man, and he winked. "We get it. Ok."

They rose to go, and he took out his wallet to pay their bill. "Don't worry about us. We won't bring anyone else."

The woman beamed at Roger. "We are just so excited to be part of the scene."

As she left the shop, her companion held the door for her and looked back at Roger. "Bye!" He dropped his voice to a whisper. "See you at practice!"

The door closed behind him with a cheerful ring, and their excited voices drifted back from the parking lot.

Roger strode across the shop to the door and locked it.

Nika and Pali had issued a punishment. Ben would write a letter of apology to his teacher, and rather than taking his usual rambles in the woods, he would have to spend a day at home doing chores for his mother. Unbeknownst to Ben, his parents had also agreed that they would think about ways to instill more structure into Ben's days this summer, believing that, perhaps, he had too much time on his own.

Meanwhile, Nika and Pali each tried separately to get Ben to tell them what was going on. After a whole day on the water, Pali had been unable to break through Ben's resistance during their fishing trip. Manly trips to the hardware store, or to Boy Scout meetings were equally ineffective.

Nika had no better luck, despite her attempts to engage her son in conversation. In the end, however reluctantly, Nika and Pali had had to accept the facts as they had been given to them.

The children's world has a set of Kafkaesque rules that block the path for adults either to learn the truth or protect a child in trouble. Ben had not meant to be rude to his mother, and he was actually desperate for advice. The plain fact, however, was that he found himself in a very difficult position, and he didn't know how to talk about it. He had a stubborn streak about handling things on his own, and his parents' well-meaning efforts had paradoxically strengthened his resolve to solve his own problems.

Ben had a boy's finely honed sense of fairness, and the injustice of his punishment rankled. He chafed at having to apologize for something he hadn't done, and he had an eleven year old's horror of writing, especially now that school was out. But to go without his Island rambles—even for a day—was a heavy punishment, indeed. He knew that his own silence had contributed to his predicament, but his new sense of maturity required that he keep his problems to himself. This, he thought, was what it meant to be an adult.

Ben tried hard to live up to the standards of the heroes in the books he read, and now he found himself asking what they might do in his situation. The answer was not obvious, but one thing was clear: not one of them would have told, or asked someone else for help. Help, in all good stories, always came, unbidden, to the deserving.

Fiona frequently pondered the incongruous mixture of delight and sheer, impenetrable boredom that made up her life on the Island. Although some of the boredom came from loneliness, much of it came from the obligations of public office. The meetings were a primary source, the other was the management of mundane administrative tasks.

Among the many things she had not considered in her rash decision to run for office, was the cascading flow of paper that gushed through her hands and into her small office at the community hall, and her guest room office at home. She vaguely recalled a nineteenth-century essay predicting that the world would soon be flooded by straight pins. In her case, she felt quite sure that it would be paper that would overtake her life. Filing, organizing, and generally being able to locate these papers was becoming an increasingly onerous task, and one for which Fiona had neither patience nor skill.

She stood, one day, in the door of her public office and surveyed the scene. It had been fewer than two months since the start of her term. Papers were piled everywhere: on the desk, the filing cabinet, and stacked on the floor in precarious piles. She thanked her lucky stars that the town clerk was responsible for important legal documents like deeds and tax bills.

Fiona had a realistic sense of her own limitations. She knew she would have to do something. More properly, she knew she would have to find someone else who would do something. A grant for harbor dredging, with all the money that would be at stake, would make this absolutely essential.

She mentioned her dilemma that night after dinner at Elisabeth and Roger's.

"Oh, Fiona." Elisabeth was in despair. "You are so disorganized. How will you ever do what needs to be done to run the Island?"

Fiona ran a hand through her hair. "I never actually planned to win, much less to run anything. This is all so unexpected."

Elisabeth sighed deeply.

The weather had taken a sudden cold turn, which is characteristic of early summer in Wisconsin. Pete, seated comfortably in Elisabeth's big easy chair by the fireplace smiled quietly to himself. Roger was pouring himself another glass of wine and gestured silently toward Pete's glass. Pete nodded gratefully.

"Thanks."

Elisabeth was in one of her bossy moods. "You have got to hire someone to help you. Is there any room in the budget for that?"

Fiona frowned. "Well, there was a woman who used to do all that, but she and her husband just retired. So, I suppose there may be some room in the budget for a replacement." She considered this, her lips twisted in thought.

"But it won't be much. Not enough to live on, surely."

"That doesn't matter," said Elisabeth severely. "It's not a full-time job." As she said this, she wondered—knowing Fiona as she did—whether this was true.

Fiona suddenly brightened. "Maybe you could do it. You're great at this kind of thing."

Pete coughed gently, and Fiona looked up at him. He gave her the kind of look she recalled her sixth-grade teacher giving her when she had made a foolish remark in class.

"Oh. No, I suppose that would be a bad idea."

Elisabeth tried to look exasperated, but she was secretly pleased. "You need to place an ad. A local ad, in *The Observer*. There must be someone looking for a little supplemental income who could be of help to you." Under her breath she added, so that Fiona could not hear, "God knows."

Pete, who was always highly attentive to his surroundings, heard it and smiled again to himself.

Chapter Eleven

His sentence over, Ben stood leaning on Nancy Iversson's fence, watching the goat he had rescued as it nudged and browsed along the tree line. His arm hurt where Caleb Martin had twisted it earlier in the week. The joy that should have been his, with all the summer stretching out before him, was tainted by his sore arm, and by his worries. He was thinking about what Caleb had said. "Could it be true?" he wondered. Could Caleb really cause his father to lose his job? It seemed unlikely, but Ben couldn't really be sure.

The goat noticed him and ambled over to the fence, hoping for a snack. Ben forgot his troubles in the pleasure of goatly friendship and the warmth of the sun on a June afternoon. He reached into his pocket for a treat, and didn't mind when the goat drooled all over his hand. He rubbed its head affectionately. He wasn't sure he should admit it to anyone, but generally speaking, he liked animals better than people. Certainly better than he liked Caleb Martin.

After much concern over the correct wording, Fiona placed her want ad in the paper. Elisabeth had suggested posting on-line as well, but Fiona was wary of attracting the attention of outsiders.

"What if someone from Chicago sees it and wants the job?" she asked. "The Islanders would never forgive me. I need to see if anyone local wants it first."

Fiona dropped off the ad copy at the newspaper office, buoyed with optimism for the results, then stopped by the grocery store to pick up a few things. She met Nika at the meat counter, and they stopped to chat.

Nika had been missing Fiona during Pete's extended visit, and the two fell quickly into confidences and personal revelations, including Nika's worries about Ben.

"I think he needs more structure, less time wandering around on his own. He's growing up fast, and I'm beginning to think we've spoiled him."

Fiona, who adored young Ben, laughed. "Ben is the least spoiled kid I've ever met. You're bound to have some conflicts with a boy his age, but it's not because you've done anything wrong."

Nika was slightly mollified. "Do you think so?"

Fiona was struck by a sudden thought. She had been feeling guilty about the work an extra animal imposed on her friend, Nancy. Even though Fiona paid for the anonymous goat's keep, she didn't really have time to do much to help.

"What if I hired Ben to do some work around Nancy's place to help with Robert—or whoever he is?"

Nika's face lit up. "Do you mean it? That would be

wonderful! He loves that animal."

Fiona smiled somewhat ruefully. "I know. If I didn't like you, I'd have given him to Ben months ago."

Nika laughed. "Lucky me. Shall I send Ben over to speak with you?"

Fiona thought for a moment. "No. Let's leave you out of it. How about I call him and see if he'd be interested?"

Nika nodded, seeing the wisdom of this. "Yes. Much better."

They said goodbye, and each went her way, feeling slightly better about life in general.

Fiona came home to find Pete reading a letter. "It's from my mother. She hasn't quite grasped the concept of e-mail."

Fiona smiled. "Have you told her I am memorizing Byron?"

"Good God, no. I want her to think that it's all entirely unplanned, and that you've been immersed in the stuff since birth. Do you think you can pull that off?"

"I endeavor to give satisfaction."

Pete smiled. "Oh, you do."

It was some time before they returned to their conversation.

"So, what does your mother say in her letter?" asked Fiona at last. "Is it all Byronic quotation?"

"Actually, no. It's quite a funny story, actually."

Fiona poured them each a drink, and they went out onto the porch to sit.

"I want to hear your mother's funny story."

"Upon reflection, I'm not actually sure whether it's funny or sad," he said. "She has a group of friends she goes to the theater with. They are quite active, and manage to see almost everything in the West End. They've been going for probably forty years. I can remember when I was quite small, being left in the care of some aunt or other while she went to the theater with these friends."

Fiona settled into the porch swing prepared to hear the story. She tucked her feet up, and happily drank her scotch. "Didn't your father go to the theater?"

"Yes, but he was in the foreign service and away a great deal."

It occurred to Fiona that the apple didn't fall far from the tree. "Keep going," she said.

"They had heard about a classic Edward Albee play being done, and they were all anxious to see it. They were in a bit of a dither about whether they'd be able to get tickets, but one of them had a nephew, or something, who was in the company, and he arranged that they could all sit together on a weeknight, so they bought the tickets and planned to make a night of it."

"Edward Albee?" asked Fiona. "But I thought—"

"As well you might," said Pete. "But just listen."

"You mean shut up and listen," said Fiona.

"I would never say that," said Pete. "So, they go to the play, which seems to have an innocuous name. 'About life on the farm, or something,' my mother writes. And after a rather sumptuous dinner at a chic, new Vietnamese restaurant—they may be elderly, but they still have a nice sense of adventure—they all take their seats, cheerful, several sheets to the wind, and buzzing with anticipation."

Pete paused to take a drink, as Fiona listened, rapt.

"The play begins innocently enough, and appears to be a traditional drawing room comedy with—and I'm quoting here—'a sort of ineffectual husband with a waspish wife.'"

Fiona gasped. "I think I know where we're going here."

"I imagine you do," said Pete. "The play, of course, was *The Goat, Or Who Is Sylvia*, which, as you clearly know, is about a man who has a—well, who has an affair with…a goat."

Fiona covered her mouth with her hands. "A goat named Sylvia. Were the ladies scandalized?"

Pete nodded solemnly. "Exactly as you might imagine. And apparently there was some dissent among those who managed to laugh and those who could not bring themselves to do so." He paused. "My mother reports overhearing a conversation on the sidewalk while they were waiting for their taxis…."

"And?" asked Fiona, spellbound.

"It was, apparently, an American man and woman leaving the theater, having a rather vehement argument about the play. The woman was saying, in an emphatic voice: 'It's *not* about the goat!' And one of the ladies, overhearing, commented loudly enough to be heard: 'I can't say I ever expected to hear that particular conversation on the streets of London.'"

Fiona sat quietly for a moment, taking it all in. "Your mother sounds a most interesting woman."

"Yes," said Pete.

Chapter Twelve ✦

Chief Gil had accepted yet another resignation from a firefighter. The situation was now so dangerous as to make him legally liable if some disaster should occur. He was the chief. He was obligated to provide emergency services within his jurisdiction, but he no longer had the personnel nor the budget to make new hires.

He was a conscientious man and a reasonable one. He knew that the town board was operating within tremendous budgetary constraints, and he also knew that their voters were outspoken and aggressive in their opposition to taxes. When Emily Martin wanted to sit down with him to discuss her ideas, he accepted, albeit reluctantly. He had encountered Emily on several occasions in the past.

"Desperate times; desperate measures," he told himself.

It wouldn't have done to meet anywhere in public. The mere fact of their meeting would have been the topic of conversation everywhere on the Island within the hour. It was arranged, therefore, that they would meet at the fire station, a shabby building of corrugated metal that had seen better days.

Emily appeared at the appointed hour, armed with a spiral bound notebook, which she removed with great ceremony from her bag, and an elegant fountain pen, which she carried in a leather case. With all the dignity of a duchess serving tea, she prepared herself to take notes, arranging herself primly on the folding chair the chief had provided.

The chief offered her coffee.

Emily noted the battered pot with the syrupy dregs left from this morning and managed to be polite in her refusal.

Having settled herself, Emily looked around with a critical eye. "This is certainly a dreary spot. In Winnetka—my home-town, you know— we had such beautiful, modern equipment." Her gaze took in the aging fire engines and the buckets placed at intervals around the room, strategically placed to catch the leaks from the roof.

"How on earth have things been allowed to get to such a state?"

Chief Gil counseled himself not to take her remarks personally, despite the fact that everything she said seemed designed to insult.

"I'm sure," he said, "you are aware of the financial chal-lenges we are facing."

"Oh, yes," said Emily dismissively. "I am well aware. But, of course, that is why we are here." She smiled brightly. "My expe-rience in civic affairs is quite extensive, you know. Quite exten-sive. Clearly, what is needed is someone who can see the full scope of the problem, and offer guidance in finding the solution."

She raised her open hands as if presenting him with a gift. "And I, of course, am just that person." She dropped her hands into her lap with an air of finality. "It's all quite simple." She smiled again.

The chief looked puzzled.

Emily sighed a little, but quickly caught herself. These people were so slow-witted. She spoke slowly and patiently, as if to a child. "We simply need to raise taxes. It's not the big deal everyone seems to think. Happens everywhere every day. Every single day," she repeated cheerfully. "When I was on the parks committee in Winnetka, we simply hired a reputable advertising firm in Chicago, and we were off to the races." She smiled her smile. "We will explain the situation, decide how much is needed, and launch a full-fledged public information campaign. Everyone will fall in line. You'll see. I've done it before, and I can do it again." Her smile was gentler now, befitting her intellectually superior position.

Chief Gil was reminded of a cartoon from *The Far Side* in which a complex mathematical formula was solved with an arrow and the notation *and then a miracle occurs*. "So, this," he thought, "is the big solution she had? I must have been crazy to agree to meet with her."

This time, he sighed, but without any attempt at concealment. Clearly, as an outsider, Emily had no sense whatever of the deep streaks of libertarian independence among the Islanders. And then there were her ideas of hiring some big-time advertising firm. Island existence was generally pretty hand-to-mouth, and there wasn't a lot leftover for new taxes, much less for advertising. If there had been, they would still oppose an increase as a matter of principle—not to mention their reaction to having outsiders interfering. Stubbornness and a desire for self-sufficiency were self-selecting traits for Island survival.

"This is very kind of you, Mrs. Martin—"

"—Emily," said Emily.

"Emily," he conceded. "I will certainly take your advice under consideration."

He stood to indicate that their meeting was over.

"Under consideration?" repeated Emily, taken aback. "Oh, no, I don't think we understand each other. No, I don't think we understand one another at all."

She summoned all her patience. Really! These people! She stood, too, so that she could speak with the chief on a more equal basis.

"What I am saying is that this is the way these things are done. I will handle everything for you. I will come up with the numbers, make a budget, figure out the tax requirements, and lead all the informational public meetings. And, of course, hire the right firm." Her bright smile returned. "We'll have everything up to snuff in no time!"

She gathered her things and prepared to leave. "And don't worry one bit about Fiona Campbell. I will take care of her, too. She'll come to see it all my way. And the board, too. You'll see!"

Waving gaily, she exited the building, carried along by her own personal wave of triumph.

Chief Gil leaned back in his chair and felt discouraged.

After breakfast, Pali, who had the day off, came into the kitchen and kissed his wife on the neck.

"Let's talk," he said.

"What about?" she asked, envisioning her mental list of the many things she had to do.

"Let's just sit down together."

With an inner sigh, Nika followed him into the next room. She never got as much done when he was home as when he was away. She sat in her favorite chair and looked at him with some impatience.

Pali looked down as he began to talk. "I think it's time we thought about leaving the Island. I've been thinking that it might be a good thing for Ben."

Her impatience forgotten, she focused all her attention on him as if her life depended on it. She forced herself to sound calm. "But we promised ourselves we'd never do that again. We love it here. It's our home."

"Nika, we need to think about this. We need to prepare Ben for his life. He's growing up, and I can't say I'm liking the way things are going. He can't hide away here on the Island forever. There's no future for him here—"

Nika started to interrupt, but Pali kept talking "—or, if there is, it's a future he can only choose when he knows what else is out there. Think about his life here. He needs to learn about the world. Ben has no experience with the worst of human character. We can't just throw him to the winds and expect him to fly."

"But we did. We left and found our way. We were okay." Her voice was low.

Pali shook his head. "It's such a different world now. This culture. The lack of values. The pace. Ben won't be able to keep up if we don't help him to acclimate. And isn't it better for him to encounter these things while we're there to guide him and protect him?"

Nika was silent. Pali could see the tears welling up.

"We don't have to decide now. We can think about it." He got up and went over to her, kneeling next to her chair and taking her hands in his. "It's our decision, Nika. Ours together. But I'm going to start looking. If something comes along, I won't say yes if you don't want me to. Just think about it, okay?"

She nodded, afraid to speak, her heart and mind in a turmoil. She hated this. When they returned to the Island they had sworn they would never move away again. And now, here he was, threatening to rip her away from everything that mattered.

"Well," she corrected herself silently, "not everything."

She felt a flash of her old passion for this man who had been her other self for so long. She had always loved him, from the first day she saw him. He was the best man she had ever known. And, when she looked into her heart, she knew, as much as she fought against admitting it, that he was right.

"Just think about it," he said again.

She nodded.

Chapter Thirteen ✣

Pali began his job search in earnest. Nika's unhappiness with the thought of moving seemed to hang over their house, but the more they talked about it, the more they both came to believe that it was the right thing to do. Ben was clearly struggling. Most likely, a change of location would help get him back on track. Maybe all the independence he had had on the Island had not been good for him.

Pali reflected on the way life has of pointing you down paths you don't expect. Not so long ago, leaving the Island would have seemed to him unthinkable.

But, here he was, searching the job markets in Green Bay and Milwaukee, and perusing the shipping pages online.

It was a grim project for him. Pali had no doubt that a man willing to work could always find a job. But, he was newly aware of how much he loved his job with the ferry, and he hoped he would be able to find something that allowed him to be on the water. The lake, its light, its seasons, its moods were a source of continuing delight and deep pleasure for him. It was the inspiration for his poetry, and it was also the spiritual home of his…muse…or whatever it was.

At odd moments on the ferry, he found himself staring off into the horizon, pondering the strange experiences he had

had. Was this…presence…based here, on the water? Would it follow him? Would it follow Ben, who had also experienced it? Or, when they left the Island, would they be leaving it behind as well? Pali breathed in the lake air and felt discouraged. The idea of being inside a factory or an office all day was deeply depressing to him, but not as depressing as the prospect of losing this mysterious bond.

There is a factor in these things, however, that Pali had failed to take into account. The human mind has a difficult time executing even the best-conceived plan when the heart is not engaged.

Chief among Fiona's concerns in her official position was implementing the new harbor dredging plan if the grant money came through. Aside from the management of the project itself, there were bureaucratic complications involving the State of Wisconsin, the Coast Guard, Great Lakes authorities, and any number of hitherto invisible entities, all with their own mountains of paperwork and labyrinthian approval processes. The ferry line would need to find a different place to dock during the work, and this, too, required preparation, paperwork, and complications.

There were questions about funds and about management; there were requests for audits; there were bonding issues and questions of authority; there were endless details required about demographics and the volume of ferry traffic, and it all went on into a distant horizon of bureaucracy that Fiona imagined had no end, to be relieved only by death itself.

The acquisition of funds seemed, by comparison, a trivial matter.

Nevertheless, with the advice of her predecessor, Lars Olufsen, and an attorney in Green Bay, Fiona had been taking the first steps toward beginning the complex process. Her inexperience with public affairs was, in some ways, an asset, because she had only to plead ignorance and others would leap to her assistance. She was not unaware that being an attractive woman also worked to her advantage.

So far, her biggest worry about the project was managing so much money, should it be awarded. She had no formal training in finance of any kind and could barely be bothered to balance her own checkbook. She would have to find help, but where? Who on the Island had sufficient experience and knowledge?

She felt as if she had started out following a tiny string, and encountered a series of massive, impenetrable knots.

When the notice of the town meeting over the fire department budget had been posted, Fiona, always impatient, had thought it seemed a very long time to wait for such a critical matter to be resolved. In preparation, she had armed herself with the budget numbers and studied them. But the numbers, she thought, were the easy part. It was what to do about them that was so difficult.

Before Fiona left for the hall on the night of the meeting, Pete presented her with a book. "Now that you're a politician, this may come in handy."

It was H.L. Mencken's *Chrestomathy*. Delighted, she opened to the section on democracy. "Giving every man the vote has no more made men wise and free than Christianity has made them good," she read.

Smiling, she put the book down and kissed Pete on the cheek. "This looks like fun. But you really can't make me more cynical than I already am, you know."

"That is not my intention, God knows. But I do think you may require some voice of reason to sustain you in office. And, by the way," he said, grabbing her hand and pulling her back. "I am quite sure that kisses on the cheek are meant for grandfathers and elderly uncles."

Fiona threw her arms around him, the better to thank him properly.

"Will you come?" she asked.

"Do you want me to?"

She hesitated. "I think I would prefer to know that you are here, ready to pour me a stiff drink when it's all over."

"Then that is what you shall have," said Pete. "Good luck."

"I'll need it."

Chapter Fourteen ❖

Fiona returned home from the meeting energized by her frustration.

"Everyone seems to blame either me, or Chief Gil, or both of us, but the situation isn't one of extravagance or malfeasance. The cost of protection is just higher than this small number of people can afford." Fiona sighed, and tossed her sweater onto a chair. "I don't blame them. Everyone is trying to keep their heads above water. But as a result," she concluded bleakly, "the whole Island is in jeopardy."

"Here's your drink," said Pete, handing her a glass. "Come on, let's sit down."

Fiona followed him into the living room, still energized, and still talking. "Everyone seems to think that if we just cut one thing there will suddenly be an extra fifty thousand dollars, but when it comes to cutting, they don't want to eliminate anything. The public's expectations are completely out of touch with reality."

She sighed and took a drink. "At least, we did manage to give the fire department a small increase." She shook her head regretfully. "I don't think it made the chief any happier."

Pete looked at her with sympathy.

Fiona caught his look and suddenly grinned. "I guess I

haven't suddenly encountered some new problem, have I?"

"Nope," said Pete, raising his glass to her. "Welcome to politics."

Pete's long leave of absence from his job had given Fiona and Pete a sense of normality they had never had before. Their confidence in one another had rapidly become an unquestioned foundation of their lives. But, they each had kept back one deep thing. For Fiona, it was her painful memories of life as a reporter on the streets of Chicago. The trauma was still too deep and overwhelming for her to encounter even in the act of recollection. For Pete, there was something else.

Fiona had a profound respect for his privacy, and a trust that he would tell her what he could, but if she had thought about it very much, she would have been more conscious of the skillful avoidance with which he handled any discussion of his work. He would tell her where he had been, or where he was going, but usually in such a genially vague fashion that the conversation would naturally turn in a different direction.

Fiona knew enough to be worried. He worked for an international energy company. She knew he was in dangerous places, and during those times when he was out of communication, she read the news with a nameless dread lurking somewhere between her heart and her stomach, expecting at any minute to see his face or hear his voice in a hostage video.

But their time together was so precious that dwelling on

ugly and even terrifying things felt wasteful, and so she did not pursue her questions, and he did not volunteer anything. When the subject of his departure arose, it was always with a regretful matter-of-factness. Fiona was not one to cling and weep, and Pete had an air of earnest good spirits that seemed unbreakable. His departure, nevertheless, began to loom for them both.

On their last night, they followed what had become their pattern: a long walk along the shoreline, watching as the day slowly dissolved into the horizon, the deepening colors of sky and water revealing the slow turning of the earth. The days were still lengthening, and the night came slowly. The soft breezes of early summer refreshed without cooling, and created a churn in the water. The lavenders of winter sunsets had shifted to rose, and the color of the lake moved to a darkening blue. There would still be another hour of light.

They walked together, talking in low voices, occasionally lapsing into silence. The lake was deserted except for one boat about a half a mile from shore, and it appeared to be moored there. They were fishing, perhaps.

At some point, as she spoke, Fiona became aware that there was a light flashing from the boat. Pete stopped to watch, holding up his hand for her to be silent. He was still for less than a minute.

"Fiona, do you have a signal?"

She looked down at her phone. "Yes."

"Call the Coast Guard." He was already kicking off his shoes, stripping off his shirt, and wading into the water. "Tell them it's a medical emergency. Tell them where you are."

As she began dialing, he dove into the water and began

swimming out to the boat. She spoke rapidly to the officer on the line while watching anxiously for the sight of Pete's head above the waves. She knew he could swim, but to be able to swim well enough in these circumstances would not be easy. It was a daunting distance, and the water was rough from the wind.

It seemed an eternity had passed when at last she saw a silhouetted figure rise out of the water and fling himself up the boat's ladder. Fifteen minutes later she heard the sound of the coast guard helicopter. She watched from the shore as the complexities of the rescue were completed. As the helicopter flew off to Green Bay, she could just catch the sight of Pete waving his arms. Somehow, she understood—even before the Coast Guard called her to let her know—that he was piloting the boat back to Detroit Harbor.

She got into the car and drove to the private marina, arriving only a few minutes before Pete guided the boat into a slip. A Coast Guard cutter was already there.

Fiona greeted Pete with all the cool casualness she could muster. He put his arm around her shoulder and squeezed hard. He was quite wet and smelled of lake water, but she buried her face into him, all of her frozen feelings thawing and rising to the surface.

The coast guard guys were there to shake Pete's hand and get more details for their report. Fiona knew one of them vaguely, and he was highly complimentary of Pete's efforts.

"Guy was a non-breather," he said. "We wouldn't have made it in time," he told Fiona. "Good thing he knew what to do."

Fiona nodded. "Why didn't they radio?"

"Some kind of system failure. Guess he was working on it when it happened. Electrical shock."

Pete gave the details to the Coast Guard with simplicity and clarity. Whereas most people would have had some impression of the extraordinary nature of these events, he seemed to take them utterly in stride, as if it were all in a day's work.

Suddenly it dawned on her that it was.

Fiona looked at him as if seeing him for the first time. She felt shaken to the core. When he had waded out into the water, she had felt sure she would be forced to watch him drown. All that fear, which she had not been able to acknowledge at the time, was washing over her in waves. She began to tremble.

But there was something else. There was something important about Pete that she didn't know, and now that frightened her, too. It was terrifying to see someone she loved put his life on the line like this, and for some reason she didn't quite understand, it made her angry.

At last, he finished his conversations, and with the coast guard blanket around his shoulders, he walked back toward her.

"Are you okay?"

Pete nodded. "I'm getting old, though. That was harder than it used to be."

Fiona studied him as if there were some answer etched on his face. "Was that Morse code?"

Pete caught her look and nodded. He seemed wary and subdued.

"Where did you learn that?"

"I was an odd child," he said, trying to be jovial.

"You didn't answer my question."

Pete, sensing her mood, dropped his usual playful demeanor.

"Yes, I did, actually. I memorized it when I was about nine, practicing on my desk to the annoyance of my History teacher. Anyway, lots of people know Morse code, including the woman on that boat. She saved her husband's life with it. I'll bet Pali knows it. And Ben, too. Besides, I work for an oil company with enterprises in remote places all over the world. You have to have basic survival skills. Morse code is an essential part of that."

"That was a remarkable swim."

He shrugged. "Anyone could have done it."

"No," she said. "Not anyone."

There was a stillness in Fiona that made it seem as if every word echoed in her head. "There is more," she said. "There is more that you're not telling me."

He held her gaze, but said nothing. Her heart twisted with fear and frustration. Why did he not trust her? Why could he not say who he was?

Suddenly Fiona could see in her mind's eye the first evening she had met him. She remembered his drawing room manners, the universally attentive smile, the ability to step into a group of strangers and make them laugh. But her mind zeroed in on one particular image. The last view she had had of him on that long, tantalizing, and disappointing evening: their exchange of glances as he left the room, and the swift, crisp, military salute that had been his parting gesture.

"Let's deal with this later. I need food. And then we'll talk."

Without a word, Fiona got into the car and started the engine. Pete got in beside her. It was a long, silent drive home.

Ben had gone up to bed, and Nika and Pali were sitting on the back porch, enjoying the June evening's long hours of sunlight. They sat together for a while in amiable silence, listening to the birdsong.

"There were some officers' positions listed on the Association website today. I sent my resume to a few places."

Nika was silent.

Pali wasn't looking at her as he spoke. "We'll see if anything comes of it."

He stole a glance at her now. She was seemingly engrossed in the view, but she nodded, her lips tight. He put his hand out, and she took it.

They sat watching the waning sunlight until the mosquitoes drove them inside and to an early bed.

In his own room, Ben lay awake in shock. His open window was directly above the porch, and he had heard his father's quiet conversation. So, it was true. His father was going to lose his job. Why else would he be looking for another one? Caleb's power to harm was now elevated to a new order of magnitude.

A tight knot of dread coiled itself in Ben's stomach, and reached up to his heart.

Fiona and Pete were sitting over the remains of dinner at the kitchen table. The meal had been unusually quiet. Seething with emotion, Fiona was unable to eat. At last she broached the subject, as he had known she would.

"So," said Fiona, ever so casually. "I have a question."

Pete nodded and took a deep breath without looking at her. "Shoot."

"Where did you learn to do what you did tonight?"

He turned to her, his eyes veiled. He had not been looking forward to this conversation.

"Through my work."

"What exactly is your work?"

"I fix things."

"What things?"

He paused, smiled apologetically and looked sheepish. "All kinds of things."

"For whom?"

He looked at her and took a deep breath, but Fiona was already speaking.

"When will you tell me the truth?" The shock and fear of the last hours were churning inside her, and now found their outlet in an anger she did not recognize and could not explain.

Pete was silent for a moment, his lips compressed into a tight line, his eyes searching hers. "I will tell you this truth: I love you. And you are going to have to trust me."

"I don't know if that's possible," said Fiona coldly.

"I hope that's not true," he said, quietly. "But if it is, I can't fix it. Trust is all we have right now."

"I would say it is the one thing we don't have at all."

She could see his eyes change. She had hurt him. She felt instantly sorry, and wanted to throw herself against him, to apologize. But she did not.

There was a long silence. Pete looked first into her eyes, and then, when she wouldn't look back, he looked off and stared into space.

Fiona rose to clear the table, and he rose, too.

Without being asked, he slept in the guest room that night.

Chapter Fifteen

*F*iona dreamed that her grandmother was still alive. In her dream, her grandmother was a tall, slender woman with short white hair, and she wore a deep gray dress that accentuated her slimness. They were in the same room together, and Fiona could see her smiling and talking with other people, but she didn't see Fiona, and Fiona couldn't seem to get to her. Fiona wanted desperately to touch her, to speak with her. She tried calling to her, but her voice couldn't be heard above the other conversations in the room. Fiona tried to cross the room, but each time she made progress through the crowd, her grandmother had drifted further away. Fiona saw her grandmother leave, and, desperate to follow her, she pushed her way through the crowd, out into a long, dim, hallway with a bright light in the distance.

At first her grandmother seemed to have disappeared, but then Fiona saw her, walking steadily, alone, down the hallway that seemed infinitely long. There was just enough light to see her silhouette as she went further away. Fiona was starting to follow her when she realized that it was too late. Her grandmother had almost reached her apartment along the hall, and Fiona knew that once her grandmother walked through that door, she would never see her again. She stood, helplessly, watching as her grandmother walked on into eternity.

The next morning, Fiona watched as Pete silently packed his few belongings. She made a bland offer of breakfast, but he declined.

In what seemed like no time at all he was standing by the door in the front hall, his bag at his feet. Fiona stood there, too: silent, desolate, and cold.

"I don't like to leave like this. But I have to go. Do you want to see me again?"

"I don't know," she said. "I don't know who you are."

"Actually," he said, "you know more now than you did before. But before you didn't mind."

"Now I do."

With a short, resigned nod, Pete picked up his bag and turned to go. His face was serious, his eyes sorrowful.

"If you are ever in trouble, call me."

He walked out the door. Fiona had half expected that he wouldn't leave. She stood frozen in place, watching him go down the path to his car. She heard the trunk, then the car doors, and the engine start. She stood in the hall until the sound of the engine faded to nothing. She imagined his drive along the curving wooded road to the ferry. She saw the ferry men waving him onto the boat, the chocks placed against the wheels, the gangway drawn up, the ropes untied. She could see the progress of the little boat crossing Death's Door, taking him away from her forever.

Suddenly weak, she sat on the floor and held her head in her hands. She sat like this, silent and dry-eyed, without any sense of time.

Chapter Sixteen ✦

It was early evening when Fiona finally stood up from the floor and looked around as if she were in a strange place. Propelled by some inner self-preservation, she grabbed a jacket and her keys and headed to the ferry. She responded woodenly to the friendly greetings of the crew, and sat staring out the windshield of her car all through the crossing.

Hers was the first car off, and she drove past Ground Zero in Ephraim, directly to Elisabeth and Roger's place.

She pulled up in front of the porch, and before she could get out, Elisabeth and Rocco, having heard the car, were at the door. Rocco leapt with joy to see Fiona, but she could only put out her hand and vaguely pat his head as she walked up the steps.

"Lizzie," said Fiona.

Elisabeth took one look at Fiona's face. "What's happened?"

Fiona was suddenly crying deep childish sobs. "I don't know. I don't know what happened. He's gone. He's gone."

Elisabeth held her friend in her arms and rocked her like a baby. Rocco, terrified by this storm of emotion, leapt frantically to reach Fiona's face with his.

"Rocco!" commanded Elisabeth. But he would not be quiet until he could touch Fiona's face, and finally, they succumbed to his urgency, and the two women sat on the floor of the porch to let the big dog lick Fiona's face, as he pressed himself against her, trying every means of deep canine consolation he could summon.

"He's gone," said Fiona quietly, holding Rocco in her arms now, comforting him and herself. "He left this morning."

"But this has been planned all along. He's coming back," said Elisabeth, pretending calm.

"I don't think he is. I don't think he's ever coming back."

"Why?" asked Elisabeth, distraught. "Why do you say that?"

Fiona began crying so hard that Elisabeth could barely make out her words. "I was so scared, and then so angry. I was terrible. I was terrible to him."

Elisabeth held her friend with her arm around her shoulder and stared off over into the distance. This couldn't be. Pete adored Fiona. He would never leave her.

"What, exactly, happened?" she asked, stroking Fiona's hair. "Tell me everything."

Chief Gil had come to a decision. It was clear to him that the town board was not going to allocate any more funding. The tiny increase that had been conceded at the meeting would not begin to cover the requirements of the fire department. Deep down, he had known that there was an option he could exercise if he had to, but he had told himself that it would never come to that.

Now, he realized, he had no choice: either the town board would reinstate his budget to the proper levels, or he would have to resign. Gravely, and with a deep reluctance, he sat down to write a letter outlining his position.

When he had finished, he sat back to think. It was a letter to the chairman of the town board, but it was also a letter to the community. Nodding to himself, he printed out two copies: one for Chairman Fiona Campbell, and the second for the Island newspaper. He inserted each copy into an envelope, and wrote the addresses in his precise penmanship. He would deliver them tonight. Grimly, envelopes in hand, he got into his truck, and headed off to finish his unhappy task.

After her storm of weeping, Fiona was enveloped in a deep silence. Roger, whose attempts at consolation were both touching and ineffectual, escaped to the living room. Rocco lay under the table at Fiona's feet, just close enough to be felt. Elisabeth made coffee for her, which Fiona couldn't drink, and dinner, which she couldn't eat. She poured a scotch, which Fiona did not touch. After sitting together at the kitchen table in silence for a long time, Elisabeth took charge. "Go and take a long bath. You'll feel better."

Obediently, almost robotically, Fiona went into the bathroom, and Elisabeth could hear the sound of the water running. But after Fiona had been there for more than an hour Elisabeth began to feel somewhat alarmed.

She knocked gently on the door. "Fiona, are you all right?"

"Yes," said Fiona, who was not all right.

Elisabeth, standing by the door, felt overwhelmed by a sense of helplessness. Grief had its own rhythm and its own time. It would be very hard for Fiona to go back to the Island now and be alone. Something had to be done.

My parents always took us on vacations in the summer. I remember the water; the waves; the pull of the undertow. Most of all I remember the fires. Every night on the beach, my father would build a fire. My mother told me they were so big that they would be seen by the ships out on the lake.

I remember one night. The flames were over my head. They were over my father's head. The smell of smoke perfumed the night air. The logs would sometimes scream and whistle as they burned. My father said it was because they were wet, but to me it sounded like the tree was screaming. I cried for the souls of the trees but I still loved the ferocity of the flames. Their cruelty frightened me, but I did not look away while they consumed whatever came to them.

My mother spread out a blanket on the sand.

I looked up and saw the white stars, and the hot red sparks from the fire drifting up to meet them, the feel of the fire hot on one side of my face, the cold of the wind on the other. But even in the sound of the wind and the lake, the wild singing of the fire was in my ears until I slept.

Chapter Seventeen ✥

Chief Gil had planned that Fiona—the chairman of the town board—and the editors at the newspaper would open their copies of his letter at more or less the same time. It had not occurred to him that Fiona might be away from the Island, so when the letter arrived at her house, there was no one there to open it. As a result, his official notice was received at the newspaper before it was read by anyone in the local government.

One of the advantages of life-long residency—which is also one of the disadvantages—is that you know everyone. Stella DesRosiers, who had been born on the Island in the small bungalow that had been the midwife's house, had roots deeper than the cedar trees on School House Beach.

It wasn't long after the envelope had been opened at the newspaper office before Stella received a phone call. What she heard about the chief gave her great satisfaction. Circumstances were playing right into her hands.

Ever since her devastatingly close loss in the election for chairman of the town board, Stella DesRosiers had been stewing in humiliation. She rarely left the house, and attended no community events. It had been a bitter pill to lose to any newcomer, but particularly to one she so thoroughly despised.

Because her defeat had been so close, however, along with the humiliation there also came empowerment.

It had been a tied vote, and Fiona Campbell had won by only a coin toss, so Stella knew she had a perfect occasion for mischief. She had, at least in theory, half the Island's support. All she needed to do was to find some flaw in the new administration, and she could rally her supporters to action. She could attack her former opponent's honesty, efficacy, policies, or morals. It didn't much matter which.

It is fair to say that Stella DesRosiers was not a happy woman. Perhaps, like the Grinch in the Dr. Seuss story, her heart was too small, or she may have had a terrible home life as a child, or, as Emily Martin frequently suggested, a hormone imbalance. But the most likely explanation came from Jake, who had known her more or less since kindergarten: she was born mean.

What her inner life might be like was difficult to determine, but her outer life was plain for all to see. Fiona Campbell's best friend, Elisabeth, was still convinced that Stella had set the fire that had burned Fiona's barn to the ground and created various goat-related mysteries, and in this realm Fiona herself had her own suspicions, none of which could be proved, but all of which were brought out and examined in great detail by the two women privately after a drink or two had been consumed.

Everyone on the Island, however, knew that Stella had set out to drive Fiona from the Island, first by spreading rumors about her morals, then by bringing the power of local government against her, and then by attempting to wrest control of this same local government to ensure that its decisions were anti-Fiona—all while still spreading rumors about her morals.

It could be no surprise then, to discover that, despite having failed in all of the above, Stella had not given up. She was perfectly pleased about the looming crisis at the fire department. It was exactly the sort of thing she needed to put to her advantage.

Despite the beauties of the Island's light and air, Stella had spent the evening in her little house with the windows closed and the blinds drawn. Her plans to thwart Fiona Campbell were not yet fully formed, but she could sense her opportunity. To assume that she had withdrawn from public life to resume a quiet place in the community would be to deny a fundamental fact of Island life: if the Island was Eden, Stella was most certainly the snake.

Chapter Eighteen

Emily Martin was in a hurry. She needed only a couple of things from the grocery store, and she planned to acquire them quickly and get on with her day. She was zooming through the store at her usual speed, when she nearly ran into Stella DesRosiers, whose cart was blocking the canned goods aisle. Stella looked up, her face its usual mask of sullen challenge.

There was no love lost between Emily Martin and Stella DesRosiers. Stella had an instinctive distaste for all newcomers, and she did not hesitate to show it. She was also fully aware that Emily Martin had been an open and very outspoken advocate in the election for Fiona, in opposition to Stella, herself.

Had any of this not been the case, Stella would still have despised Emily Martin for her unapologetic bossiness, and for Emily's confident belief that she had all the answers. And since it is so often true that people tend to dislike those who share their own most notable traits, Stella's animosity toward Emily was magnified. Although she was not conscious of it, this similarity between them, perhaps most of all, was what Stella could not abide.

Stella, however, like all manipulative people, had a gift for understanding the emotions and motivations of others. Emily

Martin, she knew, had a desperate need to be liked, and this, to Stella, was the weak spot she intended to exploit.

Emily, in her mix of tornadic activity and self-absorption, tended not to notice the feelings of anyone else, and so was at a disadvantage. She imagined herself respected for her worldly experience and good advice, and she could be easily convinced that Stella wanted to be friends because it was something Emily herself wanted.

It further worked to Stella's advantage that Emily's support for Fiona in the election had been primarily because she believed that Fiona could be more easily influenced. As she slowly realized that this wasn't going to be true, Emily's enthusiasm for Fiona dissipated. This made her even more vulnerable to Stella's snare.

Stella had quickly rearranged her expression into something resembling a smile. "Hello, Emily," she said, with unwonted cordiality. If she had had a tail, she would have been swishing it.

"Hello, Stella," said Emily, a bit primly, and instinctively wary.

"Terrible situation with the fire department, isn't it?" asked Stella, in a seductive tone. "I can't imagine how all this will end."

Emily nodded earnestly, slipping easily into the trap. "Such a shame! And so dangerous, too."

Stella pretended to look puzzled. "We all put our faith into our politicians. It *is* a shame, isn't it, that they can't be trusted with something as basic as fire and emergency service?"

"Exactly. What's the government for, if not for that?" Emily raised her eyebrows indignantly. She was enjoying this opportunity to bond over a common outrage. Stella really was much nicer than she had realized.

"Who do you suppose is to blame for the situation?" asked Stella, coyly.

Emily looked around quickly and lowered her voice, pleased to be asked. "Well, I will tell you that I warned Fiona Campbell about this problem, but she wouldn't listen. She just didn't want to hear it."

Stella nodded sagely. "Yes, I've heard that, too. It really is too bad, isn't it?"

"Oh yes. Absolutely." Emily shook her head sadly. "You know," she said, after a moment, "I have rather extensive experience in public office, but she just won't take my advice. And I have so many ideas!"

"I knew you would," said Stella smoothly. "That's why I was so pleased to see you this morning."

It was some time before Emily emerged from the grocery store and hurried on to her appointments. Stella followed soon after, looking smugly self-satisfied.

Emily drove off feeling she had made a new friend.

Fiona dreamed they were digging up trees by the roots. It was night, and the sky was filled with stars. It was cold. They went all around the yard with shovels and pulled them out, flinging the roots far away into a pile in the corner of the yard. It was not difficult work; the roots came away easily in their hands,

like pulling weeds. Finally, they had to go inside. They were being called by a distant voice Fiona did not know.

There was one tree left; one root. But someone had already put the tools away, and Fiona had to work alone. She knelt to the ground and began digging it out with her hands. This one was not easy like the others, and she dug deeper and deeper into the earth, until finally she realized that she had made a deep hole, and she was standing in the bottom of it. She looked up to see the sky with its shimmering stars, and she knew she could not get out. Oddly resigned, she stood at the bottom of the hole with towering sides, her hands covered with dirt, looking up at the sky and its impossibly distant stars.

After Fiona had dressed, Elisabeth insisted that they go out together to Ground Zero.

"It will be good for you to see old friends, and Mike and Terry are likely to be there."

"But my face," said Fiona, gazing at her swollen eyes in the mirror. "I can't go out like this."

"You look fine," said Elisabeth, lying valiantly.

The truth was, Elisabeth was nearly as devastated by Pete's departure as Fiona, but she hadn't the least idea what to do to help. At the shop there would be other people to comfort and advise. Mike and Terry were very fond of Fiona, and they would, she had no doubt, rise to the occasion in some form of masculine solace, even if it took the form of teasing and jokes.

Even Roger had a certain comforting quality, like a surly but loyal dog. She crossed her fingers that they would all be there. She couldn't very well cart Fiona around the peninsula like a parcel, but sitting here and talking about Pete would be the worst possible decision.

Chapter Nineteen ❖

Terry had been struggling with his new commitment to yoga. Months of morning practice with Roger and the Angel Joshua at Ground Zero had brought some improvement to his health, and he felt better: energized, and stronger. But, Terry had to admit that his grace and balance were not particularly noteworthy.

To be fair, this was not entirely Terry's fault. Roger's unconventional music choices could be distracting—even jarring—and they had a way of throwing off Terry's balance.

Write-ups in national publications had attributed Roger's use of Beethoven, Wagner—and others of the more tempestuous of the classical composers—to a deliberate attempt by Roger to encourage focus. But Terry—who knew him well— suspected that Roger was merely impervious to the music's effects, and therefore unaware that any sudden changes in dynamics might prove a distraction.

This morning the challenge had been particularly difficult. Roger had chosen Richard Strauss's *Ein Heldenleben*. The music—as Terry admitted to himself in tolerant understatement—was not within his grasp. It seemed to him just jumbles of orchestral noise. It jarred and jumped, lulled and pounced with such ferocity and unpredictability that Terry found himself falling out of every balance pose.

Halfway through class, Terry—whose struggles to stay upright had been as heroic as the music—tottered and collapsed, trying not to land on his classmates. His efforts, however, were in vain, and an entire row of Lutheran men in sweatpants went down like dominoes. There was no swearing, only a few grunts, and some mild words of repressed Lutheran frustration.

As was so often the case, Roger went serenely on, oblivious to any of the tumult around him. Sheepishly, Terry recovered himself, muttered apologies to the guy nearest him, and went on. The row of Lutherans returned to yogic rectitude, and the practice continued as the music crashed onward.

Joshua, whose angelic forbearance was always notable, was helpless to call out his usual warnings because the music was both unfamiliar and seemingly erratic. Its moments of sweet lyricism were so suddenly interrupted by German bombast that there was simply no time to prepare the unsuspecting.

After class, there was the usual manly teasing, which Terry bore with good humor. Joshua waited until most of the others had left, and approached Terry at the counter, pouring him a fresh cup of coffee.

"I've been watching you in class, and I think I see what you're doing wrong."

Terry smiled wryly. "Do tell."

"I don't think you have a sense of your body in space. You think you're evenly balanced, but you're actually leaning to one side. It makes you more vulnerable to falling."

"So, what do you suggest?"

"I'm not sure," said Joshua, tossing his long blond locks in a characteristic gesture. "What you need is a mirror—a way for you to see yourself and make your own corrections."

Terry regarded him with a mixture of respect and lively interest. He hadn't immediately taken to Joshua, but the guy, he had to admit, had grown on him.

Joshua's face was suddenly ablaze with inspiration.

"I know! I'll video you. I'll stay out of class tomorrow and record you, and you can watch and see what you're doing wrong."

Terry acknowledged the idea with pursed lips and a slow nod. "That could work," he said. "Sure you wouldn't mind?"

Joshua shook his head definitively, his hair gleaming in the sunlight. "Not at all."

"Well," said Terry. "Thanks. That would be great."

"No worries, man," said Joshua. "Glad I can help." He beamed with his heavenly aura.

Privately, Terry wasn't sure whether it would help at all, but he was willing to try.

Chapter Twenty

B y the time Elisabeth had gotten Fiona to Ground Zero, the daily yoga practice had finished, and although the shop was still more crowded than Fiona had remembered, there was, by this time of the morning, a place to sit. Mike had joined Terry and, having been alerted by Elisabeth that their presence was required, they were still sitting at the counter. Each, by now, was well past the usual time of departure, and far beyond their daily allotment of coffee.

They greeted Fiona with a hearty male casualness that was designed both to cajole and to protect against feminine tears.

Mike patted the stool for Fiona to sit between them, and Elisabeth, somewhat relieved to be off-duty, sat next to Terry. Mike smiled his benevolent smile at Fiona, and patted her hand affectionately.

"It's been a while since we've seen you," began Terry. "Had your breakfast yet?"

Fiona smiled weakly and shook her head. Joshua approached to take orders.

"Two more coffees," said Terry. "And how about an egg sandwich for Fiona, here. She looks hungry."

In fact, Fiona looked vaguely ill, but in Terry's view, food was what fixed things. Terry was fond of Fiona, and it was clear she needed fixing.

Utterly without appetite, she accepted his kindness for its intentions.

Mike sat silent and sympathetic. The Angel Joshua gently set Fiona's favorite café au lait before her. Roger hovered and bumbled nearby.

Fiona bestirred herself. They were good friends, and she must stop thinking of herself. To do otherwise would be churlish. "It's been too long since I've sat here with you. I've missed you all. Tell me the news."

There was a moment as they paused to collect their thoughts, looking for something to say that would be appropriate to the occasion. Surprisingly, it was Roger who spoke first.

"He'll be back," he said authoritatively.

Elisabeth and the others were horrified into perfect stillness. They had all been trying not to mention anything that could be painful, particularly not Pete's departure, and besides, there was absolutely no good response to this. Who knew what had actually happened or whether he would return? Should they say he wouldn't be back? Should they encourage Fiona in false hopes?

Fiona, however, smiled a small smile and reached out to touch Roger on the arm.

"Thank you, Roger. You are very sweet."

So far as anyone in Ground Zero knew, no one had ever said this to Roger before.

He nodded, his lips compressed, a small frown on his face. Being comforting took a great deal of effort. He had never known this about himself, but clearly, he was good at it.

"I know," he said.

Chapter Twenty-One

Nika loved watching the wild birds from her kitchen window, and she devoted time every morning to filling her many feeders with different kinds of enticing seeds, cleaning the bird bath, and making sure all was in order. It was the first thing she did after everyone left the house. Afterward, she would come back in, pour herself a second cup of coffee, and sit down to think and to plan her day. Today she sat at the kitchen table, staring out the window, watching the birds and trying to sort out the chaos in her mind.

The routine of her days was sweet for Nika. She had married the only man she had ever loved. She had a beautiful son. They lived in tranquility here on the Island. They were happy. Now Pali's plans to leave threatened everything.

Nika had grave concerns about their potential for a good life anywhere else. Both she and Pali—and now their son—had been born on the Island, and its mysteries had irrevocably entwined and enmeshed them.

In the early days of their marriage, Nika had followed Pali during his service in the Navy, and although he had been able to find solace in life at sea, she had been lonely and miserable.

She had been excited to leave at first, and had faced their

new life with joy and hope. She found a job, furnished their little apartment, and tried to be happy. But the reality of being always among strangers, away from the solitude and beauty of the Island, caught up in the rush of commuting and jostling crowds, made her feel that she had lost herself.

She tried valiantly to adjust, saying nothing to Pali about her misery. But Pali had known, and ultimately confessed to her that he felt the same. Together they had counted down the days until they could return to the Island and begin what Nika thought of as their real life together.

Nika knew that Pali's concerns about Ben were real, and that he believed he was doing the right thing. But she was not convinced that leaving the Island would be better for Ben, and she knew for certain that it would not be better for Pali and for her. She did not see how spending precious days of their lives in misery could be preparation for anything except more misery.

She thought about Ben's recent moods and the phone call from school, and she tried to be honest with herself. Did Ben need a bigger school with different friends? Would it be better to get a fresh start? How would she endure being separated again from her parents, and Pali's, and from her own friends? Would that be better for her family, for Ben?

Nika frowned and watched as a woodpecker flung seeds to the ground. She wished she knew what she should do.

That afternoon, despite Elisabeth's insistence that she stay, Fiona made up her mind to go home to the Island.

"I have a job to do," she told Elisabeth.

"Do you want me to come and stay with you for a while?"

"Don't be silly," said Fiona.

Inside, she dreaded returning to the house where Pete no longer was. The pain of it seemed beyond bearing. But Fiona was no coward.

Elisabeth studied her friend's face and made a decision. "I'm sorry, but you're being overruled. Rocco and I are going to come up for a few days."

Fiona tried to protest, but Elisabeth was firm. "No. I'll call Christine, make sure she has everything she needs at the gallery, and follow you up on a later ferry."

Meekly—and gratefully—Fiona acquiesced.

Fiona did not open the envelope from Chief Gil when she returned home that afternoon. She did not answer her phone, nor did she listen to her voice mail, even though she could see that it was overflowing. She was putting one foot in front of the other. She had driven herself home. She had walked into the empty house. But beyond that, she merely sat dully, not even thinking. It was as if her normally active mind had simply turned itself off. Pete's absence seemed to echo off the walls. She had no capacity left.

After Elisabeth arrived that night, they sat together on

Fiona's porch, rocking. A massive storm was moving in, and the wind was picking up. A dim rumbling could be heard in the distance, and the clouds were both ominous and beautiful.

Elisabeth put a glass in Fiona's hand.

"What is this?"

"'Just the juice of a few flowers.' "

Fiona took it, feeling fortunate that Elisabeth had ignored her and come to stay. She was feeling much less steady than she had anticipated. Of course, where Elisabeth went, there, too, went Rocco, and he was another source of solace.

During this crisis the big dog shepherded Fiona by his proximity, and now lay across her feet, his intuition engaged in assessing her moods. He seemed to be dozing, but he was fully on duty, prepared to comfort and protect as proof of his love. At the sound of the distant thunder, he would open his eyes briefly to gauge the danger, his long ears like antenna searching for a signal and, finding nothing to concern him, would close his eyes again, the sound of his deep breaths making a reassuring background to the conversation. Fiona gently moved her bare feet more securely beneath his softness and warmth.

That night, when they went upstairs, Rocco excused himself from his usual place at the foot of Elisabeth's bed, and moved noiselessly with his wolfish gait into Fiona's room. Touched by his attention, she invited him by patting the bed. After a moment's thought he jumped up and stretched himself out along the length of her body, not crowding, only touching.

The storm seemed to circle the Island all night, rolling in fury overhead, the lightning leaping in the sky, the thunder shaking the house. But, Rocco stayed unflinching by her side, warm and comforting, until morning.

Chapter Twenty-Two

A slim, mouse-colored young man stepped off the morning ferry. He was in his thirties and travelling alone, dressed in a pair of ironed blue jeans, a button collar shirt, a blue fleece jacket, and polished brown oxfords. He had with him a small, black rolling suitcase, of the size that would fit in an airline overhead compartment. His neat appearance was augmented by a rather fussy manner, and a tendency to take small, quick steps, which made him seem like a cartoon character doing an impersonation of a school marm.

Carefully, he placed his return ticket into a precise position in his wallet, slipped the wallet into an inner pocket, and zipped his jacket. Apparently satisfied with these arrangements, he adjusted his glasses and looked around.

He saw the ferry offices, a pizza place—apparently closed—a garage with bicycle rentals, a gift shop—also closed—and… that was about it. He had known this was a small community, but this seemed below all expectations. One of the ferry crew walked past him on his way to the office.

"Excuse me."

The crewman stopped and looked at the newcomer curiously.

"Is there a taxi service available?"

The crewman smiled, but did not laugh. "Sometimes. But you can rent a bicycle if you want."

The look on the newcomer's face was one of polite surprise. "How far is it to walk?"

"Depends on where you want to go." The reply was not intended to be rude.

This stumped the visitor. He really hadn't any idea where he wanted to go. He had assumed that getting to the village hall—or whatever it was called—would be obvious once he arrived.

"I'm looking for the town chairman—er...woman. Ms. Fiona Campbell? I understand there's an administrative position available." He held up a well-read copy of the Island newspaper, *The Observer,* folded to reveal the Help Wanteds.

The ferryman frowned, puzzled. He doubted whether anyone had expected that some outsider would just show up asking for the job. "Come on into the office," he said at last. "Heather's working today. She'll know what you should do."

He led the way to the ferry office, Oliver Robert walking behind him with his quick little steps. The crewman was too polite to express his thoughts, which were that this strange little man would not make a good fit on the Island.

"Oh well," he thought. "Not my problem."

Ben's worries about his father and leaving the Island had multiple dimensions. His guilt that his feud with Caleb might cost his father his job was of a kind he had never before experienced. His father and his mother trusted him. They believed in him, and he felt in some way that they needed to be protected. To capitulate to Caleb's bullying seemed beyond enduring, but if he, Ben, could keep his parents from humiliation, then he must do so. And yet, they were already thinking of leaving. His father was looking for a job. Had Caleb already begun to make good on his threat? Was there any way back to where this whole thing had started?

There was still another worry, even harder, that he barely knew how to think about. In the spring, he had had an encounter with an unseen something that felt like a voice in his head, a hand on his shoulder. It had led him to safety, found him help, and kept him steady in a crisis. He had no word for what it was, but he knew that it was real.

As young as he was, Ben knew instinctively that this experience was strange and rare, and not to be taken lightly. He had spoken to his father of what had happened only once, but his father had seemed to understand. Would he understand if Ben told him that leaving was out of the question? Would his father and mother force him to leave the Island and forsake this communication? Or was the whole thing now in Caleb's grubby hands? If Ben left the Island, would the presence that he trusted, that he so often felt on his walks, follow him? Or would it be lost to him forever? Ben spent many hours thinking through this problem, but the more he thought, the more tangled his thoughts became.

On the morning after her return home, Fiona decided she had better tackle the messages and mail that had accumulated in her absence. Elisabeth had risen early, made coffee and breakfast for them both, and, after assuring herself that Fiona wasn't going to throw herself off the roof, she and Rocco had gone off for a walk.

Quickly flipping through the pile of mail and tossing away the junk, Fiona turned first to the hand-addressed envelope containing Chief Gil's letter. After she read it, she sat staring out the window.

She should have seen this coming, she told herself. She had been so distracted. But, really, could anyone have predicted that the chief would go this far? Fiona thought through all of the implications, including his own liability should anything go wrong. She had to admit that she would not want to be in his position. Come to think of it, she wasn't all that keen on the position she was in, either.

She frowned, thinking about the problem. One thing was certain: she would need to go down to the office this morning and take another look at that budget, and she needed to return all those urgent calls that had come in while she'd been gone. People would be wondering what she was doing about the situation. At the moment, she had no idea.

She poured herself another cup of coffee and went upstairs to dress. It was a relief to be thinking about something besides Pete.

With the new crisis in Island affairs, Stella knew she must immediately embark upon re-establishing her presence in the community. It was the first rule of politics, and Stella, though unpleasant, was no fool.

And so, it was by a combination of design and luck that on the very day that she had decided to re-engage, she encountered her first break. Just as she was walking into the ferry office to pick up a package, Stella found herself face-to-face with the new applicant for the clerking job in the office of the town chairman. She lost no time in introducing herself.

Chapter Twenty-Three

After returning her various phone calls, Fiona turned with renewed desperation to evaluating the budget. She had to find more money to keep this fire department problem from worsening. What would she do if the chief carried out his threat? After spending her morning pouring over town finances, she was beginning to despair of finding anything to cut. The budget had been pared back so often over the years that the expenditures allotted were not keeping up with inflation.

She had shifted away from the option of relatively mindless across-the-board cuts, and was digging now into individual categories. It wasn't as if the Island had a massive bureaucracy with huge outlays for trivialities. These were lists of essentials.

She was engrossed in yet another scavenger hunt through the numbers when she heard the outer door open and footsteps coming down the hall. She sighed. She was in no mood to deal with anybody. She prayed that it wasn't Emily Martin.

Following The Angel Joshua's suggestion that Roger improve his marriage by exploring his feminine side, yoga had become both a foundation of Roger's life, personally, and, at the same time, a rather large nuisance. Roger, who fully acknowledged his inability to fathom the usual human emotions, was willing to do almost anything to please Elisabeth, and yoga seemed worth a try. He had not anticipated, however, how this simple decision would have such a wide-ranging impact.

His morning practice at the shop, which he had begun only for himself, had become a major draw in the tiny town of Ephraim, bringing crowds, traffic, and a mostly welcome boost to the local economy. Yoga-themed merchandise in the shops and get-away packages at the Inns had become a village-wide trend.

Roger had not sought out the yoga tourists, who were, largely, creatures of the culture of novelty. They had merely appeared as if by magic after a few unexpected reviews of his yoga practice in major newspapers and magazines. But Roger's little coffee shop, Ground Zero, simply didn't have the capacity for the crowds of people who were showing up, and Roger wasn't interested in expanding. He couldn't do much to discourage the participation of the Lutheran Men's Prayer Group in his morning practice—Lutherans, he had learned, could be both determined and persistent—but he needed somehow to divert the out-of-town yoga traffic away from Ground Zero. Frankly, he didn't care where.

He supposed it would have to involve some kind of marketing. This sort of endeavor was alien to Roger. He really had no idea how to begin.

The morning after their conversation, Joshua recorded Terry during their practice, and after the shop had emptied, they sat down together at the counter to watch the video.

Terry, unencumbered by vanity, watched with interest.

"See that?" Joshua stopped the video and went back. "You have all your weight on your right side. Now watch what happens."

"I know what happens," said Terry peevishly. "I was there."

Nevertheless, he watched himself attempt the pose and fall over.

Mike peered over Terry's shoulder to watch. "Not graceful, is it?"

"You try it sometime," said Terry indignantly. "It's harder than it looks."

Mike maintained a diplomatic silence and reached for his coffee.

"Okay," said Joshua, who was absorbed in his task, searching the recording for telling examples. "Let's look at this." He stopped the video again and replayed it. "See this? You need to take more time to center yourself before moving into the pose. You're in too much of a hurry."

"It's hard not to be in a hurry with that music. Sounds as if there's a war going on."

It took Mike a long moment to swallow. He pretended to be absorbed in reading the menu above the counter.

Joshua nodded sympathetically. "It's the *1812 Overture*."

"Why can't he play Enya, or something?"

Joshua, who had no answer, started up the video again. Identifying Roger's musical motivations was not within the realm of his expertise.

Oliver Robert was standing in the community building, his resume on the desk where Fiona sat. She had not slept again, and there were dark circles under her eyes. Her visitor wondered whether she was ill. Perhaps this was the reason she was hiring help.

Fiona finished reading his credentials and looked him over with ill-concealed skepticism. "Won't you sit down, Mr. Robert?"

Obligingly, he sat.

Fiona had no energy for niceties, she could only forge ahead. "Forgive me for being blunt," she said, "but what possessed you to just show up without an appointment? It's a bit…" She paused to select the right word, "…unusual."

Oliver Robert paused, too, and then took a deep breath.

"I know. But I have had it with my old job, and the city, and, well, everything. I just need to get away and to make a change." He looked around at the drab little green room with its bleak compact fluorescent lighting and folding metal chairs. "Maybe not this big a change, but a change." He looked at her with a fierceness she would not have suspected he possessed.

"People are rarely what we expect," she thought to herself.

Fiona could not help but sympathize. She didn't know why he needed to escape—she hoped not from some kind of felonious behavior—but she had been in this kind of position herself: exhausted, depressed, eager to get away and start a new life, almost without caring where, or what, or how to do it. Come to think of it, she was pretty much in that position again now.

She suspected that Oliver Robert would not be an easy person to deal with, but there was something about him she rather liked. It was his self-acceptance, she decided. He didn't seem to mind that he was different, or what anyone else thought of him.

"Are you unhappy, Mr. Robert?" she asked, suddenly.

He looked her at her directly. "Desperately," he said.

Fiona nodded. She recognized that tone. There would be difficulties with the Islanders, she knew, when they learned that she had hired an outsider. But there had been no other candidates, and she needed competent help. She thought for a moment, and made her decision. "Here's the thing: I really can't offer you very much money. It's never been more than a part-time job."

"That's okay," he said. "I really don't need much money. If I did, I wouldn't have been able to quit my job and come to the Island."

Fiona felt she had been touched by fairy dust. "I'll tell you what," she said. "I'm not convinced that you're going to like it here on the Island, I don't know whether we'll get along well, and I hesitate to make a commitment until we've had a chance to get to know one another and you get to know life on the Island. It's…not for everybody. I'm not even sure it's for me, for that matter," she added, thinking immediately that she should not have said something that could get around the Island in less time than it would take her to walk home.

"But here's what I propose: Let's agree to a trial period. Maybe a series of trial periods. We'll start with a month. If you can find a place to live, and feel happy about being here, we'll sign up for another month together. At the end of six months, if we still like one another, we'll make it permanent."

Oliver Robert nodded carefully, his lips pursed. "Yes. That makes sense."

"It's all off when we do the background check and it turns out you have a record, or something," said Fiona with a new, rather surprising candor. She said it lightly, but it was clear that she meant it.

He smiled at this, the first sign of humor he had shown. "We won't have to worry about that."

"Good," said Fiona.

They shook hands. "The next thing we'll have to do is find you a place to live."

"Oh, that's not a problem," said Oliver, much to Fiona's surprise. "I've found someone who needs a house-sitter."

"Oh," said Fiona, thinking that this guy worked fast, but it certainly wasn't through charm. "That makes things simple. I'll see you on Monday, then."

"What time?"

"Nine-thirty, ten, around then."

He looked disapproving. "I'll be there at eight-thirty. Will that be a problem?"

"Er…no," said Fiona. "No problem at all." He nodded politely and left. Fiona watched from the window as he walked with his funny little steps down to the bench in front of the school. A car pulled up a few minutes later that Fiona recognized. Oliver Robert got in, and they drove away together. The car belonged to Heather, down at the Ferry office.

Fiona didn't know Heather very well, but life on the Island was a tangled web, and even after her short tenure on the Island, Fiona did know something about Heather's family, her family history, and her many Island connections. Heather was Stella's cousin.

Chapter Twenty-Four

I *remember building my first fire. It was like building a house.*
There is a foundation. The bones. Then you fill in with the
smaller things. You want the fire to catch quickly and burn
slowly. You build the big things first. The things you will
burn longest. But the small things are important, too. Because
they are things that burn first.

I collected sticks and arranged them by their flammability. Big
logs first. Like a teepee. Underneath the sticks as thick as fingers.
Finger sticks. Then smaller ones. Twigs. As thick as pencils. Tiny
sticks. Bird nest sticks. Dry grass. Leaves. The things that will
catch first go last. What does that remind me of? Oh, I remember.
Yes. Yes, it reminds me of that. I don't want to think about that.
Later. I will think about that later.

Jim Freeberg finished his paperwork, sat back, and looked
around with dissatisfaction. His work space was also his
dining table, located in the small, but comfortable main
room of his house, which he had renovated with precision
and thoughtfulness. Jim's recipe for happiness almost always

included time spent out of doors, but today, the bureau-cratic necessities of his job as a ranger with the Wisconsin Department of Natural Resources had forced him inside. But it wasn't the paperwork—which was finished—or the house—which was in apple pie order—or the lack of fresh air that was bothering him.

Jim was not a particularly extroverted man. He loved his mostly solitary job, and was perfectly comfortable with his own thoughts, but there was a simple reality that he could not avoid. Jim was lonely.

Even though the general facts of his life were to his liking, he knew full well that a small, remote Island was not ideal for meeting new people, particularly not single women. There were, to be sure, a number of lovely widows, all of whom were old enough to be—at the very least— his mother, and a few less lovely women whose age was of less consequence than their temperaments.

But there was really only one woman who appeared in Jim's dreams and secret fantasies, and whose very presence could put his entire being into a state of alert. Although she was unmarried, it was widely understood that she was very much spoken for. And that woman was Fiona Campbell.

Jim took a deep breath, got up, and grabbed his jacket off the hook by the door. He knew himself well enough to know that no good could come from sitting at home alone tonight. He headed out to find some distraction at Nelsen's.

Even in the best of times, Elisabeth lived in a state of mild anxiety for Fiona. She had never understood Fiona's life on the Island, and now it seemed that it must be particularly painful and lonely. Experiencing life on the Island on a daily basis gave Elisabeth a fresh awareness of its challenges.

"How are you?" she asked sympathetically, when Fiona came home after a day of wrangling with distant bureaucrats.

"Oh," said Fiona lightly, "just another day in the slough of despond. Shall I open a bottle of wine?"

"Yes, please. So, I found out something interesting at the meat counter today. Do you know there's not one plumber on this Island? It's ridiculous. What are you supposed to do if your pipes burst?"

Fiona was rummaging in a drawer for the corkscrew as she spoke. "Funny you should mention it. We're about to launch a national campaign to recruit a plumber."

Elisabeth looked at her quizzically. "Are you serious?"

"Absolutely. I approved the wording for the advertisement just today."

Elisabeth smiled and shook her head. "Interesting that you should work first on getting a plumber when the Island also needs a doctor and a veterinarian."

"Isn't it? There's some deep life lesson immersed in there that I haven't had time to figure out."

"You actually sound pretty cheerful."

Fiona smiled her old jaunty smile. "I've hired a new assistant."

"Really?" Elisabeth was surprised. "Who?"

"A guy from Milwaukee. An accountant. Wanted to make

a fresh start." Fiona took two glasses from the china cabinet previously inhabited by zip code spiders, and opened a bottle of Bordeaux.

"A fresh start from what?" asked Elisabeth suspiciously, taking the glass Fiona offered after inspecting it for spiders. "What's he running away from?"

"Himself, I think. But he seems highly skilled and over-qualified. He's an accountant, so he's a very detail-y person."

"How many candidates were there?"

"Just him. Let's sit on the porch." She led the way, and Elisabeth followed, with the dutiful Rocco loping along behind.

"Just him?" Elisabeth was skeptical. "Shouldn't you have waited for a wider field?"

"I could wait for a wider field until I'm old and gray. I thought local people would be falling all over themselves for this position, but do you know how many applicants I've had for this job? One. There's need for work here, but not a lot of specialists, and I can't conduct a national search for a part-time job that pays almost nothing. Besides," she added, pausing to taste the wine, "someone will be bound to complain no matter what I do."

Looking almost cheerful, Fiona sat in her favorite place, on the step with her back against a column. Elisabeth took a rocking chair.

Elisabeth sighed. "I suppose you know what you're doing."

"Never suppose that," said Fiona, and she changed the subject to something less controversial.

When he got to Nelsen's, Jim was disappointed to find that Eddie was not there. Out of politeness he stayed for a beer, but after he had settled his bill, he headed back out to Eddie's place. It had been a while since they had been able to have a private conversation.

The two bachelors were not in the habit of calling before stopping by one another's houses. Both lived quite solitary lives, and they depended upon one another when the rest of the world seemed to have been divided into pairs. That each was always welcome to drop by was an unspoken understanding between them.

Eddie had a rare night off, and was looking forward to spending it doing some yard work. As a bartender at Nelsen's Hall, Eddie spent most evenings indoors. For the most part he didn't mind it, but he occasionally had a sense of missing the best part of the day.

Eddie rented his small cottage on the harbor, but he enjoyed being outside on a summer evening, so he didn't mind tending to the property. The work reminded him with pleasure of his childhood, and it had the added advantage of endearing him to his landlady.

Afterward, amid the smell of freshly mown grass, he would start a little bonfire and sit on the porch looking at the water. Although he would gladly have a drink with friends, Eddie was not much of a drinker. He had too many occasions to see his customers over-imbibe to find the condition charming.

But tonight, he told himself, he would have a beer. The stars would be out, and there was often the chance of catching the Northern Lights.

Jim pulled up as Eddie was throwing a large piece of an old cedar tree on his bonfire. The fire shot up, crackling and popping, and the sweet smell of cedar wood filled the early summer air.

Eddie greeted him with a nod, and brushed his dirty hands on the back of his jeans. "Hey. Come on up. I was just about to have a beer."

While Jim settled into one of the porch rocking chairs. Eddie disappeared into the house briefly, and returned with two bottles. He handed one to Jim, and sat down. As the fire crackled nearby, the two men rocked silently in their chairs, drinking their beers and watching the sky.

Eddie had a bartender's gift for psychological insights, and he guessed the reason for Jim's restlessness. Jim's passion for Fiona Campbell was a byword on the Island, and the hopelessness of his situation was a common topic at the grocery store's meat counter. Observers were divided into two camps: those who thought Jim was getting a bit above himself, and those who thought that he could do better. Both groups, however, viewed Jim with sympathy, if not downright pity. Their views of Fiona were more mixed.

For Eddie, stalwart friend of both, Jim's feelings would most likely lead to disappointment, and to the delay of any pursuit of a relationship with a better future. Fiona was in love with Pete Landry, who was not from the Island, and she showed no signs of changing her mind. But Eddie knew that only Jim could come to that conclusion, and nothing anyone else could say would change it.

Privately, despite his loyalty to Jim, Eddie could understand Fiona's feelings. Pete was a person whose talents would have been deemed extraordinary anywhere. On the Island, he had been regarded at first with some suspicion, as an outsider carrying the elitist whiff of the East Coast and beyond. But five minutes in a room with Pete's easy manners and his casual embrace of local customs were sufficient to change almost everyone's mind. Eddie had no trouble admitting to himself that his admiration verged on hero worship.

There was one detail of circumstance, however, that Eddie knew could work in Jim's favor. Unlike Pete, who travelled the world for his job, Jim had the advantage of being always nearby, and the value of this essential point was not lost on the pragmatic Eddie.

"Look," he had said to Jim one night at the bar, "your only chance is to make a move while she's alone; when he's not here."

"I thought you were friends with Pete."

"I am. But all's fair, man."

Jim gave him a look of frustration. "I'm not going to throw myself at her."

"No," said Eddie, calmly polishing a wine glass. "That never works anyway. But if you don't make some attempt, you'll spend the rest of your life wondering what would have happened if you'd tried." Eddie put the glass on the shelf beneath the bar, and looked Jim in the eye. "A broken heart is better than regret."

Leaving Jim to ponder this, he turned away to wait on another customer. "Believe me," he added under his breath, as he picked up another glass.

Chapter Twenty-Five

On the following Monday morning, Fiona realized at eight-fifteen that her new clerk was expecting to begin his day at eight-thirty. Throwing on a pair of jeans and a baseball cap, she jogged to the community hall, arriving just precisely at the appointed time. There was Oliver Robert, dressed in a perfectly starched and pressed shirt, waiting at the door, a handsome black leather briefcase at his feet. Fiona was fairly sure it was Italian.

"Good morning, er…Mr. Robert."

"Good morning," he said, primly.

"You know, it's funny, I used to have a goat named Robert." Inwardly she groaned at herself. This was not a way to make friends.

He made no response.

She found herself talking to fill the awkward silence as she got out her keys. "It was because it often sounded as if he were saying 'Bob'. You know, like Robert. It sounded exactly as if he were speaking." Brushing her hair out of her eyes where it was creeping out from under the baseball cap, Fiona struggled with the lock.

"May I?" asked Oliver Robert.

"What? Oh. Yes, thank you. That would be very nice."

And before she had finished the sentence, the door was open and he was politely holding it for her to enter first.

"Do people call you Oli?" she asked, babbling in a way even she despised.

"People call me Oliver. Or Mr. Robert."

Fiona shuddered. What had she been thinking in hiring this strange and difficult little man? "Well, which do you prefer?"

"I think Oliver would be best between us, Ms. Campbell."

"And you, of course, must call me Fiona."

There was a noticeable lack of response, but Fiona chattered on. "Everyone does. It's not very formal here on the Island."

"Life is short, but there is always time for courtesy," he said.

Fiona looked at him curiously, not quite knowing what to say. This was an unusual perspective these days. He reminded her of her grandmother, perhaps, in part, because of his fussiness. She decided it would be best to get on with the business at hand.

"Well, these are the files you'll be responsible for. On the top, here, are the ordinances and a list of your basic duties, but I thought you could spend the next few days familiarizing yourself with the budget. I'll be wanting your insights on that very soon."

He nodded.

"The bathroom is down the hall. Like almost everything on the Island, it's unlocked. The coffee pot is in that closet over there. Use any mug you find. They're all clean," she added hastily, seeing his face. "And here is your desk," she said, indicating the vintage steel colossus that was identical to Fiona's, and which reminded her of the one belonging to her kindergarten teacher. She was fairly sure that the chair that went with it dated to the 1960s.

Mr. Robert opened the top drawer and looked disapprovingly at the accumulated dust and grunge inside. He took out a hand sanitizer from his briefcase and ostentatiously wiped his hands.

"Dust of the ages," Fiona said, still babbling cheerfully. "Full of Island history."

He bit a corner of his lip. "I will bring my own lamp," he said, as if she hadn't said a word. He gazed at the outdated computer on the desk. "And, I think, my own laptop."

Fiona winced. "Have you worked in government before, Mr. Robert?"

"As you must know from my resume, I have not."

Fiona had, of course, known, but had been trying to be pleasant. He certainly made it difficult.

"Well, then, I should tell you that government transparency rules make that a very bad idea. You will want, for your own protection, to keep your own computer and computer files completely separate from the public ones. Especially," she added hastily, "your emails." A fleeting mental image of Stella with an open records request made her feel slightly faint.

Oliver Robert nodded thoughtfully. "Right." He continued to think, nodding to himself and pursing his lips. "I can purchase a decent laptop for a reasonable price and use it just for work. This...machine..." he gazed at the office computer with disdain... "is simply not up to the task." He looked at her over his glasses. "I think you will see what I mean when I finish my first reports."

Fiona looked doubtful. "That seems an unnecessary expense."

"Oh, I'll pay for it myself. After being used to a modern laptop, it would be unthinkable to go back to a computer like this. After all," he said, "once a baboon has tasted honey, it doesn't touch earth again." He gave a little chortle of satisfaction and looked around the office questioningly.

"Is there anything else you need?" asked Fiona, somewhat dumbfounded. She decided not even to bother asking what he meant. "What an odd person," she thought. "But he clearly has no money problems."

"A hanger, please, for my jacket, and, perhaps, some kind of cleaner and some paper towels. Then, I'll just get started."

Obligingly, Fiona got the paper towels and cleaner from the coffee closet, and went down the hall to steal a wire hanger from the coat rack in the community room. She returned and handed it to Oliver. He looked at it with distaste, taking it from her as if it were a relic of her most recent dumpster dive.

It suddenly dawned on her that introducing Oliver Robert and Emily Martin would be highly entertaining. It also occurred to her that their names had the same rhythmic quality. This, too, amused her. Oliver Robert. What did that remind her of?

An old rhyme from English folklore popped suddenly into her head.

Oliver Cromwell lies buried and dead. Hey-ho, buried and dead.

Yes, that was it. She cast a sidelong glance at him, lest he could read her thoughts. Had he been able to do so, his look could not have borne more disapproval.

With Oliver Robert safely ensconced at his new desk, Fiona was making one of her rushed trips to the grocery store. Since she had taken public office, shopping was no longer a leisurely or contemplative event. Now every person she met stopped her to make a comment or complaint. So far, she could not recall a single compliment. What had once been a pleasant excursion had become a source of new things to worry about, and frequently resulted in Fiona forgetting what she had come for. The controversy with the chief meant it would be even worse than usual.

To her surprise, she had managed today to get through most of the store unmolested. Feeling that she was heading into the home stretch, she whipped her cart around the corner of an aisle, only to encounter a cluster of people gathered at the meat counter. For some reason lost in the mists of time, the meat counter was the traditional place for Islanders to share local news, but this was a larger group than casual gossip would warrant.

They were all in a circle, looking down at Jake's cellphone, and hearing Fiona's approach, they looked up. Several of them exchanged glances.

"Morning, Fiona."

"Fiona."

"Good morning," said Fiona, somewhat warily and with a certain amount of false cheer. "How's everybody this morning?"

There was a chorus of replies.

"Question is," said Jake, in his usual straightforward fashion, "how are you doing?"

"I'm fine, thanks."

"You're okay?" asked Charlotte. "Not too upset?"

Fiona felt all systems lurch. "Why should I be upset?" she asked, with a calm she did not feel.

"Ah," said Jake cautiously, but with a certain amount of well-modulated excitement. "Then you don't know."

"Know what?" With a small false smile for protection, Fiona looked at each of their faces in turn, seeing varying mixtures of sympathy, concern, and glee. She waited. There was a moment of silence, then they all began talking at once.

"I suppose," said Charlotte, "it's just a sign of the times."

"Can't see any good that can come of it."

"It's a free country, isn't it? She can say what she likes."

"Anything that allows her to spread her poison ought to be discouraged."

"Not that you can stop her."

"She's a poster child for that old adage, 'if you can't say anything nice...'"

Fiona continued to look from one to another of them trying to gather some meaning.

At last, Jake noticed the look of puzzlement on her face and held up his phone.

"It's Stella," he said, showing her the screen. "She's on Twitter."

Fiona continued to control her face as she leaned in to read what was on Jake's phone.

@realstella
GOOD CHARACTER should be a
REQUIREMENT of OFFICE
#charactercounts

Fiona looked up to see everyone watching her. She smiled, and shrugged her shoulders. She was tempted to make an ironic comment about the moniker "realstella", but her few months of political experience had taught her how quotes could be twisted by repetition and, also, that dry humor was not effective in groups. She would keep on the positive side.

"Hard to argue with that. Character does count." She looked at each of their faces, knowing they were all hoping for any sign of a reaction they could discuss later. "One of life's first precepts," she added.

She pretended to look at her watch. "Later than I thought; I'd better run. Have a good morning everyone."

Still smiling what she had come to think of as her 'election smile,' she pushed her cart past the little group, skipping the produce, bakery, and dairy aisles, so she could get through the checkout more quickly. She could hear the sound of their whispers as she left the store.

"Character counts, indeed," thought Fiona.

She forgot to buy eggs.

Chapter Twenty-Six ✤

Nancy was sitting in her lawyer's office in Sturgeon Bay. Nancy and David English, Esquire, had known each other for thirty years, and although they had never socialized, their relationship was based on respect, and had grown into a kind of affectionate professional intimacy. He had a solo practice and was quite successful, but his office was modest, in keeping with the standards of the community.

Nancy noticed that the carpeting was tired, and that the woodwork could use some fresh paint. The prints of local ships on the canal had been on the wall for as long as she had been coming there. Nancy was not enamored of change, and she respected the constancy of the office décor. It was solid. Comfortable. A place you could depend on.

David took off his reading glasses and looked up from the document he had been reviewing. "You know, Nancy, you should be thinking about what you're going to do with the farm," he said. You don't want to leave these things to the courts." His gaze was kindly.

Nancy frowned. "I have been thinking about it. Frankly, it's a dilemma. No one in my family would want it. I know they'd just sell it to get the money out of it." She looked at him across the desk. "I would really prefer that it stay a farm, not be turned over to some rich summer people who will tear down the house and build some monstrosity. My neighbors would never forgive me."

He looked doubtful. "Well, in the first place, you won't be in a position to care what the neighbors think." He smiled a lawyerly smile. "But I don't know what you can do about it. Unless you can find someone specific to leave it to—someone you know will keep it intact—there's not any way to guarantee anything." He paused thoughtfully. "I suppose you could turn it into a land trust or preserve."

Nancy's frown deepened. "What would that entail?"

"Well, honestly, I'd have to do a little research. Why don't I look into it for you, and we can talk again in a few weeks?"

Nancy stood up. "Thank you, David."

They shook hands.

"We'll see you, then, in a few weeks. I'll give you a call."

Feeling hopeful, Nancy said goodbye and went to do some shopping. She hoped to catch the five o'clock ferry.

Elisabeth had found many excuses to spend as much time as she could manage with Fiona, coming back and forth to the Island, returning home when necessary, and leaving Rocco behind to provide companionship to her friend.

It was during one of their stays that the mysterious crunching creature reappeared. The creature had made itself scarce for some months, off on some business of its own. Fiona found it curious that the creature had not been in evidence during the whole of Pete's visit, but now that he had gone, it seemed to think that the coast was clear. She wondered fleetingly whether it had sensed her loneliness.

Fiona, though used to its midnight activities and secretly comforted by its presence, nevertheless felt some ongoing concern about the creature's effect on the structure of the house. The general consensus among her friends was that it was a squirrel, and they all warned her of the damage one could do.

"They'll chew right through your rafters," said Jake, "and make a big mess. Bring all kinds of nuts and things into your house, fill up the walls, and won't have the good manners to relieve themselves outside. Stink up the whole house, and then where will you be?"

Where, indeed, Fiona wondered. But still, she procrastinated. At least there was some other sign of life in the house. Once Elisabeth was gone, the emptiness of the house would become unbearable. She tried not to think about winter.

Elisabeth, although privately horrified by this lackadaisical attitude, kept her concerns to herself. She felt these days as if Fiona were made of glass, and that any new pressure would create a crack. It was all she could do to pretend not to notice that there was an animal in the house, busily—as Elisabeth thought of it—chewing the rafters into sawdust. She tried, instead, to focus on making sure that she, herself, kept up a cheerful demeanor, that Fiona ate, and that she wasn't left alone too much. On those occasions when this was unavoidable, Elisabeth left Rocco behind to keep an eye on things. His soulful presence was preferable to the company of most people.

Fiona's complacency about the unknown chewing creature's presence, however, was accompanied by an increasing
sense that she was losing her mind. She distinctly remembered
putting both of her clean gardening gloves on the dresser
in the bedroom, and now there was only one. She checked
behind the dresser, in her sock drawer, and in the cushions of
her bedroom chair. Nothing. She felt quite certain that she
had put them, together, on the dresser when she was putting
away her laundry.

It was ridiculous. There was no one else to blame, and yet,
her mind must be playing tricks on her.

"It's stress, Fiona," said Elisabeth, gently. "You're distracted
by all your emotions and your new responsibilities. I'm sure
it will turn up."

Fiona shrugged. She knew she was under pressure, but it was
unlike her to completely forget something—or, more precisely:
to remember something that hadn't actually happened. It was
very curious, and, she admitted to herself, somewhat worrying.

Fiona shrugged again. She needed to keep her life moving
along, and that meant shoving these anxieties aside. As she had
arranged with Nika, Fiona called to speak with Ben and ask
whether he would be interested in a job.

For Ben, the prospect of earning money was far secondary
to being able to spend more time with the erstwhile Robert.
Ben eagerly accepted with the caveat of parental approval, and
they agreed to meet over at Nancy's barn to talk things over.
Fiona hung up feeling that at least one burden had been lifted.

Ben hung up and danced across the kitchen. "Mom!" he
called to Nika, who was in the next room. "Guess what?"

Chapter Twenty-Seven

As soon as Fiona had made her offer of a job to Ben, he had begun his campaign for his parents' permission. But Nika, who wanted Ben to have the job as much as he did, saw an opportunity to re-structure the balance of power. His behavior of late had been both uncharacteristic and alarming, and she missed the sweet boy she had known. She would not immediately give her permission to Ben to take this job. He would have to prove to her that he would be responsible and, most important, respectful.

"But, Mom," said Ben, with a persistence that only an eleven-year-old can have. "You said you wanted me to have more structure. What could be more structured than going to work? I can save money. You won't have to pay me an allowance."

Nika preserved a neutral expression during these appeals, but she was nevertheless amused, and recounted them all to Pali. Pali admitted that they bore a strong resemblance to conversations that Ben had had with him.

"We'll sit down with him together," he said. "Fiona's in no hurry. We talked about it. It will do him good to wait a bit."

Terry watched the video of himself many times, and in the ensuing mornings of practice, he tried to think about the things Joshua had pointed out to him. He wasn't sure whether he was imagining it, or whether he might have gotten a little bit better.

"Of course, the music was calmer today," he said, as Joshua poured him a refill of his coffee after their morning practice.

Joshua nodded. Roger had chosen Chopin that morning, which had made the class feel unusually tranquil, balletic, and most un-Roger-like.

Terry drank his coffee in silence for a moment, then put his cup down purposefully. Joshua was busy steaming milk for a latte. "Hey," he said to Joshua's back. "I don't want to be a pain, but do you think you could record me in class again tomorrow? I really think it helped."

Joshua didn't even turn around. "Sure," he said with his usual good humor. "No problem."

Terry drank the rest of his coffee in contented silence, thinking about his *natarajasana*, the Lord of the Dance pose. It could use some work.

The Angel Joshua usually worked in the mornings when it was busy, leaving Roger to manage for himself during the quieter afternoon hours. Today, however, he reappeared mid-afternoon, carrying a magazine in his hand.

"I thought you'd want to see this while things were quiet," he said, opening the glossy pages on the counter. "Do you know it? It's one of the premiere yoga magazines in the country. Three hundred and fifty thousand subscribers." He spun the magazine so that it was facing Roger. "This may explain the crowds."

Joshua, accustomed to Roger, did not wait for a response. "I'm done with it. You can keep it." With a cheerful "See you in the morning," he headed back out the door.

Scowling—as usual—Roger picked up the magazine. A bold-faced headline ran along the side of the cover: 'Yoga: Why More Men Are Loving It.'"

Still scowling, he opened the magazine and began to read.

Chapter Twenty-Eight

Nika and Pali sat at the kitchen table with their son. His enthusiasm for this new job prospect was a delightful thing to behold, but his parents remained serious and, to Ben, impossibly deliberate.

"You will need to be on time every day," said Pali. "Animals don't care whether you want to sleep late, or whether you have a cold. They will be depending on you."

"I know," said Ben, trying to contain his impatience. "I wouldn't make them wait. I love them," he said, his face earnest.

"And, Nancy and Fiona will be depending on you, too," said Nika. "The Island is a small place, Ben. If you are unreliable, you will hurt your chances for another job later."

"Yes," said Ben. "I know. I know all that, Mom."

Nika raised her eyebrows, looked at Pali, and then back at Ben.

"Then let's be clear about one thing: There will be no rudeness in this house, and no disrespect. If I see anything like that, or hear another report about swearing, it's all over. You will spend the summer working for me. Is that clear?"

Ben tamped down his feelings and sat up straighter in his chair.

"It's clear, Mom."

"Remember, Ben," said his father. "We expect you to be a good man. If you do the right thing, the right things will happen."

Ben nodded. He had heard this many times before. In the silence he swallowed hard and looked from his father to his mother.

Finally, Nika smiled. "You can take the job, Ben."

Ben leapt from his chair. "Can I start now?"

With great effort, Pali suppressed his own smile. "Why don't you call your employer, tell her you'll accept the job, and ask her when she would like you to start?"

Without another moment of delay, Ben ran to the phone to call Fiona.

Nika and Pali exchanged glances again and laughed.

Smiling to herself at his enthusiasm, Fiona had agreed to meet Ben right away at Nancy's farm to discuss his new responsibilities. She arrived a little early on purpose and, as always, went straight to the barn to see the goat. Nancy was already there in one of the horses' stalls, tending to her favorite mare's hooves.

"Morning," called Fiona.

Nancy looked up, briefly. "Morning. I've just got to finish this, and then I'll be with you."

"No worries," said Fiona. "I'm not really here to see you."

Nancy laughed and went on with her task. The mare trustingly offered her foot to be examined. It was a relationship of long standing, and Nancy's affection was returned a thousandfold by this intelligent and gentle animal.

Fiona leaned over the rail of the goat's stall. It looked back at her with glittering eyes, but no sign of recognition. Fiona honestly wasn't sure whether this was a good thing or bad. It was true that she felt remorse over the terrible end of Robert, but she couldn't exactly say that she missed him. This goat, although he had a nasty habit of screaming at unpredictable moments, nevertheless screamed at some distance from Fiona's house, which, she felt, made everything a bit less difficult.

In truth, Fiona's willingness to let her own barn construction drag on had its roots in her reluctance to share her life with another goat—"If," she corrected herself, "this is another goat." So long as the barn was unfinished, she could reasonably continue to let it stay at Nancy's. Nancy, fortunately, didn't seem to mind, and Fiona considered herself safe, at least for now.

"Will you mind having Ben around?" asked Fiona, somewhat belatedly. The job having been offered and accepted, Ben would probably be starting today after their meeting.

Nancy, who wasn't quite ready to admit that she had been feeling lonely, let the question sit for a few moments before she answered.

"No," she said. "Not really. Might even turn out to be helpful."

"Well, I hope he'll be helpful," said Fiona. "That's the whole point."

"He's a pretty good kid," admitted Nancy, in what, for

her, was high praise.

Fiona nodded, even though Nancy couldn't see. "Yes. I think he's a pretty remarkable kid, actually." She picked up a handful of goat chow and offered it to the anonymous goat. "He'll be good company, too."

Nancy snorted. "If I needed company, it sure wouldn't be a kid in the sixth grade."

Fiona didn't know whether she should apologize. She just kept silent and offered the goat another handful of food. For the first time, she wondered whether Nancy was lonely. She had always seemed so perfectly content and self-sufficient. Maybe, thought Fiona, it was all an act.

They heard Ben's eager voice calling outside the barn. Fiona went out to the driveway to meet him.

The news that Fiona had hired a clerk lit up the Island gossip, and the flames were quickly fanned by Stella's tweets.

@realstella
Why hire outsiders while Islanders need work?
#islandloyalty

@realstella
No money for fire department. Money to hire strangers.
#priorities

Fiona had known there would be some pushback on her decision, particularly in light of the fire department problem. But there had always been someone in this position, and it was neither full-time, nor well-paid. There was work to be done, and someone had to do it. She simply couldn't manage the harbor dredging preparations on her own. It wasn't possible.

Probably, under any other circumstances, no one would have batted an eyelash. But with Stella there to stoke the fires of discontent, the issue didn't seem likely to go away.

Oliver Robert, however, was the least of her problems. Time was running on the chief's resignation threat, and Fiona was out of ideas. She was sadly coming to the conclusion that they would, indeed, have to inflame the voting public by raising taxes. Even as dire a prospect as turning off the street lights and closing the Island library—which consisted entirely of a space in the community building that was smaller than her living room—could not yield a sum sufficient to solve the problem.

Stella's tweetstorm on the topic was relentless. She managed to make insinuations of malfeasance, always without committing to any actual accusations. Fiona had to admit to herself that it was cleverly done.

@realstella
What will happen when you have an emergency?
#solutionsnow #fakefiona

@realstella
Island safety depends on first responders.
#areyousafe

@realstella
Tell Fake Fiona your FAMILY needs PROTECTION.
#protecttheisland

In this last slogan, Stella seemed to have struck upon just the right phrase. Her theme of protecting the Island managed to sidestep the Islanders' deeply felt opposition to tax increases, while implying that Fiona was not protecting the community; that as an outsider, Fiona was a threat to the Island; and managing generally to provoke anger without providing a solution.

Meanwhile, Stella's follower numbers were growing. It soon became clear that not only the entire Island, but outsiders, too, were catching on to the drama. Even people who had no interest in Island politics, or in politics in general, were joining through word of mouth—or through whatever tribal drumbeat drew people into virtual connections. Vacationers heard about it and continued to follow after they went home. Sometimes they told their friends and families. @realstella was becoming something of a local phenomenon.

In the context of everything else that was going wrong, however, Stella's new Twitter habit seemed almost irrelevant to Fiona. Since she had made a conscious decision not to use Twitter herself, Fiona was at first able to pretend that nothing was happening, even while she followed Stella's tweets assiduously. But Fiona soon realized that after every new @realstella tweet, there was a corresponding chill in her public interactions. People watched her. They whispered when they saw her. Fiona had to admit to herself that it was beginning to wear on her psyche.

At the post office one morning, a couple standing near the boxes had seen her come in and turned their backs so they could pretend they hadn't. During her quick trip to the Mercantile, she caught her name in whispered conversations.

The carpenter working on the barn, in a rare weekday morning appearance at the site, commented on Stella's tweets. "Chief Gil hasn't quit yet, has he?" he asked.

Elisabeth had begun her own campaign, and that night she urged Fiona to start using Twitter herself. But still Fiona resisted.

"I came to the Island specifically to get out of the rat race," she told Elisabeth. "Twitter puts me right back in it."

"But that's just the point," argued Elisabeth, her patience fading. "You *are* in it. You're only pretending not to be."

Fiona picked at the pills on her sweater and said nothing.

"Fiona," continued Elisabeth, "you know this is bothering you. And you know that everyone on the Island is following this like a soap opera. You are losing ground here. You have to fight back. Have you seen how many followers she has now? It's more than the population of the Island."

Fiona looked directly into Elisabeth's eyes. "What if I don't want to? What if I don't feel like fighting?"

"You're better than that," said Elisabeth simply.

Fiona stood up and began pacing around the room. "You're right. I know that. And I don't mind fighting. What I do mind is being followed every waking hour by a virtual persona I have to manage and maintain. It becomes an obsession that blocks enjoyment of actual life—when there is any."

She sighed. "If only I could just write letters to the editor like other crazy people."

"Maybe you should think of Twitter as very short letters to the editor."

"And what, exactly, should I write? '@realchairman I don't know what to do either #anybodybutstella?' I mean, seriously, half the problem here is that situation appears to be insoluble."

"Is that the right number of characters?" teased Elisabeth.

A small impish smile crept across Fiona's face. "Which part?"

Chapter Twenty-Nine

It was almost dusk. Fiona lay on her covers in the half light and the cool breeze, listening to the sounds of summer evening. There was a very loud robin right outside the window, along with a cardinal, some other birds she couldn't name, and the noise of the crowd at the community ball game down the street. Through the window came the scent of peonies, rich, sweet, and as light as the wind that wafted over her.

She was spent from all her emotion and sleepless nights, and the sounds of people enjoying the summer night made her lonely. She felt guilty for lying there while life went on around her, but also too tired to do anything about it. Annoyed with herself, she snapped on the bedside lamp. There had been a time when she would have reached for her current book. Instead, and despite herself, she found herself checking Stella's tweets. The most recent popped up immediately.

@realstella
Board Chairman Campbell WILL RAISE ISLAND TAXES
#sad

Fiona stared bleakly at the phone. Stella's tweets were a

far cry from Marcus Aurelius, but here she was, instead of reading a book, filling her head with meaningless jibes. That, she thought, really was #sad.

In the distance, the crowd gave up a cheer. In the soft light of the summer evening, Fiona put down the phone, turned out her lamp, and sought the escape of sleep.

*F*iona *dreamed she was visiting someone she had known from high school. They had taken a big old-fashioned steamboat on a canal to arrive at his home together. There was water everywhere: a river; a sea of some kind; and massive cliffs that reminded her of the eastern coast of Canada. He took her hand and showed her his house where his sons were sleeping, deep inside the ruins of a 19ʰ century monument. There were tall pillars, and a rotunda without walls.*

It had once been beautiful but was now marred by neglect mixed with the careless practicality that suggested public owner-ship. The pillars were crumbling, the gardens had become a jungle. There was badly installed fluorescent lighting with wires hanging everywhere, World War II era bulletin boards with papers hap-hazardly attached, and a shabby gift shop that sold postcards with strange and beautiful photographic images. Everything seemed dank and deteriorated.

Fiona tried not to express her reaction to the place for fear of hurting her friend's feelings. But then, suddenly, he flipped a wall switch, and Fiona watched as the ugliness and ruin was gradually wiped away like water from a windshield. The wires, the ugly lights, the gift shop, the bulletin boards, and the overgrown landscaping disappeared, and the beauty of the place shone as if it had been just built. Fiona gazed at it all in wonder, admiring its grandeur, but she was disturbed that it was all illusion. When he flipped the switch back again, she knew that the reality of the shabbiness and neglect would return.

Oliver Robert examined the documents in front of him, frowning. At Fiona's request, he was looking carefully into revenue to see if there were any sources they might be missing. He had been doing corporate accounting and income taxes for some years now, and nothing he had encountered in the private sector could equal the complexity of what he was finding here.

The aid from the State of Wisconsin to the Town of Washington Island, was an intricate arrangement, requiring documentation that seemed to exceed the combined lengths of the Magna Carta, the Declaration of Independence, and the Constitutions of the State of Wisconsin and the United States.

It occurred to him that something was amiss in the world when documents of deep consequence could be written with such admirable concision and wit, while these blunt instruments of regulation could be so long, and so dampening to the human spirit.

Having spent a great deal of time grimly digging through

the statutes and regulatory detail of state aid, there was still one item that troubled him.

Oliver Robert was adept at the tools of his trade, and his accounting skills were a reflection of his almost obsessive perfectionism. When anything was out of place, it nagged at him. What was bothering him in particular was this one small piece of paper. It was, in effect, a bill from the State of Wisconsin, claiming an overpayment in state aid to the Town of Washington Island. He read it again, trying to absorb its implications, but no matter how many times he read it, its message seemed to be the same: take the mean of the adult population, divided by the number of school age children, added to the distance from Eau Claire in the western part of the state and the number of milk-producing cattle, divided by fifteen percent of the acreage devoted to farming, multiplied by the number of acres farmed by women or minorities on the Island….He knew he was being absurd, but even if these were not the precise requirements, they did not seem far off from reality.

It wasn't an enormous amount of money at stake, but he knew he had to get to the bottom of the problem. Oliver Robert sighed and began once more to attempt the calculation. Same result. Twelve dollars and eighty-three cents owed to the State of Wisconsin.

He sighed again. His accountant's soul could not rest until he had resolved this thing to his own satisfaction. He would have to call someone at the State to help him understand. Even though he knew his duty, a part of him wondered whether anything good could come out of this endeavor. After all, as Oliver Robert had frequently moralized to his colleagues: a bad tree doesn't yield good apples.

Chapter Thirty

P ali had known it would take time to find a new position. If he were content to take just any job, he could have done that, but he knew it made more sense to bide his time and find the right thing. There was some sense of urgency, but he expected the process to take time, and he didn't want to uproot Ben during the coming school year. Probably next summer would be soon enough. Still, it required effort on his part not to feel discouraged.

Ironically, his search had given him a new appreciation for his work on the ferry. Knowing that it could end at any time, he now was especially conscious of the smell of the lake air, the angle of the light, the changing colors of the water.

Most of the ferry passengers were on vacation, and therefore happy and cooperative, but there were always a few whose sense of entitlement made them a burden to themselves and others. Ever patient, Pali had always taken the bad attitudes of his less delightful passengers in stride. But these experiences were more likely now to amuse than irritate. Pali caught himself reflecting that dying people were said to have a greater appreciation of daily life. Perhaps knowing that he would have to leave the Island created the same kind of sad reality. As soon as he thought it, he quickly dismissed it from his mind. He needed to keep a positive attitude for Nika's sake.

Summer was passing swiftly. The long, cool spring had merged into an unusually hot, dry summer. The leafy greenness was looking dusty and faded. Even the cold waters of Lake Michigan felt refreshing rather than bone-chilling. To those who depended on tourism the hot weather was a boon. To the farmers, it was a challenge and a worry.

After another restless night, Fiona took herself off to the town hall. Entering the little room that served as the office of the chairman of the town board, she found—not at all to her surprise—that Oliver Robert was already there, deeply engaged in some task. He looked up when she entered, nodded, and went back what he had been doing.

Fiona walked around to her desk and dropped her satchel underneath. The piles of papers that had so depressed her only a short time before had disappeared. There was one folder on her desk with documents requiring her signature, a calendar with upcoming meetings clearly marked, and an agenda for the next committee meeting lying next to it. She sighed with relief. Mr. Robert—Oliver—had certainly made himself useful.

He was also someone with some unusual personal quirks. Perhaps in keeping with his fussiness about cleanliness and his fastidiousness in all things, Fiona had noted that Oliver Robert had a very strict schedule about his clothing.

On Mondays he wore his blue shirt; on Tuesdays, his green; on Wednesdays gray; on Thursdays brown; and on Fridays lavender. At first Fiona had thought it was merely coincidence, but after a while she realized that what he wore was utterly predictable. She kept herself from asking for as long as possible, but finally, she could resist no longer.

"So, Oliver," she began, casually. "Am I imagining it, or do you always wear blue on Mondays?"

"Oh, no," he said. "You're not imagining it, and you're more observant than most people, I must say. I have a schedule that I keep. Between ourselves, I'm a little superstitious about it."

Fiona gazed at him, fascinated. "What happens if you miss a day?"

He shuddered. "I don't even like to think about it."

"Have you always done this?"

"Long as I can remember," he said, cheerfully.

Fiona wanted to ask whether the color coding applied to garments that were unseen, but she couldn't bring herself to do it.

She told herself it was a good thing that the town meeting to discuss Chief Gil's ultimatum was coming up. At least, thought Fiona, in the midst everything else, Oliver is a distraction.

Off and on, in idle moments, Roger paged through the magazine Joshua had left. There were several articles about poses that looked interesting, particularly in their advice on preparation and approach. He would read those later. But what most captured his attention were the ads. He hadn't fully realized the extent to which yoga had become a business. It was remarkable to him that so many people were apparently making money through yoga, and from so many different angles.

He was pondering the cost and effectiveness of the advertising when he came upon an article about yoga trends. The bright tone and facile language annoyed Roger, but he read it anyway.

> *In this charming Iowa town, farm animals are nothing new. But when yoga teacher Susan Miller began inviting baby goats to her classes, people noticed.*

> *"It all started by accident," she said, smiling. "It was a beautiful day, so I thought it would be fun to enjoy the sunlight and do my practice outdoors. We had half a dozen baby goats at the time, and they are really curious. Having them romping around while I was doing yoga really lifted my spirits."*

> *Susan figured that if she enjoyed it her students would, too.*

> *"I didn't include it right away in my regular class schedule. I just did it as a fun, special thing. But everyone loved it and started asking for me to do it again. One thing led to another, and…the rest is history!" she explains.*

> *It turns out that baby goats and yoga is not a phenomenon unique to Iowa. Susan soon heard from other yoga teachers around the country who were doing the same thing.*

> *Says Susan: "People are looking for ways to de-stress and have relax. Yoga is a great way to do that, but the goats just add a level of fun that makes people feel good."*

Roger stopped reading and looked off into the distance thinking. Goats and yoga. He had to admit to himself that he would never have thought of that. But goats in the coffee shop wouldn't do. He'd had enough trouble convincing the town to allow them to have bare feet at the shop. He frowned. He would have to do a little research.

Eddie rarely took time off during the tourist season, but tonight he had left one of the summer help to close up the bar, and looked forward to spending an evening reading about Antiphanes.

Eddie's fondness for self-education had made him an enthusiastic devotee of on-line great books courses. He had started out with music, but each program led him further and further astray from his original interests. As his explorations became more wide-ranging, his tastes were growing ever more sophisticated.

Over the past year, guided by some of the finest scholars in the world, his recorded courses had included ancient histories, drama, and literature. He had reached a point at which he was beginning to understand some Greek, and he was now reading the ancients' criticisms of one another.

He was particularly interested because he had recently encountered the plays of Euripides and Aeschylus. He had known some of the stories in a general way, but he had been astonished to find such ancient dramas so engrossing and moving.

There were only fragments left of the works of Antiphanes, who was of a generation later, but Eddie was intrigued when he found some criticism of the Greek dramatic device called *deus ex machina*.

> When they don't know what to say
>
> and have completely given up on the play
>
> just like a finger they lift the machine
>
> and the spectators are satisfied.

Eddie nodded to himself. Perhaps it had been satisfying to ancient audiences, but he thought the use of the technique in modern narrative was probably dead. A properly written story should resolve itself organically, through the natural development of the plot. "Modern readers," he thought, "are more sophisticated. This kind of thing would never fly today."

Eddie put down his book and looked off across the moonlit water. Twenty-five hundred years ago, when Euripides was on the earth, these waters had probably looked exactly like this. The moon had shone down exactly like this.

"Who was here," he wondered, "to see what I am seeing? What thoughts did he have? What were his worries?"

Eddie breathed in the sweet summer air and picked up his mug of tea, the steam rising into the cool night. He was glad he had taken the night off.

Chapter Thirty-One

One morning, feeling particularly low, Fiona was getting dressed and reached for a pair of clean socks she had left on the chair. There was only one. Puzzled, she looked under the chair, along the side of the seat cushion, and then began to shake out the other clothing that had been lying there. This was curious. She was certain that both socks had been there. Shrugging, she went to the dresser for another, less cushiony pair. Muttering to herself about the prospects of pending insanity, a disordered life, and many future cats, she went downstairs for coffee.

Later, as she observed Oliver Robert at work, she found that he, too, seemed rather depressed. Perhaps she was projecting her own moods on others, but she felt that she should make some overtures of welcome. She recalled her own early days on the Island without nostalgia.

"My friend, Elisabeth, and I are going to Nelsen's for dinner tonight," she said, one afternoon. "I thought maybe you'd like to join us."

Oliver looked at her with pursed lips before speaking. "No. Thank you. It would be against the rules."

"Rules?" asked Fiona, puzzled.

"Well, there are little life rules I always follow that I find helpful."

Fiona looked at him with a mixture of respect and amusement. "And they are?"

"Well, one is: 'Never confuse your colleagues with your friends.'"

Fiona laughed, unoffended. "That's good advice, generally. But it's pretty hard to pull off around here. There aren't enough people for hard lines of separation."

Oliver nodded seriously. "I have noticed that."

"There are other rules?" The light began to dawn. This would explain the odd little things he was so fond of saying.

He nodded again.

"Such as?"

Fiona had learned to recognize one of Oliver's looks: the sudden closing off of his face. It meant she had probed too far into his privacy.

"Sorry," she said quickly. "I shouldn't have asked."

He sniffed and continued with his work.

"He really is an odd duck," thought Fiona to herself. Just when she thought she was making some progress at befriending him he would retreat back into himself. It was a good thing he was so good at what he did. She recalled a remark her former editor had often made about a colleague: "He's worth the trouble," he would say.

So far, so good, but Fiona was beginning to wonder whether this would prove true of Oliver Robert. She had to admit: she had her doubts.

Roger was an MIT-trained physicist, so both skepticism and research came naturally to him. He wanted to know whether this goats and yoga thing was a real phenomenon. Was it the beginning of a trend? It didn't take long online to discover that while it certainly existed, it wasn't exactly everywhere, yet where it was being done, it was attracting crowds.

Roger was familiar with the algorithms of trends. He could see that the growth of yoga participation combined with the rising popularity of cute goat memes was an interesting combination. His research had uncovered a particularly surprising map from the Department of Agriculture, showing the numbers and distribution of goats across the country. There were 2.6 million goats in the United States, roughly equal to the human populations of Wyoming, South Dakota, Washington D.C., and Vermont.

Roger was reminded of the conditions he had observed in the coffee business just before the wild spread of hip, modern coffee shops all across the country, and then across the world. Until that moment, a coffee shop had just meant a casual little restaurant to have breakfast, where locals gathered to discuss the news of the day.

Then suddenly, it seemed, coffee shops were everywhere, and instead of being sleepy local spots or greasy spoons whose proprietors were eking out a living, they had become revenue centers, selling four- and five-dollar coffees to the very chic, while offering them a place to hang out, meet their friends, and surf the web.

Roger excelled at pattern recognition, and his keen insight at the time had put him ahead of the curve with Ephraim's first modern coffee shop. Yes, he thought, goats and yoga seemed to be a trend in the making. But was it goats and yoga together? Or was it just goats, or just yoga? He wasn't entirely sure.

Chapter Thirty-Two

Perhaps if Elisabeth had been at home to remind him of other things, Roger might not have been thinking so much about goats. But in her absence, Roger discovered that he was not as good as he used to be at amusing himself, and goats became a subject whose study helped to fill the time. As he was thinking, it had occurred to Roger that he actually knew someone who had a goat. It might not be the goat she had started out with, but it was, nevertheless a goat.

It could be useful to go and see it, he thought, to get some sense of what goats are like. He had some idea from his own brief experiences with the erstwhile Robert, but nothing long-term. Fiona, he felt sure, would be able to help him with this shortage of information. Besides, he thought, Elisabeth was there. He could see Elisabeth.

Armed with some of his research and his usual ration of insensitivity, Roger sat down to make a phone call.

@realstella
Low energy Fiona. SAD.
#accountabilityinoffice

Fiona was rather inclined to agree with Stella's assessment this morning. She felt tired and overwhelmed. Reading Stella's tweets late at night was not doing much for her sleep.

After a slightly late start, Fiona was just coming in the office door as her phone was ringing. Noting the general air of grievance hanging over Oliver, she ignored him and put her bag down on the chair.

"Hello?"

"This is Roger."

"Roger!" said Fiona, stunned. She was fairly sure he had never called her before, and she knew from Elisabeth that he did not much like the telephone.

"I want to discuss goats."

"Oh," said Fiona, who, despite having known Roger for some time now, was nevertheless surprised. She went into her private space and closed the door.

"I'm not sure I qualify as an expert."

"I want to come and visit with yours."

Fiona had a vision of Roger and the Goat Formerly Known as Robert sitting down together and chatting over tea. "Of course. You know where he is?"

"No."

That was just like Roger. Direct and to the point.

"Ah. Well, okay. Call me when you plan to come, and we can meet at my house. I'll take you there. Since the fire, you know…" her voice trailed off.

"Tomorrow," said Roger.

"Tomorrow?"

"I'll come tomorrow."

Fiona scanned her memory for events she might have scheduled. Nothing firm. "Okay. What time?"

"Ten."

"I'll see you at the house then."

The phone clicked before Fiona could ask whether he would be staying. She put her phone down and went out into the main office to see why Oliver was brooding. She had no sense of apprehension since she was beginning to learn that his moods were not discernibly related to events.

"Good Morning, Oliver." She went to the coffee closet and poured herself a cup.

"Did you see the envelope?" he asked, by way of reply.

"What envelope?"

"On your desk."

Fiona turned around to look at him, her mug in her hand. "From whom?"

"The State," he said, casually, and then went silent.

Fiona's patience was in limited supply that morning. "Am I supposed to guess what it's about, or did you want to play Twenty Questions?"

Oliver put his chin up. "Read it yourself," he said, and got up to walk down the hall.

Fiona, just short of muttering, went into her office to retrieve the letter. She skimmed it quickly, then sat fuming until Oliver returned.

"Oliver, please come in here. What is this about?"

He seated himself at the edge of one of the frowsy pink chairs that were in her office for visitors.

"Twelve dollars and eighty-three cents," he said.

"I can see that. But where did that number come from?"

"According to them, it's what we owe due to an overpayment of state aid."

"What do you mean, 'according to them'? Do we owe it or not?"

He frowned slightly. "I'm not sure."

Fiona leaned on her hand and rubbed her forehead in frustration. "This says it's a second notice with penalties soon to follow, and I don't recall seeing the first. What is this about? Please start from the beginning."

"Well," he said, "there really isn't that much to tell. I went through all the state aid files and looked at the calculations, but it's not completely obvious how they arrive at the number. I called the bureau to talk to someone, but they didn't really know, either. I can't find anyone who knows why they say we owe anything, or anyone who even knows how to figure out the formula. I just got passed from person to person. It was most provoking." Oliver looked put out at this recollection.

"Well," said Fiona, finally, "I can sympathize with your experience. Apparently, no one knows anything over there." She paused and pursed her lips. "It hardly seems a big enough figure to worry about. If we give any time to it at all, more taxpayer money will be spent than the amount of the bill in the first place. Just pay it, and we'll put it behind us."

Oliver looked scandalized. "Pay it? Even if we're not sure

we owe it? But—"

"Just pay it and get it over with." Fiona was secretly enjoying herself. "We have enough going on around here without having to deal with that."

"But—" he said again.

"It's a shortcut, Oliver. It will save us all a lot of time and aggravation."

He shook his head sorrowfully, as if he were a prophet predicting her doom. "A mile around the road is shorter than half a mile across the field."

Fiona closed her eyes for a moment. "Just pay the bill."

His lips tight, Oliver stood up and went back to his desk. Even his back looked reproachful.

That night Fiona was sleepless again, sitting at her bedroom window. Perhaps it was her stillness that gave the creature the sense that it was free to go about its business unimpeded by wall-pounding, and it began to crunch with great gusto behind the wall. Fiona wondered whether this usually went on as she slept, or if, perhaps, it was the creature's way of keeping company with her loneliness.

It wasn't loneliness, she told herself. She didn't mind being alone. It was being alone without him. That was what she minded.

She stirred and sighed, fogging the window with her breath. The creature behind the wall stopped momentarily, apparently listening, and then went back about its noisy business.

Lulled by the monotony of the noise and the companionship of the invisible animal, Fiona at last fell into a shallow, dream-filled sleep, her face leaning against the glass.

As she was getting ready in the morning, Fiona went to her dresser to put on a pair of gold earrings her grandmother had always worn. They were one of Fiona's prized possessions, and in order to protect them from rolling onto the floor and getting lost, every night she put them in a little blue pouch and left it on her dresser. Today it wasn't there.

She looked on the floor, and behind the dresser. She opened the top drawer to see if it had fallen in. It wasn't there, so she took everything out of the drawer and shook it. Still nothing.

Fiona frowned. She was under stress, and she had been getting absent-minded, but she knew she had put the earrings on the dresser last night. She knew it. The other things she had lost recently hadn't really mattered, but the earrings did. If they were gone she wouldn't forgive herself.

She shook her head to herself and headed downstairs, feeling anxious. Something strange was going on. Maybe she really was losing her mind. "Oh well," she thought. It was the perfect mood in which to meet Roger.

Roger arrived shortly after the ferry. Fiona discretely

left Elisabeth to answer the door to her husband, and spent a few extra minutes upstairs. She could hear the murmur of their voices as they went to the kitchen, but after a few minutes, Elisabeth called her down. Fiona had been hoping that Elisabeth would accompany them to Nancy's, but she quickly excused herself and left Fiona standing in the midst of Roger's silence.

Fiona almost always spent time with Roger and Elisabeth together, and the prospect of nurturing some kind of limping communication with Roger alone was not especially appealing. She took a deep breath and smiled.

"Okay if we take your truck?" she asked.

"Okay," said Roger, and without another word or backward glance, he turned and walked out to the road. Fiona followed silently.

When they arrived at the farm, Nancy was waiting for them. Roger shook hands with her and followed her into the barn. He stood staring at the goat. The goat stared back. This went on for a few minutes until Roger took a deep breath and nodded. "All right," he said. He turned his head toward Nancy without seeing her. "Thanks."

He went out the door to the barn and headed down the drive to his truck. Fiona and Nancy exchanged glances. Nancy shrugged.

Fiona raised her hands in a gesture of helplessness. "Thanks, Nancy. Guess I'd better go. Talk to you later."

Silently, Nancy raised her hand in farewell, and Fiona ran down the hill to catch up with Roger.

Chapter Thirty-Three ✦

Fiona left Roger with Elisabeth and headed over to the office. Amidst her worries, Fiona was finding that there was one thing to be grateful for: the challenges of public life were a welcome distraction from thinking about her grief. So was life with Oliver Robert. In a way she couldn't quite explain, his moods, his responses to things, and his odd little sayings engaged her mind so thoroughly that when she was with him her mind rarely turned to her personal life.

"Oh no," said Oliver tragically, after a long silence.

Fiona looked up, alarmed by the sound in his voice. "What's happened?" She expected some new conflict with the State at minimum, or perhaps the death of a family member.

"The town meeting. It's on a Wednesday."

Fiona looked confused. "Is that bad?"

"Well, normally, I would wear my good suit for an occasion like that."

Fiona waited for him to continue. When he didn't she prompted him.

"And why can't you?"

"It's blue."

Fiona continued to look puzzled, and Robert sighed in exasperation.

"Don't you see? Wednesday is *gray*. I can't wear blue on Wednesday.

Fiona paused.

"Couldn't you wear your blue suit with a gray tie?"

He gazed at her with something like disgust. "Of course not. I wear my blue suit with my red tie."

"Oh," said Fiona.

There seemed nothing more to be said.

A perfect combination of a responsible upbringing and pure passion ensured that Ben Palsson turned up at Nancy's barn every morning and afternoon, seven days a week. There was nothing on earth he would rather do than to visit his friend, and even after his chores were finished, he lingered at the farm, watching the animals, talking to them, and doing little extra chores for Nancy.

To Nancy, he was a godsend. She had lived alone nearly her entire adult life. She was used to the quiet rhythms of farm work, and to the long solitary days. It was a good life, and a happy one. But Ben's presence made clear an emptiness she hadn't known was there. He was polite, eager to be helpful— even thoughtful—and his happy chatter and many questions about the animals and their care made the busy days pleasant, and the quiet nights quieter.

"Ms. Iverssen," said Ben one day, "you need a dog."

Nancy didn't even stop what she was doing. "Don't want a dog. Don't need something else to take care of."

"But that's the thing with dogs," said Ben, shoveling hay into the goat's stall. "You don't just take care of them. They take care of you."

"I had a dog once," said Nancy. "When I was about your age."

"What kind?" asked Ben, who was always interested in animals, and who wanted a dog himself. They already had a yellow lab, but Ben was lobbying for a puppy.

"Big, scraggy mutt. Had some shepherd in him, maybe, and some retriever." Her voice began to sound dreamy. "He was a great retriever. I loved that dog."

Something in her tone of voice made Ben ask. "What happened?"

"Got hit by a car. I cried for a year." Nancy turned brisk. "Now. You say you're such a good shot. Let's finish up here, and then we can go see how many cans you can hit on the back fence."

"Okay!" said Ben, his face alight.

The look on his face and the tone of his voice gave Nancy a great deal of satisfaction.

After Roger had said goodbye to Elisabeth he drove off alone. He was thinking. It was true that he knew very little about animals, but he had confidence that he could teach himself anything. Anything, at least, that had nothing to do with emotions.

He drove aimlessly around the Island roads, barely seeing the landscape. He didn't really know his way around, but getting lost, he knew, was impossible. He was heading south along Detroit Harbor, deep in thought, and as was his habit, the more he thought, the more slowly he drove. He had slowed to a snail's pace when he came upon the old Washington Hotel. It was shuttered and a bit desolate looking. Its "For Sale" sign had been out for so long the letters had faded and blurred. Abruptly, Roger pulled the car over and got out, staring up at the nineteenth century building.

It had once been a sea captain's house, and it sat on a small hill overlooking Detroit Harbor. There was a house next door that was part of the property, and a smaller outbuilding that looked like an artists' studio on the other side.

Hands in pockets, Roger walked up the drive to get a better look.

Aside from the occasional glass of sherry, Oliver Robert was not a drinker. He did not play sports, nor was he an outdoorsman devoted to hunting or fishing. He liked classical music, some jazz, reading, and the theater, and occasionally a quiet dinner party. Finding entertainment on the Island was not going to be easy for him.

"Maybe you should take up cards," suggested Fiona one afternoon when a casual query about his evening plans was met with the title of a book.

Oliver Robert gave her one of his looks, and Fiona was instantly silenced. It was none of her business, she agreed, but she wished he wouldn't be quite so rude about it.

The truth was that, although he was, in fact, reading the book he had mentioned, Oliver had plans to meet Heather's Aunt Stella for a drink. But he had no intention of telling Fiona that.

Chapter Thirty-Four

Encouraged by his improvement, Terry had prevailed upon Joshua to do regular tapings. They had decided to concentrate on one pose at a time rather than an entire class, so that Joshua's own practice time was not completely eliminated, and Terry would have a chance to focus on one thing at a time.

One morning after class, Terry was watching the most recent video. He nodded to himself as he identified a misalignment in his position, and made a mental note to work on that particular point tomorrow.

Dave, from the Lutheran Men's Prayer Group sat down on the stool beside him and peered over his shoulder. "What's that?"

Terry looked up sheepishly. "It's a video. From class."

Dave looked interested. "Okay if I see?"

Terry hesitated a moment and shrugged. "Sure, I guess so." He made a wry face. "It isn't pretty."

Gazing over his shoulder, Dave nodded. "No," he said. "I can see that."

More or less against his better judgment, and entirely as a favor to Eddie, Jim had agreed to go on a blind date. Blind dates were a phenomenon generally made rather difficult by circumstances on the Island, since they required that everyone not know everyone else. But Eddie's landlady had a niece visiting for the summer, and, partly out of self-protection, Eddie had arranged the meeting. In the back of his mind, Eddie had a small hope that it would take his friend's mind off Fiona, but even he acknowledged that this would be an unlikely outcome.

Jim had not been on a blind date since college, and he did not remember them with any fondness. There had been one young woman who had wanted to go together to get tattoos, and another who had barely said two words the entire evening, even though Jim had scraped up his student savings and taken her to a nice restaurant for dinner.

In both cases he had been convinced that the feeling of relief when they were over had been mutual, and he had firmly resolved never to participate in a blind date again. But when Eddie had broached the subject Jim had shrugged his shoulders. "What the Hell," he thought. "It's better than sitting home alone every night."

Now, as he showered and changed, Jim wasn't so sure. He would have been happier sitting at Nelson's by himself, shooting the breeze with Eddie and whoever else showed up. He consoled himself with the knowledge that there were no tattoo parlors nearby.

Elisabeth having returned to the mainland, Fiona sat down to a solitary dinner. Looking for amusement while she ate, she picked up her phone and found a new tweet from Stella.

@realstella
Ask lying Chairman Fiona Campbell where the money is. #crimesinoffice #charactercounts

Fiona was puzzled. This was one she couldn't even be upset by. What was it about? It would have been laughable except for the impact it would probably have on the public mood. She shrugged it off and decided to make herself a cup of tea and go to bed early. She would think about this later.

She was waiting for the kettle to boil when the phone rang. Fiona answered and instantly regretted that she had. It was Emily Martin, talking, as always, very fast.

"Hello, Fiona. It's Emily. Emily Martin."

Fiona attempted to return the greeting, but Emily was already moving on.

"I'm calling because there have been some questions raised about the town's finances. We heard that there's an unpaid bill from the State. This is unacceptable. How is it even possible?"

Fiona barely listened to the onslaught, struck by the first word: "we." Who did Emily mean by "we?" A bill from the State? Surely, she didn't mean the twelve dollars and eighty-three cents? Could that be what this was about? But how did

Emily even know such an esoteric detail? The Island's budget was all online, but this kind of thing would only show up in the records kept at the office. And anyway, she had told Oliver to pay it.

Still, without waiting for a reply, Emily's voice went on ceaselessly with the driving rattle of a sewing machine factory.

"I'm very sorry, Fiona. I know you mean well. I mean, I'm sure you haven't done anything deliberately wrong. No doubt. No doubt about that I'm sure. But this money has to be accounted for. These bills cannot go unpaid. I mean, honestly, people are beginning to think there's some reason for the lack of funds for the fire department. I've discussed it with some members of the community, and we all agree we have to find out what's going on here. We've got to get to the bottom of this. I'm sure you'll agree that when all is said and done, the best thing would be to have an audit."

"An audit?" asked Fiona, incredulous. Really? Over twelve dollars?

"We can do that, Emily," she said at last, once she could get a word in. "But audits are expensive. I don't think we need an auditor to understand the problem. The books are open to anyone, and no special expertise is needed to understand them. I'd be happy to show—"

"Well, I don't know, I think we need some objective observers here. When I was on the committee in Winnetka, we had an audit, and let me tell you there were some pretty shocking things going on. Pretty shocking. Not, of course," she continued over Fiona's attempts to speak, "that you would do anything illegal, no, I know that, but not everybody does.

People need to know the facts. They want to know what's going on. Believe me, this is for the best. It will be the best for everyone."

Fiona was incensed. "Illegal? Who could possibly think there's anything illegal?"

Emily didn't even stop. "I'll be in touch once we get the process going. I really think you'll thank me for this. I really do. Well, I've got to run. Bye now."

Fiona stood holding the phone. Thanking Emily was not what she had in mind.

Standing in the kitchen, Fiona made the mistake of checking her phone one last time. Stella had been busy.

@realstella
Where is our money?
#malfeasence #character counts.

Doesn't the woman have a spell checker? Wondered Fiona.

@realstella
It's your money. Demand an audit.
#charactercounts #whereisthe$

Suddenly Fiona understood Emily Martin's "we." Stella and Emily were working together.

Chapter Thirty-Five ❖

When she went upstairs, Fiona tucked herself into bed with her tea and a book of poetry. She would not look at Twitter anymore tonight, and the Mencken book reminded her of Pete—not the content, but the fact that he had given it to her—so that was out.

The house seemed to reverberate with emptiness and anxiety. She breathed deeply to comfort herself, and was about to begin reading some poetry when the crunching began. Fiona paid it no attention. It was background noise now, and she couldn't help feeling that at least she wasn't entirely alone, no matter what destruction might be going on behind the walls.

"It is well to keep in touch with chaos," she read. Chaos certainly kept in touch with her, she thought, grimly.

Fiona put the book down and stared off into space. Her loneliness was reaching new depths.

The chewing stopped abruptly, as if the creature had been startled by something, and she heard a scurrying in the wall near her ear that seemed to be moving toward the floor and around the room. She sat listening. He seemed to be covering more territory these days. She sighed.

Suddenly she started. Across the room, peeking out from

the trim around the fireplace, was a tiny face with round black eyes and brown fur. They stared at one another. A kind of awe enveloped Fiona. Here, at last, was her secret companion, whose residency in the ceiling of the house had been a source of anxiety, and more lately, of comfort at the presence of another living creature. They had read Marcus Aurelius together, and Martin Luther, and now the poetry of Theodore Roethke—not to mention the increasingly frequent tweets from Stella.

The small creature blinked. "What could it be?" wondered Fiona. It wasn't a squirrel, she was sure of that, and it was too big to be a mouse. The shape of the head was wrong for a rodent.

A line from the poetry she had been reading leapt into her mind.

The shape of a rat? it's bigger than that....

It wasn't, though. It was a very tiny head, probably not much bigger than a walnut.

"Hello," said Fiona, gently.

The head disappeared. Fiona continued to watch the corner until she couldn't keep her eyes open, but she didn't see the little face again. In her sleep she was unconsciously comforted by the sound of the creature's nocturnal activities deep within the walls of the house.

Roger returned from the Island alight with his idea. The Washington Hotel had been for sale for several years. It was a building whose historic charm had been preserved by previous owners, and it had pained everyone who loved the Island to see the it standing empty in a long, sad, slide into disrepair.

The hotel had a few select, lovely rooms to stay in, but it had been best known for its restaurant. Fiona and Elisabeth had many happy memories of dinners there, of walking up the path across the sweeping lawn, of dining on the long, old fashioned porch that stretched along the length of the white clapboard building. There was an enormous ancient tree nearby, and a slightly obscured sunset view of Detroit Harbor, and there had been a black dog in residence who had greeted the clientele with a happy wag.

There weren't many restaurants on the Island, and none of them made any pretense about the casual style of their food. The hotel, however, had had, for a time, a chef and a cooking school and a restaurant specializing in local food in a way that was appealing to both Islanders and the upscale Chicago tourists who comprised the majority of the trade. It had been elegantly simple and very popular, often booked months in advance.

It would be an understatement to say that Roger was not a people person, and his contrarian nature did not mesh well with his newfound popularity. It was, in fact, a bit of a contradiction that a man so taciturn could have developed such a following in yoga, particularly among a group of people so well known for their gentleness, their humanity, and their easy-going approach to life.

Roger was not terribly interested in empire building, but he did not enjoy interactions with customers at Ground Zero, particularly not so many customers, and particularly not so many strangers. It was unlikely he would enjoy customers anywhere under any circumstances. He was at least as frustrated as Mike and Terry about the crowding at Ground Zero, and although the rush of business had been an unexpected financial gain, Roger preferred the old quiet.

For Roger, it was a question of the quality of his daily life. He could buy the hotel and get someone else to manage it. He could help his friends on Washington Island by improving the economy. He could pull all those people away from Ground Zero with a bigger attraction. And he could have a dedicated yoga studio for…well…anything.

He called the realtor before it occurred to him to talk it over with his wife. He was sure that she and Fiona would be pleased.

And for possibly the first time in his life, Roger got a human reaction absolutely right.

As he had expected, Jim's blind date had been, if not a fiasco, then a waste of time. The woman was the niece of one of the summer people, not a regular on the Island, and therefore an unknown quantity. He had taken her to an event at the arts center, and she had fidgeted and yawned throughout. Afterward, out of politeness, Jim invited her for a drink, but as soon as she accepted, he regretted doing so.

They drove separately, and met in the parking lot of Nelsen's. Jim held the door for her, and they went in. Eddie greeted them with a smile and a raised eyebrow. Jim gave him a look of long suffering.

The drink made her chatty, and the speed with which she downed it made Jim—who was no teetotaler—a little nervous. Unhappily, he offered to buy her a second one, which she accepted. She talked for a while about a television show she liked. When Jim mentioned that there had been northern lights the night before, she was uninterested. Jim mentioned a book he was reading about Frederick Olmstead, the great landscape designer. She yawned, and said she didn't read much.

Jim could well believe it.

After she had finished the second drink as rapidly as the first, the conversation died, and Jim was not in a mood to attempt resuscitation. They sat in silence for an interminable five minutes before she decided to end their misery, as Jim had hoped.

"I guess I'd better be going. My favorite show is on in a few minutes."

Politely, Jim stood, and signaling Eddie that he'd be back, walked her out to her car.

"Bye," she said, and drove off without a thank you.

Jim watched her go, and then went back into Nelsen's and sat down at the bar. Eddie, who was busy, came over to check in.

"You owe me for that," said Jim.

Eddie grimaced. "Sorry, man. Seemed like it was worth

a shot. At least maybe it got your mind off…you know…for a while."

"Actually," said Jim, slowly, "it kind of made it worse."

The next day Nika Palsson ran into Jim Freeberg at the Mercantile, and they stopped to exchange pleasantries.

"Thank you for bringing Ben home yesterday. He's always so filled with ideas and enthusiasm after you've talked to him. He says wants to be a game warden like you, someday."

Jim looked embarrassed. "We have good talks. He's always thinking. Usually he's about three steps ahead of me."

Nika laughed. "We feel that way, too. He's growing up way too fast."

Nika looked at Jim fondly. He was such a good man, but his loneliness was almost palpable, and finding eligible singles on the Island wasn't easy. She wished she could find someone for him. Suddenly, inspiration struck her.

"Are you taking anyone to the Island Ball?" she asked.

Jim shrugged and smiled. "Can't think of anyone to take."

"How about Fiona Campbell?"

"She's spoken for," said Jim calmly. "Her boyfriend may not be around, but she's made her feelings pretty clear."

"I wouldn't be so sure," said Nika. "Pete's been gone for some time, and she hasn't said one word about him. You must have noticed: her face is all pale and her eyes are dead. I think it's over between them."

Jim's face did not change. "I hope she's all right," he said, meaning it sincerely.

Nika smiled at him with raised eyebrows. "Maybe you should go find out."

Jim shrugged and smiled again. "Maybe."

Chapter Thirty-Six

Fiona spent some time online, searching for images of small animals native to Wisconsin. She hadn't seen enough of the creature to be able to identify it properly, but she now had a theory. She passed much of the day ruminating upon methods of enticing the little animal further into the room, because now that she had seen him, she wanted to be friends. It seemed fairly obvious that food would provide the additional incentive required. Buoyed by her mission, she headed out to the grocery store to stock up on enticements.

Ben rarely accompanied his mother to the grocery store, but Nika had forgotten something and needed to stop, and going in was more interesting than sitting in the car. He was trailing along the aisles in a bored kind of way, his hunger making everything look irresistible. He wondered idly what was for dinner.

"Nika!" Ben looked up to see Emily Martin standing with her cart at the end of the aisle. He felt his stomach clench.

Caleb's mother. He did not want to chat with her. As his mother reluctantly engaged in conversation, Ben started to edge away toward the magazine rack, but it was too late.

"Hello, Ben. How nice to see you."

Everything this woman said seemed false. Ben tried to understand why. He replied politely, and stood by nervously as the two women chatted. This was the woman who might be able to take away his father's job. He knew instinctively that his mother didn't like her. Could that be why? He studied their faces without listening to their conversation, and noticed suddenly that they were both looking at him expectantly.

"Ben?" said Nika. "Mrs. Martin is asking whether you would like to come over and hang out with Caleb."

Ben's reply was immediate and instinctive. "No!" He turned and ran down the aisle, out of the store.

Nika was stunned. She immediately began to apologize. "I am so sorry. He knows better than that. Please forgive us."

Emily Martin had a smug little smile on her face, as if rudeness were exactly what one might expect.

"Oh, don't worry about it. We all know how kids are." She looked at her watch. "I'd better be going. Don't forget about my little community meeting! We'll be expecting you!" She wheeled her cart around and hurried off.

Nika stood looking after her with mixed emotions, then she, too, looked at her watch. She would have to finish her shopping quickly. A grim expression crossed her face. She would deal with Ben when they got home.

When she got home from the store, Fiona unwrapped the beef she had bought to make herself a stew, and carefully set aside a few nice, raw chunks. She put one of the pieces of raw meat on an old jar lid, and pausing in the living room to turn out the lamp and pour herself a drink, went upstairs to the bedroom. She stopped for a moment before entering the room, hoping for some sign of her friend, but there was silence, and nothing to see.

Tiptoeing, she crossed the room to the fireplace, and set the lid down near the little opening where she had seen the face the night before. Then, settling herself on the floor nearby, she leaned her back against the wall, opened her book, and took a sip of scotch. She did not expect results right away, figuring that for now, the creature's shyness would overcome his interest in meat, but she hoped that the smell of food would encourage him. Before long, she was so engrossed in her reading that she forgot her uncomfortable position. But after more than an hour of waiting, Fiona began to feel stiff from sitting on the floor. Leaving the jar lid on the floor, she flung off her clothes and went to bed.

The next morning, the meat was gone. Fiona wondered how long the creature had waited before determining it was safe to come out. She could imagine the small black eyes, nervously peering into the dark, lured by the smell of meat. She wondered, too, whether the creature had felt any curiosity about her own presence.

It did not occur to Fiona that befriending an animal occupant of her house was eccentric. Her battered psyche had no room for the judgments of others. In her present state of emotional upheaval and duress, all she had the capacity to do was follow her instincts, and her instincts were to build a connection to a fellow creature. Any creature.

She would have to wait.

Nika's first reaction to Ben's behavior at the store had been anger, but it quickly faded. This kind of rudeness was so unlike Ben that it must have some meaning, and her concern for her son grew the more she contemplated what had happened. She decided to bring up the subject right away on the drive home.

"Ben," she began, her eyes on the road. "What was that about?"

A glance told her that he was staring out the window. He shrugged.

Nika almost smiled. "Shrugging isn't a very effective means of communication when the other person is driving. Ben…."

She paused so long that he had to look at her. "Ben, I'm worried about you. Is everything all right?" She stole another glance at him and he looked away.

" 'S fine," he said.

"I don't think I believe you," she said quietly. "Is there

something I should know?"

He shook his head briefly and dismissively.

"Ben, you know if there's something wrong your father and I are here to help you."

His quick movements were eloquent expressions of his discomfort as he shifted in his seat, and turned to look back out the window.

Sensing his increasing withdrawal, Nika said no more, but she was more alert than ever to signs of his distress. Whatever it was, she could see he was embarrassed about it. Knowing this gave her no comfort whatsoever.

Chapter Thirty-Seven

A s was typical of any of Roger's projects, once he made up his mind, he acted. The purchase of the Washington Hotel, therefore, proceeded with such remarkable speed that the deal was completed before Island gossip caught wind of it.

Elisabeth and Roger agreed that it would make sense for Elisabeth to coordinate the renovations of the hotel from the Island, so there was no longer any need for pretense to excuse Elisabeth's frequent stays at Fiona's house.

Renovation was the kind of work at which Elisabeth excelled. She had excellent taste and a keen mind for detail, and she enjoyed the chaos of construction and its demands for organization and problem solving. Previous owners had done most of the big jobs. There was a commercial kitchen, and the mechanicals were all sound, but Elisabeth had her own ideas about how things should be. Happily engrossed, she went back and forth to Sturgeon Bay and Green Bay on a regular basis, buying materials and hiring workers. She was in her element. But throughout it all, she kept a careful eye on her friend.

Fiona accepted her presence—and Rocco's—with pleasure and gratitude, but even when Elisabeth wasn't there they still talked every day. The length and substance of their

conversations varied widely, but the connection mattered to
them both. Daily phone calls were a long-established part of
their friendship, but lately they had begun to feel like a lifeline
to Fiona.

As much from mutual interest as from Elisabeth's attempts
at diversion, most of their conversations centered around the
hotel. But today Fiona was telling Elisabeth about Oliver's
peculiar dressing rules, and finding that Elisabeth was as fascinated as she, herself, had been.

"He's an odd duck, isn't he?" commented Elisabeth. "If
we were doing remakes of *Little House on the Prairie* he could
play the part of the priggish school master."

"He is a bit…tightly wound."

"Yes," agreed Elisabeth. "Although I suppose he's a good
counter to your loosey goosey approach to life."

"Loosey goosey? *Loosey goosey*? Good God. What old attic
did you find that in? Anyway, I am NOT loosey goosey. I'm…
relaxed."

Elisabeth snorted in a ladylike way. "You are many things,
my friend, but relaxed is not one of them."

"Well, you try being relaxed," said Fiona, slightly miffed.
"Did you see what Stella has been tweeting? She's implying
that I've been embezzling funds. It's outrageous."

"I keep telling you: you need to respond."

Fiona sighed. "I know. I know you're right. I just hate to
be drawn down to her level."

Elisabeth heard that she needed to back down, and softened her tone.

"You could never be on her level, Fiona. That's the whole

point. That's why you can't let her win."

Sitting at her desk, Fiona fidgeted and said nothing. Deciding to be tactful, Elisabeth changed the subject.

For the first nights after her discovery, Fiona carefully refilled the jar lid with raw meat, and positioned herself on the wall. Each night she went to bed without meeting the little creature, and in the morning, found that the food was gone. On the fourth night—partly in deference to her own comfort and partly as strategy—she decided to sit up in bed to watch. She kept the lights low, leaving one small lamp alight, enough to read, and just enough to see across the room.

About an hour went by when a movement at the edge of her vision alerted her, and she carefully turned her gaze from the pages of her book.

With small, quick movements, the little face popped out of the woodwork, and rapidly disappeared. As she watched, it popped out again, a little further this time. Its small flat head was triangular, like a snake's. She could see now that this little animal, her midnight companion for more than a year, was exactly what her research had told her: he was a least weasel, the smallest predatory mammal in the world.

Fiona mused that the similarity in head shapes between snakes and weasels might be from a similarity in environments: both snakes and weasels lived and moved in narrow tunnels. The little head popped out again, and again, each time evincing a deepening interest in the meat. All at once, he flashed out of the hole, ran to the meat, snatched it up, dropped it, snatched it up again, and disappeared with it into the hole. It all happened within a second or two. Then he was gone.

About six inches long, he was a rich, tawny brown, like a deer, with a white neck and chest and white feet. He moved like an otter: half-running, half-jumping, his body curved in an arc.

Fiona was filled with glee. She ran back down to the kitchen for another piece of meat.

Chapter Thirty-Eight

Oliver Robert realized that he was going to have to find some outlet. Going home alone every night to read or watch old television series was not a recipe for happiness. The monthly movies shown at the arts center were not sufficient. No. This was not the big city. He needed to join something, to meet people.

In his yearnings, he found himself returning to a long-abandoned habit of his youth. He started going to church.

It began as sheer loneliness. By Sunday morning on any given weekend, he had spent two evenings alone, and as much as he enjoyed solitude, the craving for human companionship began to gnaw at him. With some misgivings, he dressed and took himself off to the early service at the local Lutheran congregation of St. Thor.

Oliver was not certain, at this point in his life, what he actually believed, but the welcome he received at St. Thor was so gratifying that he fell easily into the routine of churchgoing. It all felt so familiar and comfortable that he wondered why he had even hesitated, and going to church on Sundays quickly became the high point of his week.

As a city dweller accustomed to secular values, it surprised him a little to see who and how many people were there, and he observed, with an outsider's clarity, the depth of connection among the congregants. Even so, behind the scenes, all the competitions, grudges, friendships, rivalries, and alliances of human interaction were playing themselves out in the usual fashion. They were so close to the surface as to be visible to a thoughtful observer during the post-service coffee hour, like eddies beneath the surface of the water. Oliver watched with interest, and learned a great deal about Island life.

It was during one of these coffee hours that Oliver, momentarily standing a bit off to the side, overheard a conversation between two women.

"Did you hear that Gloria isn't going to direct the play this year?"

"Yes, she just has too much on her hands with Frank's illness these days."

"Who's going to do it?"

"No one, so far. I don't think we'll be able to find anyone."

"Maybe there won't be a show this year."

The conversation paused for a moment as the sadness of this prospect presented itself.

"Oh, well. Can't be helped."

I have secret thoughts that I never tell anyone else. No one. Sometimes my thoughts frighten me. Especially now. Fire never frightens me. It soothes me. It comforts me. It compels me. It speaks to me like a friend. I am not lonely with fire… Fire eats. It

devours. It destroys. So warm. So bright. It reminds me—no. No. I won't think about that yet. Not yet. I will think about that later.

I don't think of fire as an element. I know they say that. Said that. Before. Elemental. It's elemental. Not the same thing. No. But elemental is true. It is elemental. Earth, water, fire, wind. The greatest of these is fire. "The greatest of these is love." Why does that come to me now? Fire and love? Fire and love. The greatest of these is fire. I need to think about this. I need to think about it soon. Not now. I can't think about it now. I am cold. I need fire.

I could build a small fire. Now. Right now, I could build a small one. Just for myself. Why not? It's just outside. I can go out into the night and feel safe. I don't feel safe anymore. I think. Don't think now. Just build. Don't think. Logs. Sticks. Big sticks. Medium sticks. Small sticks. Straw. Build. Burn. Make comfort. Later. Later I will think.

Yes. Yes. I could build a fire. Then I would be warm. I would be warm and I could think about it then.

Ben had finished his chores in the barn and was now contentedly leaning over the fence in his accustomed manner, watching his charge busily cropping grass. The goat coexisted peacefully with Nancy's big beef cattle, who were separated from the bulls by two pastures. Ben had a healthy respect for the cattle, along with the gentle appreciation he felt for all creatures, but he was particularly fond of this goat. He didn't mind that it was not usually a demonstrative animal. He was happy merely to be accepted by it, and acknowledged as a familiar being.

This pasture was located at the front of the barn and house, bordered on one side by the road and on the other by the dirt drive that ran up the hill from the road to the house. At the far end was another fence and the woods.

Ben was engrossed in his own thoughts when he was startled by a voice nearby, and recognized it with a sinking feeling. It was Caleb.

"Well, look who's here. It's little Ben."

Caleb sauntered up the drive to the fence and leaned against it with an air of ownership.

Ben merely looked at Caleb, his face stony. The cattle lowed mildly in the silence, and the ersatz Robert, with his usual canniness, moved away from the stranger while still continuing to graze.

"Whatcha doing, little man?" asked Caleb with an infuriating singsong.

Ben still said nothing. Experience had taught him that to engage was to lose.

"What's a matter? Cat-tle got your tongue?"

Caleb laughed at his joke and leaned over to pick up a stick. He climbed onto the rail of the fence, and played with the stick, switching it against the fence. "Whoa, that is one rasty-looking goat. You had any sense, you'd put that animal down."

Ben began to breathe fast in his anger, but he would not be drawn in.

"I can help you, if you want." Caleb switched harder with his stick. "Wham!" he hit the fence. "Right down on its head.

That ought to do it."

Even though he knew the goat would be capable of fending for itself in such an attack, Ben felt the red anger rising in him and his body roused to do battle.

"Or we could use a rock," continued Caleb. "There's a nice one right over there."

Ben rose from his slouch against the fence and straightened his shoulders to face this threat to his animals. Nancy appeared at this moment, as if out of nowhere.

"How are things going, Ben?" she asked. "Everyone here and accounted for?"

Ben swallowed, and looked Nancy in the eye. "Yes, ma'am."

Nancy knew Ben well. She had never seen him angry, and his intensity surprised her. She quickly surmised the truth of the situation, however. The methods of bullying are timeless, and she recognized them from her own youth. She turned her piercing gaze on Caleb and looked him over.

"You seem to be interfering with my employee's work. What is your name?"

Caleb's boldness had been unchallenged for so long that he made the mistake of trying to brazen things out. "Ask him." Caleb indicated Ben with a tip of his head.

"I asked you."

Caleb muttered something under his breath.

There was a long silence as Nancy looked at him, unmoved, her face calm with a country woman's open appraisal. She knew perfectly well who he was, and who his parents were.

Caleb did not have the courtesy—or the courage—to look at her.

"Not much of a farm, here," he observed. "My parents' farm is tons better."

Ben nearly gasped at this impertinence.

Nancy waited a moment before replying. "Perhaps so," she said, apparently unmoved. "But it's probably also a lot safer than this one. We have lots of accidents around here. Bulls," she added, casually, "are considerably more dangerous than goats."

Caleb's mask of nonchalance fell for a moment before he resumed his swagger.

"Well, I've got better things to do than hang around here, anyway. Guess I'll be going, Benno. Better get on with your chores."

The sneer in his voice was still in evidence, even in the presence of an adult. He jumped off the fence and started down the driveway toward the road.

"Bulls don't scare me," he added loudly, as an afterthought.

Nancy stood for a moment watching Caleb as he sauntered down the driveway. "I don't want you having friends over while you're working," she said loudly enough so that Caleb would be sure to hear. "You tell that kid if I catch him over here again we'll find out how scared he is of bulls."

"Yes, ma'am," said Ben, gratefully, though not as loudly.

"That ought to take care of the little skunk," she said, in a lower tone meant for Ben alone. "Let me know if he gives you any more trouble." She turned and headed back up to the house, calling without looking back. "I'll be making lunch in a few minutes. Come up and have a sandwich before we get started on that fence. If we get done before it's too late, we can do some target practice."

Ben looked after her departing figure worshipfully.

Chapter Thirty-Nine

Every night Fiona waited impatiently for the least weasel to come out. He seemed less interested in crunching now than he had previously, apparently preferring to manifest himself in occupations that involved the raw meat that Fiona was leaving out for him.

It was now clear to Fiona that the disappearance of her mouse problem had not been the result of her fervent wishes for their removal. This small creature was sleek and well-fed, and clearly had no need for Fiona's supplements to his diet, even though he found them enticing. She hoped she wasn't dissuading him from his primary pursuits. She had been enjoying her mouse-free status, even though she felt a twinge of pity for the mice. She had no doubt that her new friend was without no mercy.

Fiona had taken to leaving on a night light and curling up sideways at the end of her bed to watch for her visitor. Sometimes she fell asleep there and woke to find herself stiff and confused about where she was. Most nights, however, she lay awake, and the hope for the arrival of her friend brought to her sad wakefulness a small sense of consolation.

The weasel's increasing comfort with his new dining arrangements encouraged her to move the jar lid further and further from the wall, drawing him each night into greater boldness. His habits were of the eat and run variety. He would sneak up on the meat with a predator's wary focus, and once within range, would pounce and drag away his prize with a speed that often left Fiona wondering whether she had actually seen him. He never ate within her view.

After many incidents like these, it occurred to Fiona that ground meat would be harder for him to carry off. She also decided to supplement with a little bit of raw egg in half of a shell. He would have to linger for that, too. The jar lid had been too light and easy for him to tip and move, so she arranged her offerings this time in a tiny dish meant to hold soy sauce or wasabi from a set Elisabeth had brought her from Japan.

She put the dish down on the floor and climbed onto her bed to watch. She hadn't long to wait for his arrival. He appeared suddenly, as always, and Fiona realized that he must have been watching.

With quick darting movements, he approached the new food to sniff and then ran away. He approached again, intrigued, and darted away again. After a half-dozen forays of investigation, he grabbed some of the meat and carried it speedily away. But this time, there was too little to occupy his appetite for long, and she was rewarded by his quick return for more.

Oliver Robert did not see much of his landlady. Her family was happy to have a clean, responsible tenant to look after their vacant property, and he was content to have a place to stay without a long-term commitment. He had his doubts about Island life, and wanted to keep his options open.

So, when Heather appeared on Oliver's doorstep one evening after work, he was both surprised and slightly annoyed. Just because he was bored and lonely didn't mean he wanted just anyone to drop by, but he didn't see any way to avoid inviting her in. She might think he was hiding something, or she might be offended and ask him to move out.

He arranged his face into a pleasant expression and held the door open for her to enter.

"What can I do for you?" he asked, once the usual comments about the weather had been exchanged.

"I was going to call, but I was passing, so I thought I'd just stop in."

This routine feature of Island life was not to Oliver's taste. Telephones were for ignoring people if one so chose and for not answering if one didn't feel like talking.

"Ah," said Oliver, shortly.

"Yes, well, I wanted to ask you to dinner on Friday. It's nothing formal, just some people I know. Thought you might like to join us."

Oliver could think of no polite way to refuse, and besides, it might be nice to go to a dinner party. He doubted if it would be of the kind he was used to, but it would be better than coming home to watch a movie alone.

"Thank you, yes," he said, rather stiffly. "I can come."

"Great!" said Heather. "I'll tell my Aunt Stella. It's at her house, and she really wants you to be there."

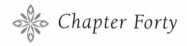 *Chapter Forty*

In the small group of men who practiced yoga at Ground Zero, news of Joshua's videos travelled fast. It wasn't long before everyone wanted to see them, and they began asking whether they themselves could be recorded.

Joshua quickly saw that this could get out of hand.

"Listen," he said, after a few minutes of good-natured jostling for first dibs among the members of the group. "Why don't I just keep doing the videos of Terry as I have been, and just post them online for all of us to watch?"

He saw the doubtful looks exchanged among them.

"It can be a closed group," suggested Joshua. "Only those of us in the class will be able to access it. "I can't do everybody, but if I do Terry, at least you can all learn by example."

"By bad example, you mean," said someone, and they all laughed.

Terry just shrugged philosophically and smiled. He was feeling too pleased by the progress he was making to feel self-conscious.

Chapter Forty-One ✤

During the days, her life went on as before. Fiona seemed, to her friends, flat and dull-eyed, but to almost everyone else she seemed as always. Her inner life, however, was plagued with dark thoughts. She did not know how to tell Elisabeth that her feelings were not merely about missing Pete. The truth was, she did not know how to understand, herself.

Fiona stared now at the bleak landscape of her life and found that her pain was too raw to touch. The deep and heavy weight she felt on her heart overwhelmed every moment, and her best way of coping with it was to hide from it. Those first tears she had shed with Elisabeth had been the only ones, and now she moved through her days as if wrapped in cotton, insulated from both the grief and from any small joys that might be found in the routine of life. Even watching the progress of her new barn had lost its charm.

There was something counterfeit, now, in the way she presented herself to the world, and her own misery gave her new insights into the people around her. She watched their interactions and wondered. What lingering unhappiness did Emily Martin have that she needed to put such a false face to the world? What had made Oliver Robert dread his daily surroundings so much that he had to move to a place unencumbered by memories? And even Stella? What about her? Was she hiding herself from some deep, daily anguish?

As the long, dry summer began to give way to fall, the water-starved trees were turning brown without their usual rich color. With the dying of the season, Fiona grieved daily over small things: the shrub withering in the yard; the fox dead and unnoticed by the side of the road; even the shells on the beach.

Death is present everywhere and always, and daily life most often brushes past it unseeing. But in her grief, it was all brought forward: primary and emphatic. Death, endings, and impermanence seemed to her to loom over everything, and she could no longer take pleasure in the small joys that were diminished now in their shadows. She did not know if she would ever recover her old self, but she knew she was in a time of deepening perception about herself, about the world. Even small things made themselves manifest as profound and important.

She was walking along the shoreline one afternoon, when she came upon a pile of shells, cracked and empty. She did not recognize the kind of mollusk, but noted wryly to herself that given the quantity of these remnants, all heaped together, they must have been tasty.

Fiona had always loved shells, but suddenly the beach seemed to her full of death; each shell representing the remnants of a life now gone. How, she wondered, had she never thought before of shells as skeletons; of the bones of the dead? How had she walked on the beach admiring its beauty without being aware that it was a cemetery for sea creatures?

She was stunned by her insensitivity, at her own blindness, but at the same time, she wondered whether she would ever be free to enjoy the shore again. Overwhelmed and alone, she turned away from the water. She took the road instead of the beach in the walk back to her empty house.

When she got home, her restlessness was unfinished. Elisabeth had gone. After prowling the house for a few hours, she tried to go to sleep. She tossed in her bed for a long time before she finally rose and went to sit on the little window seat.

She leaned her face against the cool glass of the window. She could hear his voice in her head, his laugh. She could see the looks on his face, all of whose meanings she knew. She remembered the scent of his skin when her face was pressed up against his neck, against his chest, leaning her cheek on his hand. Each particular memory caused its own pain and struck her heart with a blow.

She was spending most of her nights this way lately. Unable to sleep very much, she would rise to sit on the window seat and watch the sky. Sometimes she would fall asleep there, but mostly she stayed and just sat with open eyes. The stars were a comfort to her, as they had always been, particularly here on the Island.

Elisabeth, who watched over Fiona anxiously—and who had no way of knowing of these night vigils—had accused her of wallowing. Fiona thought, instead, that she was coming to terms with reality. She needed to face what was now, and in order to do that she needed to do…this. Whatever this was.

Maybe, she conceded to herself, it was wallowing. But she could no more resist this exercise in observing her grief than she could resist the urge to breathe.

Somehow, her loss of Pete had stirred something else already there, partly hidden since her days as a crime reporter. All of the knowledge of human cruelty, the darkness and evil she had seen on the streets of Chicago, which she had so long suppressed—first to do her job, and then as habit, and finally as a means of survival because noticing it would threaten her very existence— seemed like an acid that ate away at her heart and soul. It had no real expression, because it felt so deeply embedded in her. She could not bring herself to look at it, but she could feel its corrosion moving deeper, spreading its poisons into every corner of her being. She coped by not seeing it, by turning away from the full view of it, and yet, it would not allow her to forget its presence, always burning beneath the surface of her life.

She thought sometimes of going out to walk in the night, but she was keenly aware of how any eccentricity—whether real or perceived—might be interpreted on the Island, so she stayed at the window, sometimes imagining how it would be to walk along the paths she knew so well, or on the beach alone.

In a grief apart, she always thought of him. She didn't wonder where he was or what he was doing. She simply remembered with a reality that was often jarring, how it had been when he had been there. She thought again and again of the strange quality of time that permitted things in the past to linger in the present, of how only time separated him from her, not distance.

It doesn't pay, thought Fiona, *to think existential thoughts in the pre-dawn hours. The night has a way of twisting our minds toward the darkness that can only lead to a thwarted theology. The blackest parts of the soul, the old wounds, the deepest fears stir and stagger in the heart, and then, because you are awake, they stay with you into the daylight and bring their poison with them. In night it is best to distract the inner beasts of the human soul with the commonplace and the straightforward.*

Perhaps, she thought, *the anxieties of our dreams come to the surface whether we are sleeping or not. Why else this primal angst that comes in the night?* Nothing was different about her life in the night than it was in the daytime. She was unhappy, yes, but that was true both day and night. The magnitude of the night's anxieties had a different quality.

Looking up, she saw the thin line of light that ran along the edge of the clouds of sea smoke above the lake. Dawn was coming.

She hoped it could outrace her despair.

Chapter Forty-Two

I remember sleeping in my mother's bed because my father was away. I don't know whose comfort it was for, hers or mine, but I was not yet asleep, and I liked being in the big bed. There was the sound of fire engines coming closer, and then closer. It seemed that they must be at a neighbor's. My mother threw open the drapes to see, and gasped. The view from the windows was a wall of flame in the woods on the edge of our yard, less than fifty yards from the house. The flames engulfed the trees and towered over them.

"Quick!" said my mother. She pulled me from the bed, calling my brother and sister from their beds. It was cold out. We put on coats over our pajamas.

"The house could catch fire," my mother whispered to my brother. But I heard.

We went outside into the night. The fire engines were there, the low rumble of their engines thrumming in the night air. I could see the men with hoses, anonymous in their helmets and big coats, moving toward the flames, the spinning red lights, the puddles from the hoses, the static chatter of the radios.

"Look," said my brother, digging his toe in the earth along the edge of the road. "The plows have dug up all the sod along the road." This seemed a dire thing, and I pondered sod. Why were *the plows digging up sod? What was sod? Should I be afraid?*

"The fence is burning," said my mother, watching.

I saw the silhouettes of the men against the flames. I saw the trees dwarfed by the fire. I smelled the smoke.

I remember waking the next morning, the smell of smoke everywhere in the house. The gray light of morning showed the burned and charred fence posts, the gap in the woods where tall trees had been. I walked to school among the puddles left from the fire men's hoses, remembering what I had seen, remembering the orange flames towering over the trees.

I was not afraid.

I was glad.

Elisabeth came down to breakfast one morning grim-faced, her cell phone in her hand.

"I suppose you haven't seen it?"

Fiona yawned, and poured herself some coffee. "Seen what?"

"Stella's latest tweet."

Fiona rolled her eyes. "You know I don't want to see that stuff." This, of course, was not strictly true, but Fiona was no mood to have this conversation with Elisabeth again.

"Well, you need to. Look at this." She held out her phone and Fiona looked.

@realstella

With no fire chief UR IN DANGER.

#washingtonisland #dangerousincompetence

Fiona was silent for a moment, then shook her head. "That's not even correct. We have a fire chief. He's only threatened to resign. It's a tactic."

Even at this hour of the morning Elisabeth was in full battle mode. "It doesn't matter that it's not correct. Don't you see? People are reading it, and discussing it, and they're starting to believe it. This is bad for you Fiona. You have to do something."

Fiona sat down at the kitchen table and drank her coffee. "Maybe after breakfast."

"After breakfast, what?" asked Elisabeth.

"Maybe after breakfast I can get excited about it. Right now, I just want to drink my coffee."

Exasperated, Elisabeth went back upstairs to get dressed.

Later that afternoon, Fiona and Oliver Robert were working together in an almost companionable silence, but Fiona was fretful, thinking about Stella's latest tweets. "What do you think, Oliver? Should I start tweeting back?" Fiona looked at him frankly.

Oliver didn't even look up. "If you return an ass's kicks, most of the pain is yours."

Fiona suppressed a smile. She should have known he'd have a rule.

"Is that a no?"

He gave her a pained look, but said nothing.

At the end of the day, Elisabeth took one look at Fiona, and knew she needed a diversion. Elisabeth's resources were growing a bit thin. There weren't many diversions to be had on the Island.

"Let's go to Nelsen's for dinner. I'm not in the mood to cook."

Fiona was too tired to even contemplate dinner and readily acquiesced.

When they arrived, Elisabeth saw someone she knew from Ephraim and went over to chat. Fiona seated herself at the bar and accepted a copy of the menu she knew by heart.

It was moderately busy. There was often a pre-weekend burst of festive anticipation on Thursdays. Eddie had been alternating his work with leaning on the bar to watch a game on the television overhead. He saw Fiona come in, and came down to take her order.

"Hey, Fiona. Usual?"

Fiona smiled and nodded. She knew she probably wouldn't feel like drinking it, but she could hold the glass. "And a cabernet for Elisabeth."

Eddie returned with her order and settled in for a chat. "I was hoping we'd see you tonight. There's something I think you should know."

Fiona tilted her head in curiosity. Eddie didn't usually tell tales.

He leaned in and spoke quietly. "Your new guy, Oliver, and Stella? Last night they were in here together."

Fiona stared at him. "Stella and Oliver Robert were here? Together?" She repeated his words in disbelief.

Eddie nodded seriously, his lips tight and eyebrows raised in an expression of regret and concern.

"What were they talking about?"

"I would tell you if I knew, but they were either speaking very quietly, or very carefully, because I did not catch a word. And I did try." He acknowledged an order down the bar and turned back to Fiona before reaching for a glass. "You need to watch your back."

Fiona was left to manage her reaction to this news. What could this mean?

She took a drink of scotch as her mind raced. Just when she began to think she had a handle on things, some new predicament always seemed to arise. Oliver Robert and Stella. Now what could that be about? Obviously, nothing good. By the time Eddie had returned, she had finished her scotch without even noticing.

"Another round?" asked Eddie.

"Please," said Fiona.

Chapter Forty-Three

Since his conversation with Nika, Jim had been observing Fiona's mood from a distance. He knew she was unhappy. The whole Island seemed to know. Reluctant to pressure her, he still had no illusions about his opportunity. But it was now or never, he told himself. He had nothing to lose.

It was Ben Palsson who inspired Jim's first move. The boy's love of nature and his insatiable desire to learn frequently brought him to Jim's door for conversation or a walk in the woods. Jim didn't know it, but Ben was also in need of advice, and was desperate to bring up his ongoing problem with Caleb. If anything, things were getting worse.

That afternoon Caleb had been waiting for him after school, just off school grounds, where the rules didn't apply.

"Hey, Benno." His mocking voice had a lilting quality. "What's happening?"

Ben kept walking.

"Hey, little man, I'm talking to you." Caleb grabbed Ben's arm as he tried to pass, but Ben jerked away.

"Get lost," said Ben.

"Oh, you can't get rid of me that easy," said Caleb, reaching for Ben's backpack.

At that moment, they heard a truck approaching, and Caleb was forced to change his demeanor.

The truck slowed. Nancy leaned over the passenger seat to open the door.

"Hey there, Ben. I'm just heading your way. Hop in and I'll give you a ride."

Without a backward glance, Ben climbed gratefully into the truck, but not before Caleb could deliver a final message.

"Don't forget what I said about your daddy, little man," he hissed. "Don't you ever forget."

Humiliated, Ben pulled the door shut and looked straight ahead.

"Everything all right, Ben?" asked Nancy as they drove off.

"Sure," said Ben. "Fine."

Nancy glanced at him and let it go. "Where to?" she asked. "You're not on the schedule for the farm today."

"I was going to see Jim, if that's okay."

"Jim it is," said Nancy brightly. She would have asked more, but she figured Ben would be more likely to confide in Jim. Sensing that Ben was not in a chatty mood, she kept the conversation going with updates about the animals all the way to Jim's. Ben expressed his thanks, jumped out of the truck, and ran up the path to the house.

When Ben showed up at Jim's door, he had just about convinced himself to bring up his problem. Jim was an adult, but he was also a friend, and it was okay to ask for help from friends. Jim wouldn't try to fix things, or rebuke him, or ask too many questions. He would just listen, and maybe, give a little advice about how to deliver the right punch. That was all Ben wanted.

Jim, unaware of Ben's agenda, had one of his own. It had occurred to him that their regular walks would be a no-pressure situation in which he could spend time with Fiona. Particularly since their rescue of the goat a few months ago, the three of them had a good rapport together.

Ben was waiting for the right moment to mention his troubles when Jim spoke.

"How about we call Fiona, and see if she wants to come with us? You know, get the band back together." Jim tried to seem casual.

Disappointed, Ben shrugged. He liked Fiona, but it wouldn't be easy to talk with both of them there. "Okay."

Jim tossed the phone to him. "Her number's there. You call."

Ben's propensity for shrugging was a leading indicator of impending adolescence. He shrugged again and dialed the number.

Chapter Forty-Four

Fiona's sense of the office as sanctuary had been turned upside down by Eddie's revelation. Oliver's apparent friendship with Stella could only mean one thing. She made her way to the office less willingly this morning, and with less sense of escape.

The town meeting to determine what to do about the fire department was fast approaching, and she wanted to finalize her position. With the help of Oliver, she had identified some options to relieve the financial pressures on the town budget, one of which was a tax increase that she hoped no one would ever even see.

She pulled into the lot at the back of the building and was about to get out of her car when she caught some movement out of the corner of her eye. She watched as the door of the building opened, and Stella, carrying a clipboard and some folders, walked out, headed to an unfamiliar car, and drove off.

Fiona sat back in her seat, her mind racing. So, Eddie had been right. More than right. She would need to do more than watch her back. She would need to lock her desk and the door to her inner office. Fiona felt as if the sun had gone behind a cloud. The rules of the game were now very different indeed.

Fiona increasingly looked to her time at home as her only sanctuary. She did not know who she could trust, and every day seemed to bring some new blow. What she had come to think of as "weasel adventures" became the best parts of her days.

Fiona had heard of coyote attacks being described as having the speed of a car crash, and she mused that an encounter with weasels, too, must seem to happen without warning. She wondered if he lingered near the gap in the wall waiting for the scent of raw meat to reach him, or if the dish was merely a new stop on his nightly rounds.

As she had hoped, each time he returned much more quickly than before. And perhaps out of boldness, or merely out of an instinctive need to conserve energy, he stayed longer each time, to nibble—if such voracious eating could be described that way—on the ground beef.

But for all his greed, he had dainty habits. He was clean and sleek and, for the first time, Fiona was able to observe the fastidiousness with which he stopped to groom his whiskers. When the meat was gone, he returned with interest to the egg. With the raw meat present, he would not appear to notice it, but once that the meat was gone, he seemed to feel that further inspection was warranted.

He approached the egg with his usual wary confidence, his movements fast and furtive as he sniffed, then quickly retreated. Once he had assured himself that it was safe, he returned and began to lap delicately at the egg with a small pink tongue. Fiona marveled at the precision and grace of his movements, and at the beauty of his markings. His white belly gave the impression of racing stripes along his side, and his little triangular head was sleek and elegant. She gazed at him with delight, her other difficulties forgotten.

Chapter Forty-Five

After the first invitation, Jim called Fiona regularly to go for walks with him and Ben. Elisabeth had mixed feelings about Fiona spending so much time with Jim but she knew that it was good for her to re-engage with life. Privately, Elisabeth admitted to herself that part of her relief was selfish. No matter the depth of the friendship, there is a limit, and Elisabeth had been away from home for a long time. After so long on the Island, Elisabeth had some gallery business to attend to, and she was missing Roger. Promising to return soon, Elisabeth departed for home, taking Rocco with her. The house instantly felt empty and sad.

The evening of Elisabeth's departure, Fiona was sitting on her porch steps, absorbing the last of the day's sunshine. She had many things to do, but she was doing none of them. It occurred to her that, in the midst of so many municipal crises, her indolence was on display for the entire community, and that, as a public servant, it might not create the right image, but she was beyond caring. She thought fondly of impeachment.

She looked down at her glass and swirled its contents. Since Pete's departure, she had been curiously uninterested in drinking, which, she now realized, had always been for her a form of ritual celebration. She hadn't much interest in eating, either. She felt as if she were going through the forms of life without participating. Everything felt like dust. She had not experienced this kind of grief before.

She had not tried to reach him during the past months. He had not tried to reach her. She tried not to think of him, but the pervasive quality of her misery made him omnipresent, even when she wasn't conscious of it. Whatever his feelings, he must be less tormented than she was. He was in places she had never been, with no associations to evoke her presence in his mind, and he would no doubt be busier than she—too busy to dwell on loss, or memories, or brokenness.

She thought bitterly of whatever secret things he might be doing. Secret things that he could not trust her to know. She stared into her glass and then up at the sky. The deep blue had an intensity only seen in autumn, and the leaves were still on the trees. So much beauty was around her and, for the first time in her life, she was indifferent to it.

There was the sound of a familiar engine, and she looked up to see Jim stopping his truck in front of the house. Her heart sank. She didn't want to see anyone. She poured her scotch into the bushes, hoping she wouldn't have to ask him to stay and have a drink.

"Hey," said Jim coming up the walk.

"Hey," said Fiona.

She tried to smile, but it didn't quite work. Everything felt forced and false, and she was unable to access anything real, as if she had been frozen in ice and tucked away into some deep, inaccessible place.

Jim sat down across from her on the same step, and leaned his back against the column facing her. "I'm not sure scotch is especially good for shrubbery."

Fiona made a sound that could have been a laugh. "I don't have a taste for anything lately."

Jim looked serious and nodded, then broke his gaze and turned to look across the street. He knew exactly how Fiona felt. It was the same way he felt about her. "Summer sure went fast. Can't believe the Albatross will be closing for the season soon."

"No."

There was a long silence.

Jim tried again. "I gave young Ben a ride home yesterday. He tells me he likes working for you."

Fiona nodded and then mentally chastised herself. Jim had been a good friend to her, and on more than one occasion. The least she could do was be civil. She owed him at least that much. He deserved that much.

"It's good to have some help, what with all the meetings I have these days. He's nice to have around, and I think Nancy enjoys him."

"Yes," said Jim. "He's a good kid. Pretty excited about the animals, and he's learning a lot."

"Yes." Fiona fidgeted.

Jim did not. He was a patient man, and a highly intelligent one. He would play his cards thoughtfully.

"How is your mother?" asked Fiona politely.

"Nosy as ever," he said, cheerfully. "But at least she has a hobby."

Fiona laughed in spite of herself. "I think it's a fairly

universal interest."

"Well, yes. On the Island, anyway."

"Especially on the Island, yes." Fiona found herself softening. It felt good to be sociable, even for a little while.

"Had dinner yet?" asked Jim.

"No. Too lazy to bother."

"I know what you mean."

There was a moment's silence. Then he took the plunge. "C'mon. We'll be lazy together. Let's get something to eat. I'll drive."

Fiona had been about to refuse, but she checked herself. Saying no would take more effort than saying yes. "Okay."

"You'd better get a jacket. It will be cold when the sun goes down."

With uncharacteristic docility, Fiona rose and went into the house to get her jacket.

Jim leaned back again and took a deep breath. At least she hadn't said no.

The Island was abuzz with its many public happenings. Along with Chief Gil's ultimatum, which was still hanging fire, there was news of the auditions for a musical. Bright yellow posters had popped up on all the Island bulletin boards.

Gloria's sad withdrawal after years of directing had left a gap that Oliver Robert was only too happy to fill. He had fond memories of community theater from his youth and college days, and he had even dabbled as an adult, although his work obligations at his old job had made that increasingly impossible. Now, however, he had time, authority, and an eager audience. It was a dream come true.

Normally, the play is chosen before the auditions, but without knowing what—or rather, who—he had to work with, Oliver had decided to let his casting opportunities dictate the program. The bright yellow posters advertising the audition, therefore, said merely "Open Auditions: All-Island Musical". Oliver had blithely printed them out on the town board's printer and hoped that no one would notice.

The use of the term "open audition" was something of a misnomer, "a bit," thought Oliver, "like the American misuse of 'high tea.'" But as he had found himself doing so often these days, he had merely shrugged his shoulders and gone on. "When in Rome," he thought.

He had also made the rather extraordinary decision not to schedule a date for the performances. He had wrestled a great deal with himself about this, because it went against his nature not to have everything fully prepared and in place. But his lack of experience with the local talent made him cautious and, in the end, his caution had won out over his compulsive organizing. Not knowing who would show up at his audition or what they were capable of meant that Oliver had no confidence that they would be able to throw a show together in a quick four or five weeks.

"No," he decided. "First let's see what we have to work with."

Nelsen's was quiet that night, and Eddie stood at the bar polishing glasses in an expert manner as Jim and Fiona Campbell came in together.

"Evening, Jim. Fiona."

"Hey, Eddie," they said in unison.

"You've got the place all to yourselves tonight. What'll it be?"

As they placed their orders, Eddie showed only his professional demeanor of casual friendship. No emotion, no opinions were betrayed in his expression.

But the truth was that he felt a series of seriously conflicted emotions. He liked Jim. They were friends. He had known him for a long time. He had been encouraging Jim to take this step, knowing that not to try would mean a life of wondering. Jim was a totally decent guy who deserved love and happiness, and he had felt sorry for the turmoil of Jim's—so far—unrequited love for Fiona. That kind of feeling, Eddie knew from personal experience, was among life's most painful emotions. He could understand it, too. Fiona was an attractive woman.

But, Eddie admired Pete Landry and also considered him a friend, and he couldn't help but feel that Pete was a better match for Fiona. He had seen the spark between them many times, and he knew it was a rare thing. But he had also seen Pete in action.

After last spring's election, Eddie had begun calling Pete "*Commendatore,*" based on a character in an opera, and the nickname's combination of heroism and a love for seeing justice done seemed, in Eddie's mind, to suit Pete perfectly. It didn't hurt, either, that the *Commendatore* was a ghost with supernatural powers. That seemed, somehow, to capture the essence of Pete Landry. So far, there had been nothing he couldn't do.

But Eddie had also guessed—along with half the Island—that something hadn't gone right between Pete and Fiona. He had seen Fiona's face over the past months—drained of color and life—her eyes flat and dull, so unlike her usual sparkle. He had heard the gossip in the bar. No one understood what had happened, but that didn't stop there being a hundred different theories about it. The conclusion, though, was all the same: Pete was gone, and Fiona was unhappy.

Eddie was fairly certain that none of this boded well for Jim. It was never good to be the second choice. Even if the first choice was gone for good.

Later that night, after closing, Eddie sat on his porch. It was his habit to unwind after his shift by reading or watching the stars. Tonight, he had too much to think about to be able to concentrate on reading. He had made himself a mug of tea, and sat rocking, looking off to the sky above the harbor. The contrast in temperatures between the cooler air and warmer water made it misty, and the stars that were visible were hazy and sparse.

So, Jim had finally invited Fiona out. From his post at the bar, it had all seemed natural and light, but Eddie was pretty sure he knew what was going on in Jim's head. When they left the bar together, Eddie had been busy with some late-arriving customers, but his sharp eyes caught Jim's subtle gesture of possession as he guided Fiona through the door. It was none of his business, Eddie knew, but it felt absolutely all wrong. He sighed, shook his head, and took a drink of tea. He wondered whether Pete Landry was really gone for good.

Chapter Forty-Six

Robert's rules were a curious amalgamation of life advice and cryptic metaphor and, at first, Fiona looked forward to each new manifestation as an interesting diversion. After a while, however, much like Oliver himself, the charm began to wear. She was always careful what she said around him now, and although there were some things that couldn't be kept secret and, when she thought about it, really didn't need to be, she nevertheless felt the stress of determining which was which. She found the whole thing exhausting. She was reaching a point where she was so tired of it all that she barely even cared anymore. Increasingly her philosophy could be expressed as: let Stella do her worst.

In this uneasy atmosphere, Fiona and Oliver Robert had been working together in the town office for some time one afternoon. After a particularly exasperating phone call, Fiona put down the receiver with a bang. Her frustration did not mix well with choosing what she should or shouldn't say.

"I've got to figure out the permits we need for the harbor. Every agency I call sends me to somebody else. It's driving me mad. I suppose I'm going to have to end up finding someone in the legislature to make some calls for me."

Oliver was apparently engrossed in some bookkeeping

matter and did not look up. "Poke around in the weeds and the snakes come out."

Fiona stared at him. "What is that supposed to mean?"

Oliver sniffed. "I should think it would be self-evident."

"Well, it's not."

He continued typing sporadically, stopping occasionally and squinting at the computer screen. "Under every stone a scorpion sleeps."

"Seriously, Oliver, you are beginning to annoy me."

"If you like peace, don't contradict anybody."

"Enough!"

"An unhappy man's cart is easy to overturn."

"I'm going out. I don't know when I'll be back."

Oliver looked up and called after her. "Do good and don't look back!"

Fiona slammed the office door so hard the music festival posters fell off the wall.

Chapter Forty-Seven ✤

Oliver Robert surveyed the small gathering of people who had come to his audition and resisted a sigh. They were an unassuming assortment of theater groupie high school kids, young adults who imagined themselves would-be stars, retirees, and a few former liberal arts majors longing for cultural stimulation. As always, there were more women than men, a circumstance for which Oliver had been prepared, but which would make choosing the play difficult.

Oliver sighed audibly this time. He was all for civil society, a Tocquevillean community of voluntary associations, but still, there was a small part of him that had hoped for the joy of discovering real talent. "Ah well," he thought, almost unconsciously quoting his grandmother to himself. "We put our dreams away."

This voice from his past awoke in Oliver Robert a fresh burst of ironic self-awareness. His dreams had, indeed, been put away, but he supposed that was the whole reason for coming here. He considered himself too young to be having a mid-life crisis—"I'm only thirty-three, for heaven's sake," he told himself. But his life in Milwaukee had been a daily grind of work and despair. He had thought accounting would be a perfect career, since someone always needs to count something. He was good at it, but the work had bored and depressed him, reducing everything in life to a tidy row of complex figures. "Life," he thought, "must surely be more than that."

He had no romance to tie him to the city, a little money tucked away, and the desire to find some adventure, some mystery, some reason to get out of bed every day. So, when he happened upon Fiona's ad in the *Observer* during a weekend trip to Door County, he had simply quit his job and headed to the Island. He smiled to himself whenever he imagined the reactions at his office to this sudden decision. He had surprised everyone, he knew, and it gave him a little frisson of secret delight at the thought of the gossip it would inevitably provoke. For a day or two, at least, he, Oliver Robert, would be the talk of Greenwald, Fitz, and Keefer, LLC.

Noting the time, Oliver Robert shook himself from his reverie and stepped to the front of the auditorium to face the future cast of the all-Island musical. He clapped his hands together sharply to stop the chattering of those assembled and raised his voice. "All right, people, let's get started."

Surveying the earnest faces before him, Oliver Robert felt a little surge of hope.

"This will be," he thought to himself, "an extravaganza."

And, generally speaking, extravaganzas were in short supply on Washington Island.

The appearance of the least weasel was not predictable, and although Fiona tried to stay awake for him, she was only occasionally able to do so. Instead, she continued moving the jar lid with its appetizing contents closer and closer toward her bed. Each time, she found the food gone in the morning, and she took it as a sign of the least weasel's increasing trust and comfort in her presence.

Elisabeth listened to her account of this progress with a mixture of fascination and disapproval.

"This is a wild animal, Fiona, and you're letting it run around in your house."

"He's been living in the house for well over a year. I would say he's been domesticated by now. Besides," added Fiona cheerfully, "he's completely eliminated the mouse problem. He is a courageous and relentless hunter."

"What about all that chewing?"

"Weasels generally don't gnaw. They're not rodents. So, I don't know what he's doing up there, but I don't think he's hurting anything. Except maybe mice." She paused a moment. "I wonder if what I've been hearing is bone crunching..."

Elisabeth winced and shook her head in mock despair, but she had noticed the tone of Fiona's voice. It was a relief to have Fiona behaving more like herself.

More out of a lack of any more suitable response than anything else, Elisabeth asked, "Does he have a name?"

"I thought about Martin Luther, and Attila, and Ted."

"Ted?"

"For my favorite poet. But I think Attila feels right."

Elisabeth had to laugh. "If he's up there crunching bones it probably suits him."

"Yes," said Fiona fondly. "I think it probably does."

Fiona dreamed that she had gotten up in the middle of the night to ice skate on a river. The river was crowded with many people, all skating, laughing, and playing.

She wanted to get away from the crowds, so she moved off on her own to look at the strange buildings along the banks of the river.

All alone, she suddenly realized that the ice was rotten, and as she tried to reach the shore, she knew that she was going under. Desperately, she looked for a spot where the ice was thicker, but the cracks spread like streaks of lightening all around, and she felt the ice breaking beneath her. The water was bitterly cold as she went down, and above her head through the ice, she could see the people in their brightly colored winter clothing, skating blithely along, paying no attention to her frantic pleas for help.

In what had become something of a minor obsession, Terry sat at his computer watching the videos Josh had made for him. There was a series by now, and he had come to depend on them for assistance in his practice. He was surprised and gratified that he was actually starting to get better.

He had to admit that he wasn't fully comfortable with this whole online thing. Until now, he had managed not to have joined a single on-line network and had considered his registration for an e-mail address some time ago a mad concession to fashion. He had read the media stories about identity theft and spam, phishing, and other criminal enterprises, and had always silently congratulated himself that he had no need to worry.

But he was pleased with himself, now, for his new venture. His wife was always saying "trying new things keeps you young," and Terry was pretty sure that, between the yoga and now this, he was doing more than most guys his age. Besides, he was wearing his belt a little tighter since he had begun practicing yoga with Roger.

Glancing at the screen, Terry could see the number of views on the page: forty-one. Probably he, himself, accounted for many of those, but he was okay with the guys in his practice getting the benefit, too. After all, he reasoned, they saw him doing yoga every day anyway. He clicked around on the other videos and laughed at himself. He had a long way to go.

He caught a look at the time and realized he had gotten lost sitting here at the computer. He had a customer meeting and some supplies to pick up. He needed to get going. Quickly, he closed out the open screens and shut down the computer. He didn't notice that he had pressed the share button in the lower corner of the screen.

Chapter Forty-Eight

The day of the public meeting about the fire chief's ultimatum had arrived, and it created a great deal of excitement. Although these kinds of meetings were normally unencumbered by drama—in fact, they were usually the very definition of boredom—everyone knew this one would be contentious and therefore highly entertaining. The event had to be moved from its usual drab committee room to the equally drab community hall to accommodate everyone.

Despite its potential for diversion, the serious nature of this occasion had chilled the local impulse to provide the festive array of cookies, cakes, and brownies that were a regular feature of most big meetings. There was, in a concession to necessity, an urn of dreadful coffee at the back of the room, accompanied by an array of white powders for its alleged enhancement, none of which were successful in making it palatable.

The conversation in the room was lively until Fiona walked in, followed by Oliver Robert. Like her predecessor, Lars Olufsen, Fiona had learned to wield her gavel with speed and confidence. She took her seat and promptly called the meeting to order.

The chairman and board members sat at long folding

tables along the front of the community hall, while Chief Gil, stern and cold-faced, sat in the front row. Fiona saw, but ignored, the presence of Stella, also in the front row, with Emily Martin seated beside her. This was a partnership she did not wish to contemplate.

Oliver settled himself at the far end of the table and began typing frantic notes. This was his first Island meeting, but he barely had a chance to take it all in. Amidst all the distractions, Fiona had noted that he had solved his color problem by not wearing a suit, but merely his usual shirt and tie. Even the tie seemed overdone by Island standards, but Fiona couldn't imagine Oliver without one. It would not have surprised her if she had learned that he slept in formal attire.

Reverend Dave, from the Baptist congregation, had come up on the rota for this meeting, and he delivered a prayer calling for peace and good judgment in a voice so low that no one could hear him past the second row. Everyone stood for the Pledge of Allegiance, and when it was finished, before the crowd could begin its usual murmur of expectation, Fiona rapped smartly with her gavel.

"I know I don't need to tell any of you about the serious-ness of this situation. We are here to learn about the dire con-ditions at our fire department. We will begin by examining the budget. I will offer a brief summary. Chief Gil will then make his case, and we will open the floor to public comment. It is essential that our decision is made in the open with public par-ticipation. This concerns us all in the most fundamental way."

With care and concision, Fiona walked them all through the budget. The biggest expenses were public safety and roads.

The public utilities were operating at a loss. The salaries for the few employees were at the bare minimum. She pointed out the various lines of expense, being careful to include things like the cost of the library, and of the airport, and how cutting them—should that even be desirable—would make little difference. Short of turning off the street lights and decreeing that all baseball games be played in daylight hours, there was almost nothing to cut, and even those dire exigencies would have changed nothing.

The fire chief sat facing Fiona. The rest of the committee members were seated in their usual places, but without their customary lassitude. Fiona pondered briefly the tendency of people to choose the same chairs when they weren't required to do so.

Chief Gil made his statement. He was calm, but his bald statement of facts was an angry slap in the community's face.

The room had gone deadly quiet, and the faces of the board members were serious as they listened. There was a copy of the chief's letter at every place.

"You are, essentially, holding the Island for ransom," said one of the board members after the chief had finished.

The chief looked affronted—as well he might—but before he could respond, another board member spoke.

"That is completely unfair," he said. "You can't blame the chief for taking his responsibilities seriously. What he is telling us is that he cannot provide the necessary services on this budget. Would it be better that he wait until a crisis comes and he can't meet it?"

"If this isn't a crisis, I don't know what is," commented

another. "I don't have to tell you how bad things are on the Island. Families are already struggling. An increase in taxes like this could be devastating. Not to mention what political havoc it would rain down on our heads."

"What about the havoc of being unable to put out a fire? Or deliver emergency medical care?"

They were silent as they each contemplated this dilemma.

Oliver Robert sat quietly, assiduously taking notes.

Fiona looked down the table to try to glean the mood of the members. This was, indeed, a crisis. She turned to the chief.

"Can you give us some more time? I don't see how we can resolve this tonight. What about bringing in a third party to negotiate?"

Chief Gil looked at her, his face stubborn. "I can no longer be responsible for this department under these conditions."

"I do see that," said Fiona, with a calmness she did not feel. "And I appreciate your integrity." She did not add that she had grave misgivings about his approach. "But this is a matter of public safety. We can't just not have a fire chief."

The chief looked her in the eye. "I cannot take responsibility under these conditions," he repeated. "That, too, is a matter of public safety."

Fiona stared him down. "So, you believe it would be better to leave the Island without a fire chief? You think that would better serve your responsibilities?"

The chief's voice grew cold. "Are you accusing me of neglecting my duties?"

Fiona drew upon her old fearlessness, built out of years as a city reporter in Chicago, and tried to keep a growing anger from her voice and face. "I am simply asking a question."

Out of the corner of her eye, she could see Oliver Robert shift uncomfortably in his chair, his hands moving furiously over his keyboard taking notes.

The chief stood, his face rigid with anger. "I cannot protect anyone under these conditions. I will not be responsible." He looked each board member in the eye as he spoke. "My resignation is effective immediately." And turning, he strode out of the room.

There was chaos in the hall.

After some minutes, having gained some control of the room through aggressive use of her gavel, Fiona looked down the table at the board. Unlike their constituents, they were all unusually still.

"So," she said, at last. "We need to put some emergency alternatives in place. Who else in the department can step in as acting chief?"

The members looked at one another.

"I don't think anyone in the department will want to defy the chief by taking over."

Fiona had not thought of this. It was inconceivable. In Chicago, such a move would be viewed as a career opportunity. "Seriously? No one would want to be chief?" She looked first at the board, and then out at the crowd.

The Islanders looked around the table at one another, and across the room at their neighbors. This was more than an unwillingness to take on responsibility for the Island's protection under these circumstances. There were unspoken cultural rules at play here, of which Fiona, a newcomer, was unaware.

These were the kinds of things on which feuds were built, and the Island's factions could be vicious over even the most trivial affairs. In a situation of this kind, when so much was at stake, the potential for the creation of lifelong enmity was enormous. Stepping into the chief's place would be an act of disloyalty second only to actual homicide.

All the heads at the table were shaking no with varying degrees of emphasis.

Fiona was dumbfounded. She looked around the room and saw their unanimity.

Her eyes fell upon the assistant chief, a young man with a new family, who could probably use a little extra income. "Tyler? I would like to appoint you to the position of chief."

He looked stricken, and shook his head.

Fiona looked a bit stricken herself. She turned to another member of the fire department. "Kyle? This is an opportunity for you. I appoint you."

Kyle's lips tightened, and he should his head slowly, his eyes on hers.

"Well, we have to have somebody. We can't have a fire department without leadership. People's lives are at stake here."

From his side of the room, Oliver Robert made a small sound as he cleared his throat. All heads turned toward him.

"If I may," he began, with a formality that defined him as an outsider, "there are rules in place to govern this situation."

Fiona looked at him with surprise. She hoped he wasn't going to deliver one of his rules. Nervously, she tried to convey with her eyes that this situation required great seriousness. "Please go on," she said, with some anxiety.

He cleared his throat again. "Well," he said, "there are rules to guide us in this situation, all according to Wisconsin statute."

Fiona had known that he was thorough in his work, but that he had already made a study of the governing statutes and ordinances was rather extraordinary. She felt a sense of growing gratitude, and a realization that hiring Oliver Robert had been the smartest thing she had ever done. Perhaps, despite the cuts, it was time to give him a raise.

Oliver continued, all eyes on him. "According to Wisconsin statute, the town chairman has the authority to appoint a fire chief, but in the absence of this, the chairman—or woman, as the case may be—" he stopped and cleared his throat again— "is the *de facto* acting chief."

It was an instant sensation. All heads turned to look at Fiona, talking at once. That rising feeling of gratitude she had been feeling popped like a balloon and disintegrated into a painful combination of dread and dismay.

"Surely not," she said, trying to keep her voice steady over the renewed hubbub in the room.

Oliver Robert looked her in the eye. "It's the law."

Chapter Forty-Nine ✦

After the hall had cleared, Fiona remained in her seat. Oliver Robert was fussily gathering his papers and preparing to depart.

"Sit down, Oliver," said Fiona.

Looking surprised, Oliver stopped his fussing and sat, his hands folded on the table in front of him, as he gazed at Fiona with a look of mild curiosity.

Fiona looked at him and sighed, but then immediately switched to a different mode. "We need to draft a plan and put it into action immediately."

Oliver reached into his bag and retrieved his ubiquitous notebook.

"Find out who is on the rescue squad. I want to meet with them tonight."

Oliver was scribbling as fast as he could, which played havoc with his usual neat script.

"Figure out how to add me to the emergency call list. If I am the chief, however insane that may be, I will have to be at every scene."

"Arrange a separate urgent meeting for everyone in the fire department. It should be within twenty-four hours. Also, get in touch with the State, or whoever, and get me—and anyone else in the department who wants to---signed up for some kind of training at the first possible opportunity." She paused. "And get me an outline of the command structure. If there is one."

Oliver cleared his throat.

Fiona looked up. "Yes?"

"We will need to make a purchase."

"Of what?"

"You will need a flashing red light for your car."

Fiona laughed. "I don't think that will be necessary."

"But you will need to clear the way to get to the scene."

Fiona looked at him, a faint smile on her face. "In what traffic?"

Oliver was silent. His disappointment over this minor point was evident.

"And one more thing." Fiona watched as he prepared himself for further note-taking. "Make sure there is a bottle of scotch in my desk drawer." Despite her recent lack of interest, she couldn't help feeling it would come in handy.

Oliver was not successful in hiding his disapproval.

Fiona rose and gathered her things. "Thank you, Oliver," she said, fully aware of the invisible irony in her words.

@realstella

Fire Chief needs TRAINING. RECALL FIONA CAMPBELL.

#powergrab #protecttheisland #recall

The news of Stella's Tweet on the following day made for an unpleasant evening.

Elisabeth, who followed @realstella, had seen it before she returned from the mainland that afternoon. Upon entering the house, she found that Fiona's bad mood was almost palpable. Fiona was sitting at the kitchen table, staring at her screen, her face flushed with some emotion. Elisabeth noticed once again the thinness of her face and the dark circles under her eyes.

Although she was trying heroically not to let Stella bother her, Fiona was beginning to realize that she was losing control of events. Even at the grocery store, she could sense a shift in people's reactions to her. Stella's poison was taking effect, and now there was this new burden of responsibility that she barely knew how to contemplate. Fiona's series of meetings, as outlined the night before to Oliver, had been depressing in the extreme.

Elisabeth tried to be cheery. She had returned for just one night and wanted to make the best of it. She made a good dinner and opened a bottle of white Bordeaux. She spoke with animation about the tribulations of contractors' reliability, and the back orders of stone tile and a particular brand of plumbing fixture that were delaying her progress. By the time dinner was over, however, Fiona's preoccupation could no longer be ignored.

"Stella's starting to get to you, isn't she?"

Fiona tried to shrug it off. "She's starting to get to everyone, that's the problem."

Elisabeth studied her from across the dinner table. "I really think you can't continue to allow these things to go unanswered.

This is getting serious, Fiona. You need to respond."

"I know that," said Fiona peevishly. "But I can't bring myself to get enmeshed in a Twitter battle with Stella. It's unseemly, and stupid. And it feels like letting her win. Besides," she added with a new note of gravity, "I have new responsibilities that are far more important."

Elisabeth could see the truth in this. "Maybe so, but you are acting like Rocco, who thinks if he's not looking at something it isn't there. People are starting to believe her. You can't pretend you live in another century. This is reality. You have to exist in it."

"Do I?" Fiona's frustration was visible. "Elisabeth, they have called for a public hearing into my malfeasance in office. They've set a date. People actually think I'm embezzling money. Recall petitions are starting to be circulated by my good friend Emily Martin. I am suddenly responsible for all the emergency care on the Island and I don't even know where to begin or who I can trust." She put her head in her hands.

Elisabeth's voice was urgent. "You have to fight back, Fiona. You have to."

Fiona spoke without lifting her head. "I'm just so…tired. I don't even know if I care anymore."

"Fiona, honestly. I'm starting to think you want to be recalled."

Fiona went very still, staring down at her cup. "Maybe I do."

Elisabeth sat watching in silent distress.

Fiona lifted her head and took a deep breath. She smiled weakly at her friend. "Sorry. I didn't mean that." She grinned suddenly, looking for a moment like her old self. "I didn't come this far to succumb to the likes of Stella DesRosiers and Emily Martin. I'll fight back. I'm not sure how, exactly, but it will be on my own terms, not theirs. Let's drink a toast."

Elisabeth raised her glass to Fiona's. "To victory!" she said.

"To survival," said Fiona.

Fiona lay in bed that night, her well-thumbed copies of the Meditations of Marcus Aurelius, the writings of Martin Luther, and her books of poetry all lying nearby, gathering dust, while she stared at the blue light of her phone.

@realstella
We deserve better. Recall Fiona Campbell.
#recall #protecttheisland

Despite Stella's tweets, the upcoming hearing, and her terrifying new duties, Fiona's preoccupation with Weasel Observation had bolstered her spirits. Had she thought about it at all, she would have realized that the fact that her activities would be considered odd, eccentric, or flat-out crazy were part of what energized her, and the inconvenience of this particular truth, while inescapable, was a reflection of her contrarian nature. A love of community disapproval, she noted wryly to herself, was probably not the first attribute of a successful politician.

On the other hand, success might only lengthen her term in office, and this was an outcome she had every intention of avoiding.

Meanwhile, Attila's confidence in her was growing daily. His movements around her had grown less furtive—although his wariness was instinctual—and he seemed content to spend more time in the open while she was present. It was inevitable, then, that he should start to explore.

The next evening, Fiona was sitting at the small writing desk in her bedroom, when she heard a small scrabbling sound. She looked up to see Attila, creeping furtively but with his usual grace, along the edges of the room. His eyes were bright, and his nose was quivering with interest. Fiona was reminded of a furry slinky.

He must have known she was there, but all at once he stopped and froze, raising the front half of his long body in the air to look. They gazed at one another for a moment. Fiona remembered the uneaten plate of cheese and sausage on the desk, which she had intended for her dinner. Moving slowly and carefully, she took a piece of sausage and dropped it as far away from herself as she reasonably could without making a big movement.

Attila ran back to the wall and disappeared, but in a moment, he was back. He peeked out for a split second, his black eyes sparkling with interest. All at once, he sprang out into the room, dancing across the floor, his back arched, making tiny leaps in the air, all while he moved toward the sausage. Suddenly, he darted back to the wall. He repeated this test several times, always getting closer to the sausage, as if he were teasing it. Soon he was back, dancing in a circle around the sausage, leaping into the air with all four feet, spinning, twisting, and rolling on his back, all with blazing speed and agility. He continued to move closer to the sausage and dart away until finally, in one swift strike, he seized the sausage piece and dragged it off to the wall in triumph.

She smiled to herself and flung another piece into the room. She knew he'd be back.

Fiona received official notice that a delegation of state auditors would be arriving the following week just as she was preparing to leave the Island for a few days of fire department training. The letter instructed her to give the auditors work space and full access to all town records.

Fiona had to admit she almost felt relieved that they were coming. She had been waiting for this particular shoe to drop for some time now. Her relief, however, lasted only until she started thinking about Oliver Robert and Stella. Oliver knew far more than Fiona did about bookkeeping, and Fiona knew nothing whatsoever about accounting, or audits. What if the auditors found irregularities that he had created? What if, in her ignorance, she had accidentally done something that was prohibited? Worst of all: what if Oliver Robert had somehow made it look as if she had embezzled money? What then? She prayed they would find evidence to exonerate her and wondered whether she should hire a lawyer.

She tried to gauge Oliver's innocence or guilt by his reactions. Did he seem smug? Did he seem nervous? But, she could determine nothing from his demeanor. He seemed just as annoying as always.

She looked forward to being away for a few days and thinking about simple things like fire, disaster, and death.

Chapter Fifty

Jim and Ben's walks now routinely included Fiona. She no longer enjoyed her own company much, and the increasing public pressure on her made every walk an escape and a relief. If Ben minded her presence, he didn't show it. Jim, for his part, was thoroughly delighted, and he did everything in his power to make their time together interesting.

Shortly after she returned from her training, Jim called Fiona after dinner.

"I have a team of scientists coming up tomorrow to band the young eagles on the northern bluff. I've already invited Ben to come. Would you like to join us?"

Fiona felt enthusiasm for the first time in a long while. "I would love to. What time?"

"We'll pick you up at six-thirty tomorrow morning."

Fiona laughed. "Okay, that's pretty early, but I can take it. Shall I bring coffee for you, too?"

"Sure," said Jim happily. "That would be great."

The next morning, Ben rang Fiona's bell at precisely six-thirty, and they clambered into Jim's truck and headed toward the northern edge of the Island.

A white SUV was parked at the end of a dirt road leading to some private property. Three men, carrying quite a bit of gear, got out and met them as they got out of Jim's truck. The property owner was walking up the drive.

"Hey, Mick, Dale, Bob." Jim was already talking as he got out of the truck.

"These are my friends, Ben and Fiona." They all shook hands, and then turned to greet the property owner. Everyone helped to carry the gear, and they set off down the dirt track toward the woods.

The nest was pointed out. Secretly, both Ben and Fiona already knew where it was, since their frequent rambles in the woods often led them to remote places. Fiona had the landowner's permission. Ben did not.

"We need to be pretty quiet," Mick explained. "We'll wait for the parents to do their morning hunt, and while they're away, we'll climb up the tree and bring down the eaglets."

"Won't that make the parents angry?" asked Fiona.

Dale grinned. "You'll see. They will be watching us and protesting pretty loudly. Actually, though, once they've been safely returned, eagles don't seem to mind when their babies have been handled. There is no rejection as there can be with other species."

"How do you get them down?" asked Ben.

"We climb."

Ben's eyes gleamed with excitement. "Can I climb?"

Dale and Jim caught one another's glances. "No," said Jim. "I have to answer to your mom."

"But maybe you can help with the bands," said Mick. "You will have to be very gentle. These little guys are as fragile as glass."

The adventure of the climb was almost as thrilling to Ben as the eaglets themselves. The tree was easily one hundred feet tall, but it was clear that Dale had done this before. With the help of ropes, crampons, a climbing saddle, and spikes, he began the laborious process of scaling the tree.

At the top he called down. "There are two!"

He took some photos of the fledglings in the nest, then, using ropes, and pulleys, he carefully lowered the backpack to the ground. Bob gently opened the pack and revealed the first eaglet, squawking loudly, its mouth open. Bob cradled the big baby bird against his body so that its wings were folded, holding its talons together in one hand. The eaglet was already about eight pounds, and at this stage of life resembled a mix between dinosaur and bird. His enormous eyes were wide open. Fiona was surprised at how big he was already. His brilliant yellow talons were large and sharp and reminded Fiona of puppies, whose big feet are indicators that they will become big dogs. Even so, they were not yet full-size.

"We have to make the ankle bands big enough for them to grow into. The bands need to fit them their whole lives."

"He is so strange and beautiful," said Fiona in an awed voice. "Look at the expressiveness of his eyes."

"They won't get their white heads until they're about four, four-and-a-half years old," said Ben, eager to show his knowledge.

Bob smiled. "That's absolutely right."

He held the bird gently as they measured his beak. Ben was allowed to peer in and report the numbers on the calipers.

"Thirty millimeters."

Bob nodded.

They carefully arranged the backpack around the baby's head to help keep him calm, and placed him on his back to take a blood sample. The undersides of the eaglet's wings were peppered with blue spiky tubes, like straws, that encased what would ultimately become his flight feathers.

Mick got the band ready. "I'll put it on, Ben. You watch. Then you can help tighten the fasteners. Okay?"

Ben nodded eagerly, too excited to speak.

As they worked, they could hear the screams of the parents overhead, circling and calling.

Working steadily, they replaced the first eaglet in the bag and carefully sent the bag up to the top of the tree, where Dale was waiting. He put the first eaglet back into the nest and sent down the second one.

Ben had overcome his excitement by now and reverted to being the steady, calm, worker Jim had known he would be. Ben was a quick study, and he made himself useful by staying out of the way, fetching things that were needed, and following directions. He had been well trained by his father to watch and learn, and his passion for wildlife made him eager.

After the second eaglet had been returned to the nest, Dale climbed back down, and they began packing their equipment. The parents were already there, checking on the well-being of their family.

"Ben," said Mick, "you need to promise that you will not reveal to anyone the location of the nest, do you understand?"

Ben nodded solemnly. "Yes, sir. I wouldn't tell anyone. They might hurt the babies."

Mick and Jim exchanged glances, and Jim nodded his reassurance.

"I can vouch for Ben," he said, smiling at the boy. "He is a man of his word."

Mick looked over at Fiona.

She raised her hand in affirmation, also serious. "Not for the world," she said. "Thank you for allowing us to come."

Mick nodded, satisfied.

Afterward, they all went to lunch together. Ben fired questions at a rapid clip and had to be reminded that his burger was getting cold.

Chapter Fifty-One

Each fire is different. There are different kinds of fire. There is hot and slow. There is hot and fast. There is the white-hot ash that lingers long after the first flames are spent. The colors are different. Sometimes green flames. They come from copper in the ink when you burn paper. My grandmother had special logs for Christmas. They burned in colors. Green flames. Blue. Purple flames. But I didn't like them. Fire should be hot colors. Red. Orange. Yellow. White. Hot. Too hot to touch.

"So," asked Nika one afternoon when Jim was dropping off Ben after one of their walks. "Have you asked Fiona to go to the ball?" Nika knew that Fiona had been accompanying them, giving Jim plenty of opportunity.

Ben, horrified by this topic, had said his thanks to Jim, and headed off to do his chores.

Jim ducked his head sheepishly and shrugged. "I'm thinking about it."

"Maybe you're too cautious," Nika said to him. "Most

women aren't drawn to hesitancy. Maybe you need to be bold."

"Maybe," said Jim. And, feeling nearly as horrified as Ben, he found a way to extricate himself from the conversation, said good-bye, and left as quickly as he could.

But as he drove toward Nelsen's for a beer and some company, Jim thought over what she had said. Nika was right. He had been cautious, tiptoeing around her, treating Fiona as if she were a shy animal in the forest. He shook his head at himself. Fiona was a strong, intelligent woman, not some eye-batting ingénue. And she was alone. He definitely needed to change his tactics.

Eddie looked at Jim questioningly as he walked into the bar.

"Something on your mind?" he asked, pushing Jim's beer toward him.

Jim shrugged. "Maybe. I don't know. Just…nothing."

Eddie eyed him silently. He was too discreet to say so, but he knew exactly what was on Jim's mind, or, more precisely, who.

"Need a menu?" he asked, returning to his professional demeanor.

"No. Thanks. Just another beer."

Attila's boldness accelerated at a remarkable pace. Intrigued by his wild behavior over the cheese and sausage, Fiona did some more weasel research. This was, she learned, his war dance, used by weasels to distract and confuse their prey before an attack, and she soon recognized that he behaved this way on the kinds of occasions when a cat might stalk and pounce. It was a weasel's clever way of conquering animals much larger than himself.

He now regularly performed his dance across the bedroom floor, leaping and twisting in weasel gymnastics, usually just before he dashed toward some choice morsel of food and dragged it speedily away. As time went on, he seemed to delight in more and more elaborate displays of valor, and Fiona, enthralled, looked forward to each new expression of his character.

Getting ready to go back to the office one afternoon, she found Attila curled up into a tiny, furry ball, sound asleep in one of the many canvas tote bags she had lying around the house. She breathed a silent prayer of thanks that she hadn't followed her usual practice of dumping something into the bag without looking. A heavy book would have crushed him.

She spoke to him in a gentle voice, and his eyes opened to watch her. He didn't seem nervous about her presence, and Fiona wondered whether he had become accustomed to the sound of her voice or perhaps her scent.

Struck by a sudden idea, she put her papers in a different tote and, taking both bags with her, headed back to the office. She recalled the old line in politics: "If you want a friend in Washington, get a dog." She supposed a friendly weasel would do in a pinch.

Chapter Fifty-Two

Normally, Joshua entered Ground Zero quietly in the morning, his heavenly aura emanating calm and well-being. Today, however, his entrance was less tranquil.

"Terry. Dude." He said. "You're famous."

Terry, who had been sitting on the floor taking off his white athletic socks in preparation for class, looked up, puzzled. The Lutherans ceased their murmured conversations. Even Roger stopped what he was doing.

"Look at this," said Joshua, holding out his phone. "Since we went public, there have been over a hundred thousand views."

"What do you mean 'went public?'" asked Terry.

"Well, I thought it was you, man. Didn't you put the videos out there?"

Terry shook his head in utter confusion. "What do you mean 'put them out there'?."

As they listened in awe, and Terry in something close to horror, Joshua explained that the formerly private videos of Terry practicing yoga were now visible to anyone.

"How?" asked Terry.

"You probably clicked the wrong button. Or someone did," added Joshua, helpfully. "You haven't quite gone viral, but

100K in twelve hours? That's really impressive."

Terry sat stunned. "You mean anyone can see them? Anyone? In the world?"

"Listen," said Joshua, seeing Terry's expression. "You have two choices: either you take this seriously and get all weirded out and embarrassed or you have fun with it." His face was sympathetic. "Frankly, I recommend the latter. I mean, why not? We can all have fun with it."

Suddenly, the same thought occurred to them all, and they turned to look at Roger. He had a distant look on his face, and did not appear to be listening. Fun did not seem an experience that Roger would be likely to have. Particularly not with this.

Chapter Fifty-Three ✤

Fiona dreamed that she was working in an enormous, old warehouse. The structure of the building was all wood, and falling apart. There were piles of boxes everywhere, and old machines. In the midst of the disarray, she had a desk full of disorganized papers. People she had known from her days at the newspaper were there, and her old editor. Some of them were glad to see her. Others turned their backs.

The offices were arranged on balconies around a center atrium, and the floors seemed somewhat precarious. Fiona had Rocco with her, and she could sense his uneasiness, but at first, she didn't know what was wrong. Together, they were trying to leave the building, but they kept finding themselves on the wrong floor, no matter how many different staircases they tried. The old wood of the floors was splitting, and her feet kept partially breaking through.

Rocco was urgently pulling her forward to get out, and she felt that somehow he knew the way. But, suddenly, she broke through the floor, and by the time she had extricated herself, Rocco was gone. Fiona knew instinctively that someone had taken him, because he would never have left her. Desperately, she began to search for him as the old wooden building began slowly to crumble all around her. She clung to the sides of the building with nothing beneath her feet, afraid to move, afraid to look down, dangling there with no escape.

@realstella
What does Fiona Campbell have to HIDE?
#timetofindout #protecttheisland

Jim and Fiona sat at the bar. He had demolished his burger while she had merely picked at hers, trying to pretend she had interest in eating. They had been having dinners together pretty regularly now, and Fiona had come to feel very comfortable with him. Jim was good company, and easy to talk to.

"I suppose you saw what Stella tweeted out today?" Jim asked. "Man, that woman is a piece of work."

Fiona stared at him. "You follow @realstella?"

He was utterly unabashed. "Of course. Who doesn't? How else would you know what she was up to? Besides, it's irresistible. Best entertainment on the Island."

Fiona was stunned into silence.

"As far as I can tell," he continued, "there is not one bit of human kindness in her."

Fiona grimaced. "That much has been established."

Jim looked at her curiously. "I have to admit, I'm a little surprised you aren't following her."

Fiona sighed. "I am, of course. But I don't want to give her the satisfaction of knowing I am, so I have an alias."

Jim laughed. "I had no idea you were so duplicitous."

She gave a rueful shrug. "It's politics, I guess. Seems I'm

just getting started."

Eddie, spoke up. "Sorry. Couldn't help overhearing." He grinned. "Occupational hazard."

Fiona smiled back, and Eddie noticed how sad and tired her smile was compared to her old radiance.

"But listen," he continued. "You need to start answering her." He gave an expert twirl to the glass he was polishing. "I do my best to counter when I can, but I'd say public opinion is starting to move in her direction."

Fiona looked at him, surprised. "You're doing that for me?"

He put the glass away and picked up another. "Sure. I have to use an alias, too. Bartenders can't take sides." He grinned and raised his eyebrows conspiratorily, but quickly turned serious again. "But we can't have that woman getting her way. She's a menace."

Jim was having second thoughts. He looked at Fiona. "Doesn't it bother you? Seeing all the mean things she says?"

"Bother me?" Fiona laughed. "It's my day's entertainment."

Jim relaxed, and gazed at her admiringly.

It was, however, a lie.

Ben's comment about a dog had made an impression on Nancy, and she repeated the scene in her mind many times over. She told herself that her entire being rebelled against the notion of one more creature to take care of, but way back, glimmering on the edges of her consciousness was a different reason; one she was not yet ready to acknowledge.

She found herself reminiscing about her childhood dog, Rex. He had been a beautiful puppy, a gift from her father. He had had a German Shepherd's ears and soulful affection, but the long coat and bounce of a retriever. She had loved him. He had followed her everywhere, except school, and even then, he was always waiting when the school bus brought her home. She remembered the warm crush of his slightly pungent doggishness in her bed at night and his gleeful spinning when she agreed to play.

Nancy sat in her chair at the end of the day, quietly recalling those happy days. One slow tear rolled down her cheek before she caught herself and brushed it away. "Enough of that!" she said aloud.

With a great deal of unnecessary bustle, she went to the kitchen to finish clearing up before bed. She turned on the radio, telling herself that she wanted to hear the end of the ballgame, and poured herself a nip of brandy.

Without exactly meaning to, she engaged herself in a protracted exercise in re-arranging the pantry that went way past her usual bedtime. "Long overdue," she told herself. She decided, when it was finished, that she would begin clearing out the hall closet next.

Jim drove Fiona home from Nelsen's. When they got to her house, instead of simply dropping her at the path to the house,

Jim got out and walked her up the steps to her door. She had been enjoying their familiar, easy friendship that night, but suddenly her old anxiety about his expectations had reappeared. She was on edge, and now, all her alarms were going off.

When they got to the door, Jim smiled a little. "I've been meaning to ask you something."

She started to speak, but he interrupted her. "Let me finish." He looked off into the distance for a moment, then at the ground, and then into her eyes.

"I know you're going through a hard time right now, and I don't want to complicate things. But you need to take care of yourself. Get away from the politics, and from…everything. You need a distraction."

He shrugged, as if it was the most casual thing in the world. "Come to the ball with me. It will be fun. We'll get dressed up and dance a little." Fiona looked away for a moment, confused. "You don't have to answer me right now. Just think about it."

He leaned down and kissed her quickly on the cheek, and before she could respond, he was down the steps. He stopped when he got to his truck. "I'll see you tomorrow." And with a cheerful wave, he got in and drove away.

After he had gone, Fiona leaned against the front door and sighed. She had to admit to herself that she was tempted by his invitation. It would be nice to go out, to have some fun, to stop thinking so much. But she was worried that she would hurt Jim, and that was something she told herself that she absolutely could not do.

Going inside, she hung her jacket and bag on the hooks by the door. She hoped Attila would make an appearance tonight.

Chapter Fifty-Four

Fiona's tote bags had become Attila's favorite napping place, and she quickly became accustomed to checking before putting anything in them. One day, to her surprise, she found him curled up in a little nest he had made from one of her missing socks. She watched him sleeping. He looked so sweet, not at all like the deadly predator he was.

She was puzzled by the sock. There was no reason for her to put a sock in a tote bag. Suddenly light dawned. She hadn't become absent-minded. It was Attila who had put the sock in the tote bag. He liked soft things, and when he found something that pleased his weasel sensibilities, he took it. He was the reason for her missing gloves, the jewelry bag, and all the socks. He was a thief. He had made his own bed with his own soft things, or rather, hers.

She saw, in her mind's eye, the delighted way he leapt, carrying back some delicious treat she had left for him. She imagined he danced the same way carrying away her socks.

"You little weasel," she said, enchanted. "Have you been stealing my socks?" He opened his bright black eyes and blinked sleepily.

"Come on, Attila. Let's go to the office."

He nestled himself deeper into his soft, fuzzy sock and went back to sleep.

When she got to the office, she put Attila in his bag next to her desk, and became absorbed in her tasks. Sometime later, she felt the pull of tiny nails. Attila, having awakened, was climbing up the leg of her jeans. Fiona held her breath as he made his way to her lap, and up the sleeves of her sweater to her shoulder. She was afraid to turn her head for fear of scaring him, or of receiving a sharp weasel bite, but he was content to snuffle at her hair, at her earring, and to investigate her collar. It was dark under her sweater, a perfect weasel place. With some trepidation, she watched as he disappeared down the inside of her sweater against her blouse and felt him settling in with what she imagined was a little weasel sigh.

She hoped he wouldn't bite.

In a short time, however, she had completely forgotten he was there. She finished her work and began putting things away for the day when she felt him stirring. She put her hand over the little bulge he made and patted him gently.

"You little weasel," she said, softly.

Suddenly, she was aware that Oliver Robert was standing in the door.

"I beg your pardon?" he said, highly offended.

Fiona tried not to smile. "I wasn't talking to you."

Oliver's lips were tight. "That much seems clear."

"No," said Fiona, "I really wasn't. I meant it literally. He really is. A weasel, I mean."

"Who?" asked Oliver, mystified.

Attila, who had awakened, now popped his head out of

the neck of Fiona's sweater.

"What is that?" he asked. "A ferret?"

Fiona could no longer hide her smile. "Sort of," she said.
With that, she picked up her bag and headed out the door.

It was, she thought, the best moment of the day.

Chapter Fifty-Five ✤

Terry's videos had gone viral. One moment, he had been a carpenter in a remote part of the Midwest, and the next, he was seeing himself everywhere. He might not have known the full extent of his acclaim if The Angel Joshua hadn't sent him all the links, set up a Google Alert for him, and made sure he was signed up for all the latest forms of social media. A late night comedian mentioned him in a monologue.

The unfortunate result of his fame, however, meant that Ground Zero was now more crowded than ever, and not just for morning yoga. People were everywhere at all hours, taking selfies, tweeting, and, as Terry put it, "generally clogging up the works."

"You should tweet, man," Joshua told him one morning after watching one of the yoga tourists who had been so engrossed in his phone he hadn't looked up once during his entire visit. "You'd have thousands of followers in no time."

Rather than being embarrassed, and despite the crowds, Terry was rather enjoying his notoriety. "What would I tweet about?" he asked. "I wouldn't know what to say."

Roger was standing behind the counter polishing the big Italian machine. In the face of the onslaught, Roger was slightly less cordial than usual.

"Goats," he said.

They all looked at him.

"You should tweet about goats. It's a yoga thing. Goats and yoga."

Mike smiled his gentle smile into his coffee, but even the Lutherans stopped to hear this conversation.

"What about them?" asked Terry.

Roger stared off into the distance, still polishing.

"Do you want to be funny, or serious?" asked Joshua.

"That ship has sailed," commented Mike. "No one expects him to be serious. What would be the point?"

Roger returned his gaze to his work and spoke again. "You could do photos. You doing yoga with a goat."

He reached under the counter and pulled out the magazine Joshua had brought and opened it. "Like this." He lay the article about goat yoga out on the counter.

The members of the Lutheran Men's Prayer Group looked at one another and wondered whether they were in danger of drifting from their faith. With some misgivings, their prayer leader slowly turned his eyes toward the magazine, mentally planning the conversation he would have later with his pastor. To his relief, however, he saw nothing sinful, only some cute baby goats and a class of people doing yoga.

"Oh," he said. "Now I see what you mean." He gave quick nod to the other members of the group, signifying his approbation. They clustered around the counter to see the article.

Relieved, he moved his gaze to the opposite page, featuring an attractive woman in a leotard. Staring at it, he sighed. He would have to have that chat after all.

Even though she could no longer trust him, Fiona felt that firing Oliver Robert could only stoke the fires against her. She decided, instead, to act as if everything was fine, and she gradually returned to their familiar patterns of work. She admitted to herself that she had come to depend on him, and in any case, couldn't think of anyone who could replace him. She even, when she was honest with herself, had to admit that she rather liked him. "The devil you know," she thought, and realized with some chagrin that she was even beginning to sound like him.

She stopped to pick up a late lunch one afternoon and brought it back to the office, just to check in. Oliver was there doing one of the mysterious tasks that always absorbed him. He didn't look up when she came in, but Fiona was used to that.

"I got some extra fries," she said. "Do you want some?"

"Avoid fried foods, which angry up the blood."

"Ah!" said Fiona. "I know that one."

"What do you mean?"

"I mean, I recognize the expression."

"Which expression?"

Fiona sighed. "The one you just used."

"That's not an expression. It's one of my rules."

Fiona ahemmed gently. "I think that's Satchel Paige."

"Well, he got it from me."

"Interesting. Why do you say that?"

"Because he did."

"Oliver," began Fiona patiently, "Satchel Paige predates you by more than seventy years."

Oliver Robert began humming a show tune.

"Did you hear me?"

He looked at her over his glasses. "What?"

"He probably died before you were born."

"Who?"

"Satchel Paige."

"Never heard of him."

Fiona doubted this was true, but she looked at him with more curiosity than exasperation. "Are you going to the ball?" She asked more to change the subject than out of any particular interest in his answer, which she was certain she already knew.

His answer astonished her.

"Of course."

"Mind if I ask who with?"

"Yes," said Oliver.

Duly chastised, Fiona disappeared into her office with her lunch. She wondered whether the color code would apply to special events.

The thing I like about fire is everything. I like the danger, the cruelty of it. I like the beauty and the primal power of it. I like its colors: the red, the orange, the white, the blue, the purple, sometimes the green. I like the snapping and crack of the flames

on dry wood, and the slow creep of white ash as wood burns. I like its contradictions, that it warms and burns, heals and destroys. A big fire purifies me. It frightens me. I like that. Especially now.

Chapter Fifty-Six

"If you are ever in trouble, call me." That sentence echoed through Fiona's days. Did it mean he would come back to her and that things could be as they were before? Or was it simply a remnant of affection that he would honor in the breach? That he merely wouldn't want harm to come to her?

She heard the words again and again, wondering each time what kind of crisis would be sufficient to ask for him. An illness? A death? Or something less categorical? "What," she thought, "if my heart is broken?" Would he come then?

Even though school had begun again, the pattern of Fiona's walks with Jim and Ben had been essentially uninterrupted. Ben would stop by Jim's on his way home from school, and once a week or so—but not every time—Jim would suggest to Ben that he invite Fiona to join them. Ben would shrug and make the call, and more often than not, Fiona would say yes. More than anything else, walking was the thing that helped Fiona create some sense of normality for herself, and usually it didn't really matter whether she walked alone or with someone else.

But her loneliness was beginning to feel etched into her soul. Elisabeth was busy with the hotel, and Fiona looked forward to the walks with Jim and Ben as the best part of her days. Ben frequently drifted off to explore various things of interest, occasionally calling back for them to come and see what he had found. His explorations often left Jim and Fiona momentarily alone.

It was a cool, blustery day in September, making for a cold walk. The wind was blowing, and the sun was mostly hidden behind the clouds. A pair of crows called earnestly to one another. Small eddies of leaves swirled on the path ahead. The trails were usually empty, but this weather guaranteed it.

"Thanks for including me on your walks, Jim," Fiona said as they scuffed their feet along the trail together, leaving trails in the piles of leaves. "I have to admit, I hadn't realized how lonely I'd been feeling."

"Actually, it was Ben who suggested that we call you today." He looked over at her. "We both enjoy your company."

She smiled without looking at him but was relieved when Ben came running back urging them to see the fox den he had discovered.

"It's best to leave that den alone, Ben," said Jim. "Animals need their privacy."

Ben nodded seriously and, joining them on the trail, began peppering Jim with a series of earnest questions that occupied their conversation all the way back to the truck and until they dropped him off at his house. Nika waved at them from the door as Jim drove off to take Fiona home. The silence in the truck was welcome after the chatter of an excited boy, and neither Jim nor Fiona felt inclined to break it.

To Fiona's dismay, when they arrived at her house, Jim

turned off the engine and walked up to the porch with her.

"You really don't have to be lonely, you know," he said, picking up their earlier conversation where they had left off. Fiona stood with her hand on the doorknob, looking down. "There are plenty of things to do and people who enjoy your company. You shouldn't be sitting home by yourself. Why don't you come to the Island Ball with me?"

Fiona continued to look at her feet and then, taking a breath, she looked up into Jim's eyes.

"I can't, Jim. I'm sorry. It wouldn't be right."

He held her glance. "Why not? What wouldn't be right about it?"

Fiona was silent, trying rapidly to collect her thoughts.

"Seriously," continued Jim, without waiting for her answer. "What is so terrible about two friends spending an evening together? Why can't you just let yourself have some fun? You look like hell. You never laugh anymore. He's not worth it, Fiona."

He paused, wondering if he'd gone too far, then smiled mischievously. "Are you afraid I'll seduce you?"

Fiona smiled at this, too, but she looked away again, embarrassed.

"And if I did, would it be so terrible?" Jim made a fist and affectionately bumped her under the chin. "Think about it."

Leaving her standing on the porch, he ran lightly down the steps along the path to his truck. Waving cheerfully, he got in and drove off, leaving Fiona to wonder whether she was meant to think about his invitation or the prospect of seduction, and whether the two were separable from one another.

More depressed than ever, she kicked off her shoes in the front hall, where she would be sure to trip over them in the morning, and wandered toward the kitchen in search of something she wouldn't find there.

*F*iona dreamed she was walking along the beach. It was daylight, but the sky was dark and filled with stars. One meteor after another shot across the horizon as she watched, and she marveled at them and wondered how she had never noticed that this happened every night. Suddenly, there was a boom in the night as one broke through the sound barrier. Before her eyes, with the rapidity of a car crash, there was a fireball. Flaming debris fell to earth among the cedar forests along the beach. Almost immediately, the Island was being consumed by flames. She watched in horror, unable to speak or scream or run, the cedars making an eerie popping sound as they caught fire and burned.

Chapter Fifty-Seven

The morning came. Sunlight streamed in through the windows of Fiona's kitchen, where she sat drinking coffee and taking an assessment of her life. She hated being in public office—as, had she thought about it for more than two minutes before deciding to run, she would have known—but in her usual fashion, she had impulsively made a decision that she had learned to regret.

Still, what could she have done except run against Stella? Had she gained power, Stella would surely have found a way to drive her off the Island.

"And would that have been so bad?" she asked herself. Wouldn't her life have been better?

Would she be waking up with Pete instead of here, alone and miserable?

Fiona got up and poured herself a cup of coffee. Her irritation was energizing her in a way she had not felt since the breakup.

Well, she had to stay in office. She had made a commitment, and she would keep it, and, what's more, she would do her job well. But she wouldn't have to run again, that was for certain. And meanwhile, she needed to get in control of her life again. She could not wallow in her grief. Pete was gone. She was alive. She had a brain and a heart, and she would use them.

And while she was at it, by God, she would go to the Island Ball with Jim.

"Why ever not?" she asked herself aloud. And putting her coffee down with a clunk, she went to the phone and dialed his number.

It was another one of her impulsive decisions.

After her call to Jim, Fiona was feeling cheerful. Jim had been delighted, and his happiness had pleased her. She wasn't quite sure whether her mood would withstand an encounter with Oliver, so she stopped by to see Elisabeth instead.

"Oh, good. You're just in time. How's this?"

Elisabeth was standing on a ladder in the front hall of the historic Washington Hotel, adjusting the chain on a vintage light fixture she had installed herself. Fiona, who had just come in, stood back and looked.

"I'd say it needs about six links more length."

"It won't be hitting anyone on the head?"

"Only if they're ten feet tall. That ceiling is pretty high."

Elisabeth gave a brief laugh. "You're right. I just want everything to be perfect."

Fiona smiled indulgently. "It's beautiful. Everything is beautiful. It will be wonderful to have the hotel back, and I'm so excited to have you here on the Island full-time."

Elisabeth frowned. "It won't exactly be full time. We'll

have to close for the deepest part of winter, and then we'll go back to the gallery. But we'll be here probably from May through October."

"Better than nothing!"

Elisabeth smiled. "Yes. Much better." She began to climb down from the ladder. She was remarkably agile, and her eagerness to see the results made her quicker than usual. She stood back to admire her work.

The project was almost finished. Elisabeth had added historically appropriate touches, having haunted auctions and consignment stores for period fixtures and vintage furniture. She had tweaked the style of the guest rooms, and the dining room, and added luxurious touches throughout. The result was a place both beautiful and restful. She and Roger would be moving in and having a grand opening soon.

"Where's Roger?" asked Fiona.

"He's out at the studio, getting things set up. Want to see it?"

"Of course," said Fiona, somewhat disingenuously. She wasn't completely certain her mood could withstand Roger, either. "Will you open before Christmas?"

"We'd been planning to open in the spring for tourist season, but with all the crowds at the coffee shop, we're re-considering. Come on. I'll show you what he's up to out there. You'll be surprised."

It occurred to Fiona that being surprised by Roger wasn't a particularly new phenomenon, but manners forbade her saying anything aloud.

Elisabeth took one more look at her gleaming new fixture

and led the way out to the new studio and Roger. Fiona followed, prepared, as she thought, for any contingency.

Day after day, the state auditors showed up at Fiona's office. Each morning, Fiona found the two of them waiting politely for her to unlock her door. They were dressed casually and seemed, to Fiona, incredibly young.

"That's because they're probably just out of school," explained Oliver. "It's a miserable job, so their seniors assign these things to the newbies."

"I don't really mind them being here," said Fiona, "but I do get tired of the constant requests for things. I wouldn't have thought we had so many things to investigate."

"Ah," said Oliver, getting a look on his face that Fiona recognized. "One grape, many wasps."

"You could say that about my political life, as well," said Fiona pointedly. "What I'd like to know is how the whole matter became public in the first place."

Oliver shrugged. "The walls have mice, and the mice have ears."

"Are you implying that we have a spy?" asked Fiona, hoping to rattle him.

Oliver appeared unmoved.

At that moment, one of the auditors appeared in the doorway. "Excuse me, we have a question."

Fiona and Oliver both looked at her.

"We're wondering about this bill for twelve dollars and eighty-three cents. Why hasn't it been paid?"

Fiona slowly turned her head to look at Oliver. "What do you mean it hasn't been paid?" she asked, looking directly at him.

Oliver was suddenly fascinated by an invisible spot on his sleeve.

"Oliver?" Fiona's voice was insistent.

Oliver sniffed and spoke to the auditor, avoiding Fiona's eyes. "We have been unable to get a rationale for the calculation. We are waiting for word from the State."

The auditor murmured something technical that Fiona interpreted as Sanskrit.

"Exactly," said Oliver. He opened a file cabinet, pulled out a neat stack of papers, and handed it to the auditor. "You'll find my calculations here."

The auditor accepted the file and went back to her work down the hall.

"Oliver," said Fiona crisply, "I explicitly told you to pay that bill."

"Oh, did you?" he said, with an air of unconcern. "I don't remember that."

Too furious to speak, Fiona turned to go into her office. She would deal with him when she had calmed down. Oliver, meanwhile, went to his desk and began preparations for departure.

"Are you leaving?" asked Fiona, surprised. "It's only nine o'clock."

"Yes," said Oliver simply.

She watched in disbelief as he gathered up his things and headed out the door. He closed it behind him before she could ask where he was going.

Was this, she wondered, a reaction to her question? She knew he remembered her telling him to pay that bill. Did he feel embarrassed about such a patent lie? Or was he avoiding having to admit his complicity in some scheme?

Left alone in the office, she was forced to come to grips with all of the implications of his behavior. None of it made her very happy.

Chapter Fifty-Eight

After three days, Oliver still hadn't returned to work. Despite her complete lack of trust in him, Fiona found herself wishing he were there. Sitting alone in her office waiting for the auditors to strike some kind of felonious gold was threatening to drive her mad. At six o'clock on the third day, she decided to track Oliver down and went to look for him at rehearsal.

The performing arts center was a relatively new building, built by a local benefactor and the contributions of the Islanders. Fiona slipped into the darkened theater and looked around. There was activity on stage, but it seemed somewhat disorganized, with people milling about, and not much in the way of scenery. In the audience section, there was a large piece of plywood placed over several rows of seats, serving as the director's table, with one work light hovering over it to make reading possible. Oliver sat there looking important, and consulting the sheaves of papers in front of him. Several tech people hovered nervously nearby, hoping not to draw his ire.

Fiona strode down the aisle to his table and stood looking down at him.

"Oliver, I need your help."

Oliver was distracted by the stage blocking diagram in

front of him and wasn't listening. "Mmm," he said.

"You can't just walk off and leave like this. It doesn't look good."

Without acknowledging Fiona's presence, Oliver looked up and pursed his lips briefly, and then shouted suddenly toward the stage.

"People! You need to speak audibly! I'm in the tenth row and I can only hear every other word!"

The actors looked at one another nervously and began again.

Oliver looked back at his notes as if Fiona weren't standing there looking down at him.

"Oliver?"

Nothing.

"Oliver!" Fiona summoned her most peremptory tone, and Oliver Robert looked up as if he had only just noticed her presence.

He gazed at her with disapproval. "It would look even worse if I were there in the middle of everything, looking as if I were trying to influence the audit. The best thing we can both do is stay away."

"The drums are beating, Oliver. The natives are restless. Pick a rule. Any rule. There will be a mob outside my door one of these mornings. I can't just disappear and act as if I'm guilty of something."

"Be visible, then," said Oliver dismissively in a rare direct answer. "Surely that can't be difficult around here."

He sniffed and looked back at the stage where the rehearsal was limping along. "No, no, no, NO!" he shouted.

The actors all froze as if they had encountered a ray gun.

"Begin that scene again. If I've told you once, I've told you a thousand times: You must act surprised when James enters the room. For Heaven's sake, people! Now once more, with TALENT!"

Breathing deeply to suppress her anger, anxiety, and frustration, Fiona stalked from the theater.

Chapter Fifty-Nine ✣

Fiona had returned to the house after her confrontation with Oliver utterly spent, her anger having changed to exhaustion. It was early evening on an Indian Summer day, and she was taking in the air. She felt old, and tired, and drained of ambition. Even the prospect of an evening with Attila held no charm. She sat moodily on the porch steps, listening to the tree frogs, when the wind blew a sudden scent of the lake, slightly fishy, that reminded her of her other life.

Without warning, like being caught in an undertow, Fiona was swept into a memory of her days in Chicago. It had been a day like this had been, unseasonably warm with the scent of fallen leaves and the water. She had been running from the train, only a few blocks from the Lake, assigned by her editor to cover yet another shooting.

As she arrived on the scene, she could see a small boy lying on the pavement. He lay with one arm flung out over his head, his hand in a tiny fist as if he had been thrust into a restless sleep. He was dressed in a freshly laundered blue shirt and khaki pants, the uniform of his school. He had been walking with his grandmother, his hand clinging to hers on his way to his first day of kindergarten, when the shots had been fired.

Now, he lay with a tiny trickle of blood beneath him as his grandmother wailed her agony to God.

Fiona had been dry-eyed then, toughened by so many scenes of death and grief, and she had written her story with the professional coolness that her journalistic training required. Now, far away from that place on a remote Island, the sound of the night beginning to sing around her, she stared unseeingly into the distance, tears pouring down her face. She could not forget that baby's fist.

After Ben had gone to bed, Pali and Nika sat down together on the porch swing. It was a warm autumn night, and the tree frogs were singing. They swayed together in silence for some time, breathing in the air. At last, having waited for the right moment, Pali spoke.

"I've been offered a job," he said.

Nika felt as if her head were spinning. This was the moment she had been dreading all these months.

"What kind of job?"

"As a mate for a shipping company. For a freighter."

In her silence, Pali just kept talking. "It would mean moving. Probably to Chicago." He heard her little catch of breath. "I know it's not what we've always planned, but it would be a lot more money."

Her impatience forgotten, Nika focused all her attention on him as if her life depended on it.

"You'd be gone a lot," she said, quietly.

"Yes. A lot during the season. But in the winter, I'd be home more."

Nika was silent, thinking. This was her last chance. She had to speak up. "When we came back to the Island, we said 'never again.'"

Pali looked grim. "I know. But it's an opportunity. It's not a factory, or an office." He turned to look at her. "We need to consider it, Nika."

She nodded.

In their silence, Nika could hear the night world going on around them, the sounds of other creatures involved in their own business of living. There were frogs singing, a whippoor-will, fox calls, and owls, and the rustle of something in the tall grass nearby. It was that feeling of being so far away from everything else that she loved so much. They had their own little planet here, where it was safe, and real, and the people—if not all exactly kind—were, at least, a known quantity. Life was simple, as if stripped down to all the most essential things. This was her life, her family's life. She did not want to live any other way.

Up until now the focus of the conversations had always been on Ben and how he would be able to adapt to life away from the Island. But now, she was thinking about herself, about the way it had felt to be a stranger all those years ago when she had gone away to school, and later, after they had been married. It had been an exercise in misery.

"When?" she asked. "When would we go?"

Pali stirred uncomfortably. There had been a part of him

that had been hoping she'd refuse.

"I'm not sure yet. A few months. Next season, maybe. There's some training involved."

Nika said nothing. It was so soon.

F iona had been so drawn into her memories that she had not seen or heard the familiar truck pull up, nor Jim's steps as he came quickly up the walk.

Looking closely at her face, his entire being went quiet, and, without a word, he sat next to her on the step, near, but not too near.

Normally, Fiona would have felt dismay at weeping in front of anyone, but she could not stop the waves of grief that were pouring from some long-hidden depths, and she was so overwhelmed she had no ability to experience any other emotion. She made no sound, there was only the pouring of her tears as her shoulders shook, but it was, to Jim, more wrenching than anything he had ever experienced. He did not dare to speak or to touch her, any more than he would have thrust his hands into an open wound. He could only be near.

When her tears began to ebb, they sat together in silence for a long time. The frogs were still singing, but the birds had long gone silent. There was a faint breeze.

Fiona began to shiver uncontrollably. Jim went to his truck and brought back a thick wool blanket. He slipped it around her shoulders and knelt before her, a step below, studying her face. She looked back, for once unguarded.

He had thought he knew the reason for her weeping, but now he wasn't sure.

He took both her hands, which were cold, and still trembling. He began to wonder whether she was in shock, but gradually she steadied herself, and he could feel her relax through her hands. He did not let go, however.

"Tell me," he said. "If you want to."

The dead images paced slowly through her mind once more, each intimate and unbearable detail. She did not have the strength to live it yet again. She closed her eyes and shook her head. "Can't."

Jim looked steadily into her eyes, suddenly aware that he was angry, and hoping it didn't show. "Where is he?"

Fiona didn't ask who he meant. "I don't know." She looked up at him, her face open. The grief had somehow changed her face as if she had been purified by it.

Jim was silent, looking at her with great sympathy. He skipped over the obvious next question and went to the easy one.

"You don't have to be in love with me. Let me just be your friend, okay?"

She nodded. Jim saw her vulnerability, and whereas in the past, he would have restrained himself, this time he did not. Brushing her tears away gently with his thumbs, he held her face in his hands and kissed her.

Chapter Sixty

As had become her custom when she was at home, Elisabeth showed up at Ground Zero after the yoga crowds had diminished. Although, on the philosophy of shared marital interests, she participated in classes with Roger elsewhere, she had decided as a general rule to forego the experience of morning practice at the shop. Mike, too, generally preferred to arrive afterward, although every now and then, if he were feeling at all in need of amusement, he would turn up in time to watch the proceedings with a carefully neutral expression.

Elisabeth and Mike sat together one morning amid the post-practice bustle of people coming and going. The scene was almost surreal in its busyness, but Elisabeth was sitting quietly drinking her coffee and staring into space. She had missed this routine lately while she was on the Island.

Mike looked at her sideways.

"Everything all right, Elisabeth?" he asked in his gentle voice. "You seem worried."

Elisabeth sighed and put down her mug.

"It's Fiona."

"She'll be all right," said Mike placidly. "Fiona's got a lot of spunk. She'll get through this."

Elisabeth shook her head doubtfully.

"If it were just spunk it would be okay. It's just that it's all getting so…peculiar. I'm starting to think she's going completely off the rails."

Mike drank his coffee as he listened.

"Moving to the Island and living in that vermin-infested house was one thing. Frankly, I never thought she'd stick it out. Then the goat—"

"—which was not her fault," interrupted Mike mildly.

"No, no, I know; I suppose that couldn't be helped." No one knew better than Elisabeth the intricacies of life with Roger, who, for reasons not fully understood, had given Fiona the goat in the first place. "But then, this political craziness and now, a weasel." Elisabeth sighed again. "She just seems to be a growing collection of eccentricities."

"Well," said Mike, in his genial way, "she doesn't ever seem to concern herself with convention, and you know how she loves animals." He smiled with affectionate reminiscence. "She is very soft-hearted."

Terry plunked himself down on the stool next to her. "Probably read *Rascal* as a child, and it had a bad influence."

Elisabeth ignored him. She had grown up with brothers.

Terry took a drink of coffee. "She's always been a bit of an odd duck. Only thing that keeps people from caring is her looks."

Elisabeth glared at him.

"It's true," he said, as if Elisabeth had engaged in a debate. "If she were a homely woman, people would notice more. How different she is, I mean." He leaned back from the counter, enamored of his own idea. "But as it is, you hardly notice at all." He looked over at Mike.

"She is, in many ways, like a small child, surprising and endearing," said Mike.

Unable to conceive of a response, Elisabeth continued on her own train of thought. "The thing is, these habits seem to be growing and intensifying. Did you know she carries that weasel around with her? It's so thoroughly odd. Not to mention risky. What if it has some kind of disease? Or fleas?"

A new idea suddenly occurred to her. "What if Attila turns out to be a she? Fiona could be inundated with weasels."

Everyone paused to consider this intriguing possibility.

Terry leaned over to Mike and spoke in a low voice. "Frankly, I keep hoping she'll bring him—or her—down here. I'd love to see a least weasel. Elusive creatures."

Mike nodded in agreement. He bent his head closer. "You know, 'Inundated with Weasels' would be a great band name."

Exasperated, Elisabeth shook her head and looked to Heaven. She wished they would take this seriously.

"More coffee?" asked Joshua, appearing out of nowhere and beaming with empyrean light.

Elisabeth held out her cup. She would have taken whiskey had one been offered.

Clearly, none of them was going to be any help whatsoever.

As Fiona left the office after another solitary morning, Jim was waiting for her in the empty parking lot.

"How are you doing?" he asked, with the same concern he might have shown to someone at a funeral.

She smiled a small smile of mortification.

"I seem to be making a habit of crying on people," she said, trying to be light. She saw the worry on his face. "I'm okay. Thank you, Jim. And I'm sorry. Please forgive me. I was overtaken by…something, and I couldn't shake it."

He half-smiled. "I was there. And you don't have to be sorry."

She gazed frankly at him, wondering whether he would apologize. It would be like him. But he did not. He just looked at her for a moment, and Fiona was struck by a new feeling. She was shocked by it, but it was a whole lot better than misery.

Jim's blue eyes shone with warmth and concern. Fiona wondered whether he was about to kiss her again. She realized suddenly that she wanted him to.

"Ben and I are going rambling. Meet us at the dunes at three-thirty if you want to come." Without waiting for an answer, he got into his truck.

She gazed after him, her thoughts spinning. It was as if she were seeing him for the first time. He was intelligent, kind, and good-looking. God knew he was patient.

Could she trust what she was feeling? Or was this the pure definition of a rebound? One thing she knew: her walks with Jim and Ben were her lifeline of sanity. Even though she didn't know where she was heading, she wasn't going to give them up.

Nancy had gone into town and left Ben in charge for the day. He felt a deep sense of pride and responsibility as he walked into the barn that morning.

He looked around. Everything was exactly as it should be. There was the ancient desk in the corner with its old brass lamp, a marmalade jar pen holder, the farm registry, and leather folders stuffed with papers. In the drawer, he knew, along with files for each animal, was a bottle of whiskey for a farmer's night vigils with births and sick animals. The big clock on the wall was ticking along as always, and the calendar from Mann's hung on the wall with Nancy's firm red cross marking off the days past.

The barn smelled of healthy animals and fresh hay, and its occupants were already awake and stirring in their stalls. They knew Ben and trusted him, and he spoke affectionately to each as he filled their water and fed them. He took great care with his tasks, but, as always, he saved his favorite for last: the big brown and black goat that ostensibly belonged to Fiona Campbell.

Ben knew that the goat returned his affection in its own way. He stroked its ears as it ate, and the animal tossed its head occasionally, whether with pleasure or irritation Ben did not know.

A startled whinny from one of the big draft horses woke Ben from his drifting thoughts, and he went to see if anything was wrong. The goat stopped eating and lifted its head to watch him go, its yellow eyes glittering in the dim morning light. Ben found nothing amiss in the horse stall and spent some time stroking the animal's long muzzle, speaking words of endearment and proffering a lump or two of sugar from the store in his pocket. The goat tossed its head and stamped its feet, but Ben did not notice. He was too engrossed in the comfort of the massive animal now affectionately nuzzling his neck.

The goat seemed dissatisfied with this arrangement and strove to find some way to regain Ben's companionship. After a few minutes of impatient stamping and snorting, the Goat Formerly Known As Robert was able to apply his wily intelligence to solving this vexing problem and, with very little effort, quickly succeeded in attracting Ben's full attention and confirming all his hopes.

Ben came running and stood gazing at the animal with delight. A great lover of secrets, Ben felt enormous joy and satisfaction. He now had a beautiful one all to himself.

Chapter Sixty-One

Islanders, whose amusement is left entirely to their own devices, tended to be broad-minded in their choices of entertainment, particularly once the cold weather came on. When there was a Lutheran church social, Catholics went, and contributed to the refreshments. If there was a dance, it was attended by everyone. To the disgust of the teenagers, their parents attended the monthly movie nights. The meetings of the Boy Scouts, the American Legion, the Ladies' Aid, and the Historical Society all were well-attended. So, it was no surprise that opening night for Oliver Robert's production was greeted with enthusiasm and brisk ticket sales. Whether skeptic or well-wisher, no one could resist the novelty of an Island musical.

Oliver Robert, wearing his lavender shirt and a yellow bow tie, peered out at the audience from behind the curtains. It was a packed house, as he had known it would be. He attempted to calm his nerves. As badly as last night's dress rehearsal had gone—and it had gone very badly indeed—according to theater lore, a terrible final rehearsal was an omen of success.

Furthermore, he told himself, it was only Washington Island. How high could the standards be, for Heaven's sake? He tried not to think about the effect of his outsider status on the reviews. Had he been Island born and bred, the production would have been received with the highest praise no matter the level of fiasco.

It was his concern for this last factor which led him to decide that the curtain speech at the beginning should be made by someone else, and he had duly assigned this thrilling task to a local stalwart, despite some rather aggressive lobbying by Emily Martin.

"I don't think you should give the curtain speech, Oliver," said Emily, coming up to him late one night during the last weeks of rehearsal. "It's going to be better received if you have someone local do it."

Oliver smiled his obsequious smile. "Great minds, Emily. I had come to the same conclusion."

"Well, at the risk of seeming immodest," she said, as if he had asked a question, "I think I just might be persuaded. I mean, with my background in theater, it really would be rather perfect."

Oliver frowned and looked puzzled.

"But I thought you only came here last year," he said.

Emily laughed her merry laugh. "Well, that's true, I did. But, you know," and she leaned closer to Oliver and lowered her voice a bit. "Some of us have a gift for fitting in. It's probably connected to theatrical talent, you know. But I am just as much an Islander as if I had been born here, I assure you. Everybody loves me, and," she added with a wink, "I love them!"

Oliver knew he had to think fast. "If only I had thought of you sooner, Emily, but I'm afraid I've already asked someone." He tried to look apologetic.

Emily's face went through a rapid series of changes as she tried to keep her true feelings from showing.

"Oh? And who would that be?"

Oliver's mind was racing, and it leapt upon the first name that came to mind. "I thought I'd ask Jake. His family has been here for generations."

"Jake?" Emily looked annoyed. "What has Jake got to do with the theater?"

"Well," said Oliver, struggling to keep up, "he...likes it."

He took a deep breath, glanced at his watch, and smiled brightly at Emily.

"Oh my, is that the time? I'd better be getting on. It's a school night, you know!"

And he turned to gather up his things, managing to leave the auditorium with a speed that Lars Olufsen would have admired.

He had to call Jake before Emily did. Out in the parking lot, he couldn't help noticing the bumper sticker on Emily's big, German SUV. It read: "If you think YOU are the solution to all the Island's problems, DO US ALL A FAVOR and go back where you came from".

Sometimes the most important decisions don't come after long debates or carefully balanced lists of pros and cons. Sometimes they come in a flash, and the ensuing wave of calm and clarity is proof of rightness.

Nancy had often found this to be true in life, and she found it true now. She hadn't been waiting for a revelation, but it had come to her as she was closing the pasture gate one evening.

Ben had gone for the day after a solid two hours of work after school. He had been in a cheerful mood, happily chattering about things in class, and his upcoming Boy Scout project, and Nancy, although pretending to be stern, had thoroughly enjoyed his company.

He had learned a great deal since he began work last summer and was now, she noted to herself, far more help than hindrance. He could throw hay and mend fences. He knew how to run all of the machinery. He had common sense and kept his head in a crisis. Most important, he could manage the animals, feed and water them, soothe and direct them. He had an absolute gift for understanding them, and Nancy sometimes wondered if he had some kind of telepathic connection with other creatures.

She looked down at the tiny puppy gamboling at her feet and shook her head. "Who am I kidding?" she asked herself. "He's even better at understanding me." The puppy was beginning to chew the grasses by the fence. "Come on, Rex," she said gaily and, breaking into a trot, she urged the puppy with little terms of endearment she would have denied even knowing as they frolicked together up the driveway to the house.

Chapter Sixty-Two

In the aftermath, Oliver had to admit that he should have known doing a show with magic would present some daunting challenges. He had tried to talk everyone out of the scenes from *Cinderella*, but given his already nearly insurmountable casting problems, he had to go with the enthusiasms of his actors.

Cinderella was played by a pretty girl with a pretty voice whose idea of acting consisted of striking poses as if for a magazine. Thanks to her looks, she was just able to pull it off. Prince Charming, however, was more problematic. He was an adequate actor and singer, but he had an odd personal habit of keeping his arms straight at his sides as if he were a toy soldier. This tended to mar the delicate nature of the love scenes, and no amount of coaching could tempt him to change. Still, the two made a handsome couple, which, Oliver supposed, was, if barely, sufficient to requirements.

All went well enough. Cinderella was lovely, and Prince Charming's stiff arms were less apparent while dancing. Oliver had a bad moment when, after the flash pot went off, the fairy godmother's wig got caught in the scenery, and she reappeared in a different place without her hair. The audience tittered, briefly, but the show went on.

Oliver felt grateful that everyone remembered their lines.

In the second scene from another show, the acting went well enough, and even the singing was relatively pain-free, but the gun did not go off when fired, forcing a group of actors to take a different cue for their entrance. This would not have been so bad if any one of them had had the wit to extemporize a replacement of the written line: "We heard a shot."

The unintended comedy of the scene was followed by some singing which even Oliver, in the privacy of his own thoughts, felt compelled to label "hideous," not merely for its utter tunelessness, but for the smugly confident lounge lizardry of the actor who attempted it.

Then came the famously difficult song from *Guys and Dolls*, which Oliver had feared would be beyond the capabilities of his middle-aged singers, and which had been rehearsed diligently with Oliver's utmost patience and determination. The stage fright of the performers sent all the careful practice out the window, and although it was presented with good voices, not one shred of the driving syncopated rhythms that distinguished the piece remained. Oliver was reduced to watching in the dark from the back of the house in the utmost frustration, spasmodically jerking his head to mark the correct beats as if the singers could see him and follow his lead. One theater patron silently observed his behavior, and assumed he had a medical condition.

These events were the worst of the evening, however, and once past, the rest of the production—whose cast members were quite talented—helped the audience to forget the miserable start.

The final curtain came down, and the audience leapt to its feet, voicing its appreciation with cheers and bravos.

These, Oliver felt, were unwarranted, but he was pleased nevertheless, and he breathed a sigh of relief. Next time, they would do better. Even as he hurried backstage to congratulate his cast, he was already planning his next production.

He was stopped, however, by a voice from the stage.

The polite audience was quiet immediately, and Oliver looked back to see that Emily Martin had taken the stage and was holding a mic with a look of perfect serenity.

"Good evening, ladies and gentlemen, and thank you for coming to Washington Island's first Musical Extravaganza!"

Chapter Sixty-Three ✦

It was the day of the public hearings on the allegations of misappropriation of funds. Fiona decided to stay away from the office. She did not want to see Oliver. She did not want to read any of Stella's triumphal tweets, and she was in no mood to sit in her dreary green office pushing papers around her desk.

She rose early, drank an entire pot of coffee, went for a long walk where she was unlikely to meet anyone, and then spent the rest of the day reading Dostoevsky with the kind of focus she had had as a teenager: carrying the book with her through the house, reading while stirring, reading on the back steps in the cool sunshine, reading while eating, reading while in the bath. She did not check her emails, and when the phone rang several times, she ignored it. It was luxurious and thoroughly distracting.

As the meeting time approached, Fiona at last relinquished the book, and began her usual last-minute flurry of preparations. For a moment, she wished she had asked Lizzie to come, or someone to sit with her during the coming ordeal. She shook her head at herself. She was a grown woman, an office holder. She did not need anyone to hold her hand, but still, the prospect of facing a room filled with antagonists did not appeal.

As she shuffled through her files to make sure she had everything, Attila made one of his increasingly common daylight appearances and was gaily dancing across Fiona's desk. She smiled absently at his leaps and was drawn into playing a mild game of tag with him, using her hand to pretend to chase him, while he darted in and out of the cubby holes, rolling on his back to allow her to tickle his furry belly.

Over the course of the past few months, she had been amazed at how quickly Attila became accustomed to hiding beneath her sweater. He never bit, but seemed, instead, to be calmed by the dark safety of his new place. Gradually, they came to trust one another, and in no time, he was scampering up her arm or hiding in a pocket. She knew it was odd, but she didn't care. It was comforting to have his warm furry presence and to know that he trusted her.

She watched fondly as he darted in and among the papers on her desk, and wondered suddenly why she should be nervous about the meeting. What could they do to her? She had done nothing wrong, except try to do her job. She had acted in good faith. If they didn't want her in office, so be it. She would welcome a recall—or even an impeachment—with relief.

Emboldened by her new momentary philosophy of not caring, it suddenly dawned on her that she would bring Attila. Delighted by this idea, she ran down to the kitchen, and using a scrap of leftover bacon as incentive, she encouraged him to climb up her arm and under her sweater. Attila would be a silent witness to today's proceedings. She would take her comfort where she found it.

Nancy had asked Ben to wrap things up at the farm for her. She was going to the meeting and wanted time to, as she put it, "get the barn off."

She was meeting some people at Nelsen's first and checked in with him before she left.

"You all set?" she asked.

Ben nodded. "I just need to check on the water in the stalls, and then I'll be done."

Nancy smiled. "You do good work, young Ben."

Ben smiled. "Thanks, Ms. Iverssen."

She waved as she drove off, and Ben went back to the barn to finish up.

It took him about an hour to finish his chores. He locked the desk, turned off all the lights except the one by the door, and picked up his jacket. He was warm from his work, so he stuffed it into his backpack. After one more careful look around, he said good bye to his favorite animals, lingering a bit with the goat, and headed out. The days were getting shorter, and he was happy to be going home while there was still plenty of light.

He was whistling and didn't notice at first that Caleb was standing in the middle of the driveway. He had a long piece of twine in his hand, and it was attached to an eaglet. It was not yet mature enough to have its white head, but it was nearly full grown. The young bird rolled on its back and cried piteously as Caleb tugged at the string and laughed.

"What are you doing to that bird?" Ben could see that the eaglet was banded, and he wondered whether it was one of the birds he had held that day in the woods with Jim and the research team. It was much bigger, but then, it would be.

Ben took one step forward. "Did you do this? Did you hurt him?"

Caleb sneered. "What a little sissy lala you are. Poor little birdie," he mocked. "Might hurt the little birdie."

Ben found himself filled with a fury he had never known.

Caleb was not prepared for what happened next. Hurtling at Caleb with all his strength, Ben brought him hard to the ground and, straddling his chest, began pummeling him with his fists. Caleb fought back mightily, but despite his larger size, he could not match Ben's determination, nor the advantage of his position.

Caleb got in some good hits, but Ben was not giving up, even though he could see his own blood falling on Caleb's face.

Caleb struggled to roll Ben off, but Ben was too quick. He leapt to his feet, keeping his balance, and struck blow after blow on Caleb as he struggled to stand. Unable to gain supremacy, Caleb managed to extricate himself and get away.

Ben watched him stumbling off with grim satisfaction. He called after him, shouting with all his might.

"Don't you ever let me catch you hurting an animal again Caleb Martin, or I will break your hands."

Ben didn't even know where he had heard such a threat. It had come out of his mouth from nowhere.

Kneeling to the terrified and crying bird, he wrapped it tightly in his jacket to cover its head and protect its wings in case it was injured, and, without removing the twine, cradled it in his arms and ran to find Jim. Jim would know what to do. The bird struggled in his arms, cackling ceaselessly in fear and pain.

Ben did not know that his nose was broken and that his eyes were blackening. He didn't have time to care.

Based on his long experience and impartiality, Lars Olufsen had been chosen by acclaim to run the proceedings. After the usual formalities were observed—the Pledge of Allegiance, and a blessing by a local pastor—Lars banged his gavel and called the meeting to order.

He looked at the assembled community over the tops of his reading glasses.

"This is a meeting extraordinary for the purpose of determining whether there is any evidence of wrong-doing in the office of the town chairman. We will call witnesses, and, after they have testified, the community will be invited to speak or ask questions."

There was a murmuring from the crowd, and Lars banged his gavel. "I will not tolerate any disruption or disorder from the observers. Anyone attempting to do so will be removed by Sergeant Johnsson." He indicated one of the Island's two policemen standing in the corner at the back of the room.

Stella stood up. "Mr. Chairman! Mr. Chairman!"

Lars looked at her mildly over his glasses. "The chair

recognizes Stella DesRosiers."

"Mr. Chairman, what about citizen testimony? I haven't been asked to testify. As a former candidate for the office—"

Lars pounded his gavel for silence. "I have already explained that there will be time for the community to speak afterward."

Stella was indignant. "But—" Lars pounded his gavel again.

"Please sit down, Stella," said Lars with the same unruffled demeanor. "You will have your opportunity."

Stella sat, fuming.

He took another appraising look around the room and found everything to his satisfaction.

"Let us begin." He looked down at the papers before him. "I call Oliver Robert to speak."

Oliver Robert approached the long table carrying a bulky brown file folder.

Ben was running down the hill to the road, when a white pickup truck slowed and pulled into the driveway. A tall man in a uniform like Jim's got out.

Ben did not know this man, and he had an Islander's distrust of officialdom. He did not intend to stop for him. He could feel the young eagle's fearful heartbeat beneath his jacket, and Ben felt helpless in not being able to convey to the bird his good intentions.

The man stood and blocked his path. His face was hard.

"What have you got in that bundle?" He demanded.

"I can't stop. It's an emergency," said Ben, attempting to pass.

But the man put out a hand and grasped Ben's shoulder.

"Please!" begged Ben. "It's urgent."

"I will take that," said the man, reaching for the bundled eaglet.

"No! You'll hurt him!" Ben was desperate.

But the man would not listen. He unwrapped the eaglet, which continued to struggle in its fear and pain. The man's face was hard. He re-wrapped the baby bird tightly in his own jacket. "Get into the truck."

Ben thought of running away. But he did not. "Please," he said, again. "I've got to get him to Jim Freeberg. He'll know what to do."

The man looked over at Ben, sizing him up. He knew Jim. He noticed, now, the boy's bloody nose and blackening eyes, but said nothing. He started the truck and drove at high speed toward the Rock Island ferry station on the west side of the Island.

Fiona moved restlessly in her chair. She had no idea what Oliver was going to say. He had been so maddeningly tight-lipped that she had been tempted to fire him, but that, too, would have become a scandal. One part of her wished the auditors had filed their report, but she had no idea what they would find.

Once again, the doubts began to swirl. She was no book-keeper. What if money had been skimmed off, and she had been too oblivious to notice? What if she really were answerable to some kind of misuse of funds? Who was Oliver Robert, anyway, and why had he come here? What had she been thinking when she had so blithely decided to run for office? What sane person would want to participate in government when the only thanks from the public was ridicule, scandal, and disgrace, and the general attitude was that you were some cardboard figure without feelings or dignity?

She watched as Oliver, with great seriousness and calm, made a little beckoning motion to the town clerk, who approached with an easel and a dry erase board. It was a green day. Beneath his tweed jacket, his shirt and his tie matched. There were some restless whispers as he took his time setting up the easel, placing the board just so, and laying out a set of colored markers on a chair within his reach.

He stood, straightened his shoulders, and shot his cuffs in a manner that reminded Fiona of a magician at a children's party. "Nothing up my sleeves," she thought, irrelevantly.

Then he picked up a marker and began to talk. He drew columns and figures in one color. He made lists of applicable rules in another. He drew arrows. He explained the requisite formulae. He showed his work. When he was finished, the white board was filled his notations. He turned to face the long table at the front of the room.

"So," said Oliver in conclusion, "The bottom line is this: we do not owe the State of Wisconsin twelve dollars and eighty-three cents. We owe them exactly nothing. The State, however, has been miscalculating our state aid for years. They, in fact, owe us."

There was a sensation.

When the truck carrying Ben and the eaglet arrived at the Rock Island Ferry landing, there was another white truck in the parking lot, and several men standing nearby. Ben immediately recognized the eagle banding team—Dale and Mick—and relief flooded through him.

The driver of the truck rolled down his window and called to them. "We have an injured eaglet here."

Instantly, the others were gathering up the jacketed bundle. They didn't even look at Ben, but the driver behaved as if he expected Ben to run away. He held Ben by the collar and pulled him along to stand watching as Dale and Mick did their work, assessing the bird's injuries. As soon as it saw light, the eaglet began a frantic crackling.

As Ben stood watching, Dale looked up and recognized him.

"Ben!" he said with dismay in his voice. He shook his head slowly in disgust and disbelief.

Mick noticed but said nothing. He got a backpack from his truck and began removing medical supplies. He thrust a cold pack at Ben. "Put this on your nose."

Ben did as he was told, never taking his eyes off the eaglet.

Mick gave the bird an injection, and Ben watched with horror as it ceased its writhing and drooped its head.

"You killed him!" he cried, struggling for the first time to keep back tears.

"Of course not," said Dale impatiently. "It's a sedative to keep him still and relieve some of his pain while we look at his wing."

"Is it broken?" asked Ben anxiously.

The men looked at one another and then at Ben. Their faces were serious.

Suddenly, Ben understood the truth. These men thought he had done this.

"I found him," Ben said. "I didn't hurt him. I wouldn't hurt him."

He saw them exchange grim glances.

Mick shook his head as he worked. "We should never have trusted anyone with that eagle's nest." He looked up at Ben with cold eyes.

Ben was solemn and silent. His face was beginning to throb, and he was scared. He would never hurt an animal, but these men didn't know him. He could see that he would not be believed. Ben longed for the familiar faces of Jim and Fiona, who knew him and trusted him. He longed for his father and mother. He suddenly felt very alone, and his fear grew. He was beginning to tremble.

"Why did you do this?" asked Dale, sternly, looking at Ben. "Did you think this was fun? Is that it? Is it fun to hurt an innocent animal?"

Ben shook his head silently. Studying the faces of the men

around him, he could sense their fury and their distrust. His fear for the eagle mingled now with fear for himself. Would he go to jail?

"You need to answer me," said Dale. "This is serious."

Ben looked at them all. He was in the midst of a moral struggle. He knew the code. He was not supposed to tattle. But it was dawning on him that there was something bigger here than children's rules. He knew that human beings need to protect animals from other human beings. He knew he could not look the other way when someone did harm to anyone. He also knew he was in the worst trouble of his life.

"Whoever did this," Dale continued, observing Ben's silence with barely concealed anger, "is going to be in some very hot water. Messing with an eagle is a federal offense. A felony. People go to jail for it, and they pay a very large fine."

Ben could hear his father's voice telling him: "If you do the right thing, the right things will happen."

He took the ice pack off his throbbing face and looked each of the men in the eye. "Yes, sir," he said, turning to Dale. "I know."

"Do you know who did it?" Dale looked as if he already knew the answer.

"Yes, sir," said Ben again. "I do."

Chapter Sixty-Four

It was with some effort that Lars was able to restore order to the room. He pounded his gavel repeatedly, calling for order. At last the room was quiet.

Fiona noted the faces of Emily and Stella. Emily looked uncomfortable, as if she would like to disappear into a hole. The chairs were too tightly arranged for her to be able to move hers, so she was leaning slightly away from Stella in a manner that Fiona thought must be rather uncomfortable.

Stella sat with her arms across her chest, her face purple with rage, her notepad, unnoticed, on the floor. Fiona felt some concern that she would have some kind of an attack.

Having conquered the chaos, Lars turned his attention back to Oliver Robert.

"Mr. Robert," he said, would you please explain your last remark? What, exactly, do you mean by a 'miscalculation?'"

Oliver raised his eyebrows. "Well," he said, looking around the room and finding every eye on him. "I have only been able to look back ten years so far, but let's stick with that for the moment. When you look at the amount of aid that was legally owed by the State to the Town of Washington Island and calculate that amount over ten years, it's already a rather large figure."

"However," he said, raising a finger to stave off further murmurs while he made his larger point, "if you understand that the State is required to pay interest on unpaid aid, and you do the calculation of compound interest over ten years, the total amount comes to…" he broke off to look down at his papers, "Five-hundred-and-one thousand and fifty-three dollars and forty-seven cents."

There was silence. Even Fiona was shocked.

Oliver cleared his throat. "If I may point out, as a matter of context, that the total amount paid for the fire department's wages last year was less than fifty thousand dollars."

"Thank you, Mr. Robert." Lars looked around at the board members, and at the audience, and cleared his throat. "Half a million dollars," he said, as if to himself. And then, in a voice meant to be heard, "This certainly puts quite a different picture on things."

He frowned suddenly and looked back at Oliver Robert. "But, wait a moment. Could you please explain how this whole business about our owing money to the State began?"

"Well," said Oliver again.

Fiona could see that he was enjoying the effect of his little bombshell.

"The State's miscalculation had led to their sending us a bill."

"For twelve dollars and eighty-three cents?" asked Lars.

"Exactly," said Oliver cheerfully. Oliver was always delighted by precision.

"Then how did all this," Lars waved his hands, "become such a major public outcry?"

Oliver pressed his lips together and looked uncomfortable. "I'm afraid I may have mentioned it to someone."

"And who was that?"

Oliver's tone was casual. "Stella DesRosiers."

The murmuring in the room began again.

"I shouldn't have, I realize. It was indiscreet. But I do want to say that when she came to the office, I did not allow her access to my files." He looked at Stella, who looked back at him with loathing. "Though she tried."

He sniffed. "The fox knows well with whom he plays tricks."

"Thank you, Mr. Robert. You have been very helpful."

Oliver smiled slightly, gave a little bow, and began organizing his papers.

Fiona stood for a moment watching him. What a strange little man he was, she thought, for the thousandth time. Then, still smiling to herself, she turned to see Stella bearing down on her.

It seemed to Ben that he had been there for hours. After he had told his story to Dale and Mick, Dale had gone off in his truck, but Mick stayed, watching over the injured bird. Ben had been allowed to call home, but no one answered, so he had called Jim instead.

Ben was miserable with anxiety for the bird, and for himself, and from the pain of his injuries. He didn't know whether anyone had believed his story. He didn't know what would happen next. He wanted to go home.

All at once, there were footsteps on the wooden porch, and the door to the little building burst open. Jim came in to find Ben, whose face and shirt were caked with blood.

"Ben!" he exclaimed. "Are you okay?"

Relief flowed through Ben. He could feel the tears rising again, but he fought them back. Jim wouldn't cry. He knew it. So, he wouldn't cry, either. He nodded without speaking.

"Come on," said Jim, putting his arm around Ben's shoulders. "Let's get you to your mom and then to a doctor. That looks like a broken nose."

Gratefully, Ben went with Jim to his truck and climbed in.

Stella walked menacingly toward where Fiona was seated. Suddenly alert to the threat and unwilling to be caught in an inferior position, Fiona slowly turned to face her.

Most of the crowd hadn't noticed, but several people jumped up to intervene.

Stella leaned in and drew a breath.

In one of those odd moments of the mind, Fiona's thoughts drifted off as if she were watching from a distance and all of this were happening to someone else. Was this, she wondered, what people actually meant when they said "picking a fight?" Fiona hadn't been in a physical fight since second grade, when Paul Meyer had insulted her father during lunch.

She had flown at him, and the punch she had delivered had meant an entire week of standing at the wall during recess. He had hit back, and Fiona remembered with great clarity the smell of blood in her nose.

This was the kind of situation she would have once reported on, she mused, with a certain above-it-all journalistic tone that now seemed to her condescending and without compassion. Apparently, people could get themselves into these situations without having been small or stupid. She understood now with absolute clarity what it meant to be in the wrong place at the wrong time.

Her thoughts had flashed through her head in an instant. She could feel Stella's hot breath. Fighting a sense of revulsion, and out of natural self-preservation, Fiona backed away until her legs were up against the chairs.

Stella began to speak. She had built her fury to a perfect pitch, and she reveled in having an audience. She poked Fiona in the chest with each sentence for emphasis, her face a mask of vicious fury.

Poke. "You think you're so smart."

Poke. "You think you're so wonderful."

Poke. "Well, I've"—poke—"got"—poke—"news"—poke—"for"—poke—"you…" Poke.

Beneath Fiona's sweater, Attila had been keeping his peace amid the noise around him, contentedly dozing in this cozy, familiar place. But when Stella's fingers began poking, he was alert to new possibilities. What was this thing? Was it a delightful new game or an enemy threat? The distinctions were merely philosophical to his weasel mind, because his reaction to either circumstance was the same.

After briefly observing the situation with his usual intelligence, he lay in wait until the thing poked again, and, then, with his perfectly sharp little weasel teeth, he bit.

Stella screamed and jumped away from Fiona. She stood clasping her finger in her other hand, her mouth open in shock and pain. She looked at Fiona, then down at her painful finger in disbelief.

"What was that? What was THAT? She has an ANIMAL! She has an animal hidden! Something bit me! It BIT me!"

She turned to Jake, who had, along with Eddie, rushed to Fiona's aid.

"See that?" She held up an apparently uninjured finger to the room at large. Attila's usually lethal bite had been buffered by the heavy knitting of Fiona's sweater. "See that?"

She turned on Fiona like a viper. "I could get rabies! I could lose my finger."

She spoke slowly for emphasis, but this time without poking. "I. Will. Sue. You. For. All. You're. Worth!" Her eyes now gleamed with triumph. She had Fiona where she wanted her. She had the upper hand at last, and she had an audience.

Stella's voice had become meaningless sound to Fiona. She was more concerned about the safety of Attila. Was he hurt? What if someone tried to take him away? In the storm of her recent emotions, this tiny animal had become her comfort. She sheltered his body with both hands over her sweater, and, for once, he stayed still.

Stella stood breathing in Fiona's face, but, by now, Fiona was encircled by friends, and although no one laid a hand on

Stella, she was forced to step back.

Without missing a beat, Stella turned to the onlookers, still holding up her finger. "See? See what she did? You are all my witnesses!"

The crowd, momentarily silent, all seemed to be holding their breath.

"Oh, Aunt Stella," said Heather into the silence. "The skin isn't even broken."

There was a split second as the onlookers absorbed this information, but Stella recovered quickly, even as small titters of laughter began amidst the crowd.

A smug grimace crossed her face. "She can't prove it," she said, defiantly.

"No problem," said Eddie, holding up his cellphone. "I have it all on video."

The growing laughter in the room exploded now all at once in a release from built-up tension.

The one thing Stella could not endure was humiliation. She froze for a moment, then turned with a sliver-eyed glare that encompassed the entire room. She stood for a second amid the laughter, then, with what dignity she still retained, turned and stalked out.

Eddie and Jake exchanged glances and grinned.

"Ta ra ra BOOM de ay!" whispered Jake.

Lars Olufsen pounded his gavel for silence, but the noise in the room diminished only slightly. He raised his voice. "Seeing no evidence of any wrong-doing, the chair will entertain motions for adjournment."

"So moved," called Mary Woldt.

"Second," said Tom Sumner.

"All in favor?"

There was a chorus of "Ayes," accompanied by the scrapings of chairs as members of the audience began their preparations to leave.

Lars Olufsen looked over his reading glasses to take in the faces of the board.

He was shouting now, so he could be heard. "Opposed?"

There was plenty of conversation and laughter to be heard, but not a single "Nay."

"The 'Ayes' have it. Meeting adjourned."

Lars pounded his gavel three times, and moving with his familiar alacrity, was away from the table and out the door in the blink of an eye. Feeling a bit dazed, Fiona watched Lars with renewed appreciation. He had not lost his touch.

Mary Woldt sidled up to Fiona and leaned in to whisper in her ear. "After all that, you have re-election in the bag."

Other members of the crowd approached to congratulate Fiona with varying degrees of sincerity, and she thanked them in the same spirit. She felt Attila stir and nestle in for a nap. Fiona patted the lump under her sweater affectionately.

Chapter Sixty-Five

After the crowd had thinned, Fiona found Oliver in their office down the hall. He was putting away his papers, tidying his already tidy desk, and preparing to go home.

Fiona stood in the door for a moment, watching him.

"Thank you, Oliver," she said. "I really don't know what would have happened if you hadn't been here."

Oliver looked up, his usual expression of censure softened somewhat into mild distaste.

"A good rooster will crow on any dung heap."

Fiona looked at him. "It worries me that I know what you mean well enough to be insulted."

He noticed the small lump that was Attila, now snoozing peacefully against Fiona's ribs, and pursed his lips.

Fiona caught his glance and patted Attila softly. It wouldn't do to startle him and be bitten. "It would have been nice, though, if you had told me what you had found." There was a tone of query in her voice.

As usual, his answer was cryptic. "A good deed is never lost," he said primly, then added, "But it was nothing the average accountant couldn't have done."

Fiona was about to point out that in ten years the state

accountants hadn't figured it out, but instead she grinned suddenly.

"Ain't no man can avoid being born average, but there ain't no man got to be common."

Oliver Robert looked at her with respect and was about to say something, but Fiona was already speaking.

"Satchel Paige."

She headed out the door and closed it smartly. Whistling, she fairly skipped out to her car. She was meeting some people at Nelsen's for a drink.

The Palssens had a lot of time to wait for Ben's nose to be set at the hospital in Sturgeon Bay. As they waited, first in little bits, and finally in a flood, Pali and Nika got Ben to tell his story. When he got to the part about why the family was planning to leave the Island, they listened in bewilderment.

"What, exactly, did Caleb say?" asked Nika.

Ben took a deep breath. "He said I had to keep quiet. He said his parents would take away Dad's job."

Pali saw the whole thing. In an instant he was transported back to being eleven years old: seeing adult business going on without understanding its inner workings, believing that what you saw was everything there is, and feeling as if the whole world depended on your thoughts.

Pali looked at Nika and then back at Ben. "Now, Ben," he said calmly. "I want you to listen to me."

Chapter Sixty-Six

After many hours at the emergency room, Pali and Nika drove back to Northport. There would be just enough time to catch the day's last ferry.

They drove in silence for some time while Ben, filled with a sedative and pain killers, dozed in the back.

"You will have to speak with him about fighting, Ver," said Nika at last. "We can't have this kind of thing going on."

Pali shook his head. "No. Sometimes you have to fight. Ben needed to stand up for what he thought was right. I won't be angry at him for that."

Nika said nothing, but she was thinking she wouldn't mind hitting Caleb herself.

"But, you're right. I do need to talk to him about it." Pali glanced at Nika and then back at the road. "He needs to understand how to pick his battles, but he did fine with this one. I want him to hear that."

They were silent for a while. "You, know," said Pali, "here I was worrying about how he would learn to face the hardships of the world, and he's been figuring out all kinds of things on his own."

Nika listened silently.

"Today he faced a moral dilemma that lots of adults would

when she came in.

Almost unwillingly, she smiled back. "Sorry. I couldn't have you looking at me in that condition."

"You're always beautiful," he said simply.

Flustered, she sat across the table from him and picked up her coffee.

In the silence of the kitchen, the refrigerator whirred and the radiator pipes clanged.

Pete leaned back in his chair, looking into his cup, and then, looked up at her.

"You know, I learned something important these last few months."

Her eyes met his. "What was that?"

"I learned that I can live without you."

Fiona took a breath and looked away. This was not what she had expected—nor had wanted to hear. Now, she stared out the window.

"I can do it," he went on. "But I don't want to."

She continued to look out the window, not knowing what to feel. "Was that what made you come back?"

"It was Elisabeth. She told me you needed me." The silence beat in the little kitchen. "Is that true?"

She couldn't lie to him. She remembered one of the few pieces of relationship advice her father had given her many years ago. "Never put your pride ahead of something you love." She realized suddenly that was exactly what she had been doing. She looked across the table at him.

"Yes."

He nodded. "Well, that's a start anyway." He stood up.

shrink from, and he took it head on." Pali shook his head musingly. "He stood up to defend an innocent life at great risk to himself. He coped with deception and wickedness. He accepted responsibility, and he faced injustice and authority with courage." Pali shook his head again in wonder. "We've always said we had it all on the Island, and I guess we do. Even the bad stuff."

Nika bit her lip.

"So, what I guess I'm saying is—we don't have to go anywhere for Ben to learn about life. He's doing just fine learning about it here." He paused. "I'm turning down that job, Nika. We already have the life we want."

A wave of relief swept over her that was more intense than when she had realized Ben was going to be okay.

"Oh, Ver," said Nika.

He reached over and patted her leg affectionately. Suddenly, life felt sweet again.

"If you do the right thing, the right things will happen," said Nika quietly, half to herself.

They smiled at each other, and drove back to the ferry dock in happy silence, Pali's hand on Nika's, while Ben slept in the back seat.

That evening, Emily Martin answered a knock on her door while still on the phone, but the sight of a uniformed Game Warden and a police officer inspired a hasty farewell.

"I'm sorry, Betty. I have to go. I'll call you later."

She looked at the two men. "Can I help you?"

"We have come to talk to Caleb, Mrs. Martin."

Emily frowned. "Why? What for? Why do you need to speak with him?"

"Is he here?"

Emily hesitated. "Yes. No. I don't know. I'll check. Caleb!" she called over her shoulder.

A surly voice answered from the next room. "What?"

"Come here, please," Emily's voice became crisp in the presence of the two officers.

"I'm watching something."

"Caleb!" She turned to the visitors. "I'll be right back."

The sound of a low-voiced, but intense conversation could be heard in the next room, ending in Emily's "Caleb Martin, you stand up and get in there."

Chapter Sixty-Seven

The story of Ben and the eagle was all over the Island, and in a chance encounter at the Mercantile, Nancy pulled Pali aside. "You must be very proud of that boy."

"I am," said Pali, frankly. He had been hearing a lot of this kind of compliment, and was finding it difficult to keep his pride in check.

"Sometime when you have a moment, I'd like to speak with you."

"Sure," said Pali. "What is it?"

"Not here," said Nancy. "I wonder whether you can stop by my place sometime on your way home." She noticed his puzzled look.

"What's this about?"

"It's about Ben," she said, and then, seeing the sudden look of concern on his face, "but it's nothing bad."

Pali still looked worried. "He hasn't done anything wrong?"

Nancy shook her head. "Not one thing," she said seriously. "He's been perfect."

To her credit, Emily Martin was horrified and ashamed at her son's behavior, and this was without even knowing what had been going on at school. Her conversations with him about shaming her in front of the entire community left little room in Caleb's limited imagination about what would happen if he were to embarrass her again.

In the privacy of her own mind, she worried about his capacity for cruelty, and wondered whether, perhaps, she had been a bit too indulgent.

But human nature being what it is, her worries about her own culpability did not last long, and within a very short time she had convinced herself that the Island influences were very bad for her children. She needed to do more to change the way things were done in this backwater. They needed more culture, more civilizing activities on the Island.

It occurred to Emily that her own culture and sophistication could truly be a gift to the community. It could be an act of friendship; a gesture of magnanimity. She was intrigued by this idea of public service to her fellow creatures, and began immediately to ruminate on what this could be. It would be, she was quite certain, something truly impressive.

Ben had been allowed to stay home from school, but by the end of the day he was restless. Nika had hesitated for a moment before agreeing to let him go off for his usual walk, but it hadn't taken much wheedling for her to give permission.

He made his way to his favorite place, the better to experience his feelings in private. His face still hurt, but his talk with his father had left in him a certain amount of pride.

After a day inside it felt good to be moving outside in the fresh air. Ben's casual stroll down the road to School House Beach became a trot and then a full-out run. He felt the force of youth surging through his arms and legs. It was an expression of animal vitality and joy that had no other outlet but movement.

The naked branch of the old beech tree hung above the path, its ancient branches tantalizingly low, but still out of reach of most passersby. His joy surging through him, in one splendid motion, Ben leapt toward the branch, his arms outspread, and feeling that he soared, he reached out to clasp the tips of the tree, his young heart full of dreams, the joy of triumph exploding into a vision of all that would be his.

Chapter Sixty-Eight

A small plane came into the distance above the Washington Island airport. Landing on grass requires skill and practice, but for many a farm-grown pilot accustomed to crop dusting, it was as natural as breathing. For those trained to land on pavement, it was occasionally necessary to make more than one attempt. Today, the blustering wind presented particular challenges to a small craft.

This pilot, however, brought his plane down cleanly and landed as smoothly as possible on a grassy field. He taxied to the designated location, and shut down his craft. Tossing a modest sized bag from the cockpit, he jumped down, settled the bag on his shoulder, and looked around questioningly. Seeing the car he was looking for, he strode in its direction.

Elisabeth leaned over and opened the door. "Hey!" she said. "Welcome back."

"Thanks." He tossed his bag into the back seat and got in.

With her public ordeal behind her, Fiona felt fairly cheerful the day of the ball. She spent the morning finishing up an article that was past its deadline, and for which her editor had been sending increasingly irritable emails.

With that done, she decided to take a long walk that ended with a stop at the office.

Oliver was there, perpetually occupied with his computer screen. His interest in numbers seemed genuine and unfathomable.

He looked up when she came in.

"What's happening, Oliver?" Fiona picked up the mail and thumbed through it. There didn't seem to be anything pressing.

"I'm just doing revenue projections for next year. The budget is coming up soon."

"Seems as if the budget is always coming up."

He smiled a rare smile. "It will be a little easier this time."

Fiona smiled back. "Why, yes it will. Thanks to you."

He shrugged modestly. "Glad I could help."

Fiona was in an expansive mood. "I'll admit, for a while there, I wasn't sure whose side you were on. Your little visits with Stella were not all that secret, you know."

"Ah, well. A foreign land is a land of wolves." He made a little noise of satisfaction, but looked down, apparently embarrassed. He seemed to make a decision, and looked up again at Fiona. "I didn't realize, at first, what she was up to. I thought she was trying to be friendly." He shrugged. "Got that wrong."

Fiona looked at Oliver. "What made you come to the Island?" she asked suddenly. She expected a cryptic rule, but he surprised her.

"I suppose, loneliness." He paused for a long moment, and looked at her again. "I've never been in love," he said, at last. "And there was no one anywhere near my life that I would ever be able to fall in love with." He shrugged. "So, I thought I'd try someplace new."

Fiona looked at him with sympathy. Loneliness could be a terrible thing. She had experienced it as actual pain.

"You have time," she said. But she wondered privately whether the Island was the right place to meet anyone.

"I don't think I do. It feels like time is running out. That's why I'm here."

He stared off into the distance. "It's poetic to say that our love is never ending. But it's not. Love dies with us, whether spent or unspent, like money left in the bank. No value or meaning remains."

"That is a dire view," said Fiona quietly.

"The more so because it's true."

"No," she said. "Love changes things in ways that are not limited to the people concerned. The world is better because of it, even if the relationship is only observed by others. It's like that peculiar theory in quantum physics called 'spooky science at a distance.' Do you know about that?"

Oliver shook his head.

"In experiments, it's been shown that if you split a beam of light, and do something to change one part of the split, it changes both parts, even though they are far distant from one another. No one knows why."

She paused, looking out into the distance.

"I think love is like that. Its power to change is not limited to those who are in it." She smiled at him. "Every act of love changes the world."

He gazed at her, a faint, rather mocking smile on his face. "You are a romantic."

Fiona smiled again. "Perhaps. And you are not?"

"I am a cynic."

"Then you must know that the definition of a cynic is 'a disappointed romantic.'"

He nodded slowly. "So," he said, "you have not yet been disappointed."

"Oh," said Fiona, lightly, "I wouldn't say that."

Among Fiona's tasks for the day was to meet the carpenter at the house and make the final payment on the barn. It was finished at last, just in time for winter. She walked through its fresh, raw beauty, savoring the scent of the wood and paint. Soon it would be filled with new smells: animals, and hay, and manure, but for now it merely gleamed in the late autumn sunshine. Eagerly, she climbed the ladder-like steps to the loft and, reaching the top, she rested her chin on the floor, just as she had on the first day she had seen the place.

It was all exactly as she had remembered, two windows on either end of the barn—these slightly larger than the old ones—and a single beam of sunlight slanting across the fresh, wooden planks of the walls and floor. She sighed at its perfection and wished it could remain always as it was, pristine and sculptural.

She thought of her first days on the Island, when she had come in a flurry of impulse, and stayed out of sheer stubbornness. She hadn't known then that she needed the loneliness of being here. That she needed to find some missing thing. She recalled a line from Wendell Berry, "One returns from solitude laden with the gifts of circumstance." She looked at the glowing sunlight in the barn and felt, at last, whole.

The voice of the carpenter hailing her from below brought her back to reality. She backed down the steps, holding the rope railings, and went out into the yard to meet him. They went up to the porch to conduct their business.

"It will be strange not to see you here every weekend," she said, smiling and handing him the check.

"Ah, well," he said cheerfully. "When the barn is built, the carpenter is forgotten."

Fiona caught her breath and laughed. "Don't you start."

Chapter Sixty-Nine ✤

Even though she had known Jim for some time now, Fiona had a case of first-date jitters. She and Jim had been out together on a regular basis, but this felt completely different. It felt, somehow, purposeful. She studied her face in the mirror as she finished doing her hair. She felt thoroughly ridiculous getting all dressed up like this, and also, strangely shy. She had been trying all day to figure out why, but now it suddenly struck her: she didn't want to be beautiful for Jim.

She put both hands on the sink to steady herself from the intensity of her feelings. It felt false, and unkind, and wrong. What was he expecting from her that she would not be able to give?

She knew the answer perfectly well. She also knew, however, that she couldn't back out now. She lashed herself in her thoughts. She had been selfish, and stupid, and weak to accept. She pressed her lips together and took a deep breath. But, it was done, and she was going, and she would not spoil the evening for Jim. Unless, of course…no. She shoved her misgivings aside.

She would go. She must go. She would be gracious, and warm, and cheerful, and fun. But she would also be clear. This could go no further. Jim deserved her respect, not her pity.

Feeling resolute, she put a few things into her satin evening bag and smiled at a fleeting thought, wondering whether Attila would fit inside. She stopped for a moment listening for him, but he must have been off on some pressing least weasel business. Snapping the bag closed, she checked the mirror one more time and went downstairs to wait for Jim.

"*Commendatore!*" Eddie's joyous greeting was involuntary when he saw Peter Landry walk in. A few heads turned. Chiding himself, Eddie knew that this news would be all over the Island in less than half an hour, not that, come to think of it, it would have traveled more slowly had he said nothing.

Pete smiled and held out his hand in greeting. "Hello, Eddie. Good to see you."

"Same here," said Eddie, shaking his hand. "Usual?" He asked this with a more studied casualness as he reached toward the shelf behind him for his best bourbon.

"Thanks," said Pete, sitting down at the bar.

Eddie's diplomatic skills had been honed during his years of bartending, so he did not ask the questions on his mind. Instead, he expressed himself in the meaningless banter of his trade. "When did you get in?" He asked, pouring Pete his drink and sliding it to him across the bar.

"About a half an hour ago," said Pete, with the same quality of superficiality. "Rented a plane."

Eddie nodded. There were only two methods of getting to the Island, and flying in was not uncommon. "Been a while."

"Yes. Everything okay with you?"

"Yeah, it's all good. You?"

"Yes. Good. Thanks." Pete took a long drink and plunked the glass on the bar.

Eddie, who was hovering, refilled it without asking. Pete drank again, swiftly. Eddie watched him silently, weighed his words, and spoke.

"She's not doing well."

Pete was utterly still except for his eyes. He looked at Eddie and said nothing.

Eddie met his glance and threw caution to the wind. "That's why you're here, right? I mean, why would you come here if it weren't for her?"

Pete smiled in spite of himself. "That's why I'm here. That's always why I'm here."

Eddie took a deep breath of relief. This was all as it should be. Finally.

"You want some advice?" he asked.

"Sure," said Pete. "Give me your best shot. But let's keep the opera references to a minimum. I don't have a lot of time."

"I'm into Greek drama now," said Eddie.

Pete smiled. "I don't find that particularly reassuring."

When they arrived at the school gymnasium, Fiona had a flashback to high school prom. This, she realized, was precisely the intention. The event was somewhat tongue-in-cheek, an opportunity for Islanders, who lived, for the most part, in a very casual environment, to have a chance to dress up. Some of the women had taken the event seriously and dressed nicely, but many were wearing old prom or graduation dresses, or even old wedding gowns if they were lucky enough to fit into them. The men either wore ties or pastel tuxedoes from their misspent youth.

Fiona, oddly shy about Island social events, did not feel comfortable with trying to be funny. She was wearing the silk dress she had purchased for Elisabeth and Roger's wedding. She had lost a lot of weight, and it hung on her a bit, but she hadn't thought to try it on until it was too late to fix. Jim didn't seem to mind.

"You look nice," he said, mildly, when he picked her up. He was wearing a plain suit and tie. She had never seen him in anything except jeans or his ranger's uniform.

"Thank you," she said. "So do you."

Jim brought them both a glass of wine, and they stood along the edge of the crowd, hoping the drinks would make them less uncomfortable.

"Hey, Fiona."

Jake and Charlotte, some of Fiona's first Island friends, were suddenly at her elbow. Jake was bursting the buttons of a pale blue leisure suit, and Charlotte was wearing a blue polka-dot granny gown from the 1970s and lots of blue eye shadow. It occurred to Fiona that nothing stopped these two people from finding the fun in life.

"So, it finally took," said Jake cheerfully.

"What do you mean?" asked Fiona, puzzled.

"Don't you remember?" asked Charlotte, her sweet face wreathed in smiles. "We were the ones who introduced you two right after you got here. The night you joined the Bitters Club."

Fiona and Jim exchanged an embarrassed glance.

"I had forgotten that," admitted Fiona.

Jim smiled. "I hadn't. I remember it very well."

Fiona was holding her evening bag tucked under her arm and she felt its vibration. It was a moment before she could get out her phone to look. Jim's phone apparently had gone off at the same time, and he realized a split second before she did. They looked at each other, their faces drained, and spoke at once.

"Fire."

Chapter Seventy

The fire signal had come in on multiple phones at Nelsen's, and there was a rush for the door.

"It's all hands on deck, boys," called out one of the remaining volunteer firefighters as he headed out. "We need everybody."

Pete did not hesitate. "You coming?" he asked Eddie.

"As soon as I secure the bar."

At the ball, the buzzing of phones and texts began a ripple across the gymnasium. The word spread quickly, its passage among the guests was visible, and the whispers turned to shouts.

"Grass fire, everybody! There's a fire! All volunteers are being called in."

"It's started up at Beeman's. The whole woods and pasture are burning, and it's moving fast!"

Fiona and Jim were already out the door. All around the room, men were racing for their cars. Those remaining began to cluster to form teams for the work necessary to support the firefighters with water, food, and first aid. In a small community, all hands respond to emergency, and within minutes, the hall was emptied.

"This sounds bad. I'm going to need your help, Jim," said

Fiona, once they were in the truck.

"Don't worry," he said, even though he was worrying himself. "You do have some guys who know what they're doing."

She nodded, filled with dread. The scenario she had most feared had come true.

The drive was short, and the truck was still moving when Fiona jumped out. She had no time to worry that she was inappropriately dressed.

The whole hill was burning. The woods were next in the path of the fire, and then the Martin's farm. Smoke made it impossible to see exactly what was happening, but there were segments of red-orange flames dotting the hillside.

Until now, Fiona's understanding with the first responders had been that she stay out of their way and let them do their jobs. This situation, she knew, required more than that. It required strategy and a knowledge of command, and her weekend of training would be of little use. It was the moment she had prayed would never come. But she knew she did not have the luxury of delay or indulgence. She must act.

She looked up to see Pete Landry standing there as if he had dropped from the sky. In that moment, it did not seem surprising. It was as if he had always been there.

"Who's in command?" he asked.

She appeared calm and looked at him with tightly controlled emotion. "I am."

"Do you have any training?"

"Only enough to be scared."

He nodded grimly.

She didn't have time to feel anything. "You know what

to do, don't you?"

He nodded again. "Military training."

Fiona was fierce and solemn in her responsibility. "Then you're in command," she said loudly enough for everyone nearby to hear.

Without hesitation, Pete looked at Jim, who was standing nearby. "Come on. Help me figure out our escape routes and safety zones. We'll have to take into account the possibility that it could change directions and go back toward that house."

"Got it. I'll do that," said Jim. I know the terrain. You show the greenhorns how not to get killed."

"Do any of them have experience?"

"Some."

Pete was already turning toward the volunteers gathered around the trucks and began shouting directions to the firefighters.

"There's no such thing as 'just a grass fire.' These things are fast and furious. "Put your gear on and listen to my command. Do not run in without a tactical plan."

They began to put on their heavy bunker coats, boots, breathing apparatus, and finally, gloves, as Pete continued to bark instructions. He did a quick survey of their numbers and hastily devised a strategy.

"Divide yourselves into teams of three and make sure at least one of your team is a veteran. Choose one of yourselves to be a lookout and make sure you're in communication with your team at all times. Before you step in, make sure you know your escape plan and your safe zone."

Most of the men were in gear by now and stood around

Pete in a semi-circle listening. They were already silently assembling their teams as Pete spoke.

"Look for the fastest moving smoke. Black, thin, fast moving smoke is the head of the fire. When you see it, before you tackle it, make sure you can get to your safety zone. Keep reevaluating your escape routes and safety zones."

"Don't let your guard down. Distractions are everywhere. You lose track of where the fire is, and you can become trapped before you know it. Don't think: 'I'm just a little ways out here, I can run back.' If there's a wind shift, everything can change in a second. What looks like a flank fire can change almost instantly into a head fire."

"Remember: if you're standing in fuel, you are part of the fuel. Stay inside the black where the fire has already burned."

Jim stepped forward with his assessment for assignments. He explained them quickly to Pete, who waved him on.

"Go ahead and tell them."

Pete stood back, watching that their orders were being carried out.

"Wait!" He rushed forward suddenly, grabbing one volunteer who was moving toward the fire, and practically shaking him. "Get your head straight! You need to have your gear on."

From behind his mask, the young firefighter, clad in his boots, helmet, and bunker jacket, looked confused and scared at the rebuke, not understanding what he had done wrong.

"Gloves!" snapped Pete.

"Think first," he said sternly, as the young man hastened to follow orders. "Then act. Your life depends on it."

The fire was creating its own wind. There was smoke and chaos and confusion, and people moving everywhere. It was difficult to tell what was happening, and where the danger was.

Jim approached Pete. "The barn is in the burn path. Someone needs to get the animals out."

Pete glanced at the advancing wall of flames and the now burning woods with flames two stories high. In the pasture, there was a column of thin, black, fast-moving smoke. It was the head of the fire, and it was advancing at about eight miles per hour, faster than many men could run.

"Is there anyone from the family?"

Jim's look spoke volumes.

Pete looked at the teams of men around them, all engaged in the assignments he had given them. "Okay," he said to Jim. "I guess we just volunteered."

"Who will be our lookout?" asked Jim.

They both saw Fiona standing silhouetted at the edge of the hill.

"Does she have a radio?" asked Pete.

Jim was already sprinting toward her.

Chapter Seventy-One ✤

Jim and Pete ran toward the barn. There was a narrow dirt path around it surrounded on all sides by thick, dry grass.

"They don't let the goats graze here, apparently," said Jim drily.

They looked at each other. The entire area was a tinder box, and the barn was fuel. Pete spoke first.

"We don't have time to dig a buffer. We need to get the animals out."

They looked at each other again, and Jim nodded his agreement.

"What do you know about goats?" asked Pete.

"Not much. You?"

"The same. Probably less. Think they'll follow us, or stampede, or what?"

In spite of himself, Jim almost laughed. "I don't think they'll stampede, but they may wander. We could lose more to the fire that way than by leaving them here. Goats have minds of their own."

They looked at each other for a moment evaluating their decision.

"I say we go in," said Jim at last.

Pete nodded.

After a brief survey of the fire's position, they radioed Fiona that they were entering the barn.

S omething happens to the human mind in an emergency. Life becomes simplified into the tasks of survival. Pick up this tool. Do this task. Solve this problem. Fear creates an impenetrable ring of priorities in the brain that does not permit meandering. Every action, every thought, every purpose is focused on survival: clear, simple, clean, and slow.

Inside the barn it was hard to see. The animals were loud and restive, instinctively afraid of the smoke and fire. Jim spotted some garden tools in a corner near one of the stalls and grabbed them to help direct the movement of the herd. He handed one to Pete and then stood at the barn door while Pete ran down the length of the barn, opening doors to the stalls and checking to make sure there were no animals cowering in corners. Jim kept looking back at the fast approach of the fire and kept a running commentary with Fiona over the radio. He heard her send two of the rearward teams toward the head of the fire, and saw them as they moved into position.

Pete had begun to force the goats toward the door. Jim stepped aside, and then the two men acted like shepherd dogs, running from side to side to head off those who were tempted to stray to either side. As the animals crossed the road, Jim ran ahead to open the gate.

When the goats were finally safely in the pen across the

road, Pete leaned on the fence for a moment to catch his breath.

"You okay?" asked Jim.

Pete nodded, even though it was too dark to see. "Yeah, thanks. That's a lot of goats."

"I guess we should be grateful it wasn't bulls."

Chapter Seventy-Two

At last the fire was out. They had saved the house, the barn, and the animals, but the woods and pastures lay in smoking ruins all around. Water from the tanker truck was being sprayed on the last hot spots. The men were covered with grime and sweat, their faces blackened with soot, their legs tired from wearing their heavy gear. There was the sound of restless goats coming from the pasture.

As if they had been called to order, the men all seemed to stop at once, standing for a moment to look at the scene before them and then, as if hearing the same call, turning wearily to the work still before them.

Jim happened to be standing nearby during that brief hiatus, and he looked over at Pete as he stood for a moment in the circling light of the fire engine. Pete looked up and their eyes met. Jim nodded and started to turn away.

He straightened his shoulders and went to begin the slow process of coiling the fire hoses.

"Hey," said Pete, moving toward Jim, away from the light. He reached out his hand. "Thank you. Thank you for what you did tonight."

Jim nodded, his lips tight, and reaching out, he took Pete's hand and shook it.

"We should thank you. We don't usually get much help from visitors around here."

Pete shrugged. "You do the work that's put before you."

Jim nodded, and the two men looked one another in the eye.

There was a pause—just a heartbeat or two—and a voice called out.

"Hey, Jim! Do you have the tool box for Engine Two?"

"Yeah, it's next to my truck. Hang on." Jim turned to get the box, and Pete went to help with the hoses.

Despite having relieved herself of command, Fiona's sense of responsibility had driven her to stay, and she felt satisfied that she had at least made herself useful. She had relayed orders, helped to distribute equipment, and monitored the radio communications. She now watched wearily as the last of the hoses were coiled and the equipment put away.

The shock of seeing Pete had been lost in the crisis, but she now realized that her awareness of his presence had been in the background of everything that had just happened. She saw him now, talking to Jim, and her heartbeat flickered for a moment. Seeing them together and unharmed made her want to drop her head and weep. But she wasn't ready to talk to either of them. Not now.

Instead, she spoke quietly to a few of the men, and as the last of the fire trucks drove off, she walked past the open fields they had saved—still fresh and unblemished, filled with the rustling grasses of autumn—and headed home. She knew that there would be a wind-down at Nelsen's, but that was not in her plans. She was not tired. She was empty, like a shell, brittle, fragile, and weak.

Her shoes dangling from one hand, Fiona walked slowly home, feeling the cold ground beneath her feet, and the presence of the stars above the smoke-filled air, while the sights and sounds of that night played over and over in her head.

"So," said Eddie, leaning across the bar talking with Pete and Pali. It was some hours after the fire, and they were all filthy and smelling of smoke, but no one minded.

"Wouldn't you say this qualifies as *Deus ex Machina*?"

Pete inhaled his bourbon and put his glass down, laughing and choking.

Pali, alarmed at first, pounded him on the back.

But Eddie was in earnest. "I mean, technically, the term means 'God from the machine,' or 'God in the box,' and in Greek drama, it literally meant that an actor playing one of the gods was dropped—from the sky, as it were—onto the stage from some kind of mechanical contraption to intervene in the play."

"Don't kill me," gasped Pete to Pali, who was still pounding. "I've only swallowed wrong."

Pali ceased his ministrations with some reluctance. They

exchanged glances as Eddie continued with pedantic enthusiasm. He was on a roll.

"But it's used nowadays to mean an unexpected—often improbable—resolution in a plot. And what could be more improbable than Pete flying in unexpectedly and helping to put out the fire?"

Pete dropped his head onto his hands, laughing harder and still coughing, and Pali just shook his head.

"My friend," said Pali. "A little change from the Greek classics might be a good thing. Maybe some Vince Flynn or Dick Patterson."

Pete looked up, still holding his head in his hands. He cleared his throat emphatically. "No. No, definitely not that. Maybe some Charlotte Brontë."

"Actually," said Eddie, undaunted, "I just downloaded my newest course. It's French poetry. Baudelaire, actually."

Pete chuckled and ran his hands through his hair. "Well, we have that to look forward to."

Eddie was secretly delighted with himself. "Another round?" he asked, holding the bourbon above their glasses.

"Definitely," said Pali.

"Please," said Pete. "And keep them coming."

Jim sat on his porch that night, looking out at the water. He knew the others had been headed to Nelsen's, but he wanted to be alone to experience what felt like liberation from some form of bondage.

Tonight's brush with disaster had shifted something within him. He wasn't thinking, for a change, of a woman who didn't love him. He was thinking, instead, about the stars, and about how lucky he was to be here, on this porch, on this Island, on this earth, rocking in this chair, and looking at the sky. The events of the past hours seemed like an odd and unnatural dream, and yet, even in his exhaustion, Jim felt an all-encompassing sense of gratitude and relief.

Tonight had awakened in him a new sense of duty. He loved this place. He felt a responsibility toward the Island and to the people who lived here. It was as if the tumblers on a lock had fallen into place, exactly where they should be, and the lock had opened with a small, definitive click. Jim knew that he was the right person to step forward and run the fire department. He couldn't solve all its problems, but he could serve.

An owl called and, lazily, Jim called back. The owl responded, and they kept up a conversation for some minutes before a second owl intervened. Jim sat and listened as the two laid their claim to the night. The stars were out, sparkling in a heavy blanket over the Island.

Jim sighed a deep and contented sigh and leaned back, counting the meteors as they raced toward oblivion.

It was almost dawn, not quite dark anymore, but not yet light. What there had been of the night had been wakeful, but at dawn, Fiona had finally drifted off when she heard a knocking on the front door. Deep in the molasses of heavy sleep, but inured by now to all kinds of official exigencies, she dragged herself from bed, pulled a hoodie over her tee shirt and sweat pants, and went down the stairs, still barely awake.

Seeing Pete standing there, her entire being gave a jolt, and as the events of the past hours flashed through her mind, reality rushed in at last. Running a hand over her hair, she opened the door and stood silently before him.

"I know it's early, but I waited as long as I could. May I come in?"

She opened the door wider and stepped aside for him to enter.

He stood, politely, in the entry. The grime from last night was gone, but he still smelled faintly of smoke.

Fiona, now fully awake, sought refuge in the mundane. "Come into the kitchen. I'll make coffee."

He followed her, and she gestured for him to sit down. They were both silent, and she was acutely conscious of her appearance. She had showered last night when she got home, as much to calm down as to clean up, and fallen into bed. *I can't very well go to bed fully dressed every night, expecting early visitors*, she thought. Once the coffee was brewing, however, she excused herself. "I'll just go upstairs and throw on some clothes."

He nodded.

When she returned, he had poured two mugs of coffee, hers with milk, exactly the way she liked it, and set them on the table. He was seated there, just as he had been on the first day he came. He was staring out the window, but he smiled when she came in.

Almost unwillingly, she smiled back. "Sorry. I couldn't have you looking at me in that condition."

"You're always beautiful," he said simply.

Flustered, she sat across the table from him and picked up her coffee.

In the silence of the kitchen, the refrigerator whirred and the radiator pipes clanged.

Pete leaned back in his chair, looking into his cup, and then, looked up at her.

"You know, I learned something important these last few months."

Her eyes met his. "What was that?"

"I learned that I can live without you."

Fiona took a breath and looked away. This was not what she had expected—nor had wanted to hear. Now, she stared out the window.

"I can do it," he went on. "But I don't want to."

She continued to look out the window, not knowing what to feel. "Was that what made you come back?"

"It was Elisabeth. She told me you needed me." The silence beat in the little kitchen. "Is that true?"

She couldn't lie to him. She remembered one of the few pieces of relationship advice her father had given her many years ago. "Never put your pride ahead of something you love." She realized suddenly that was exactly what she had been doing. She looked across the table at him.

"Yes."

He nodded. "Well, that's a start anyway." He stood up.

"I would like to invite you to dinner tonight. Will you come?"

In a flash, Fiona saw all the places they could go on the Island and all the eyes that would be watching them, but she knew that coming here to the house wouldn't be a good idea either.

"Where can we go?"

"I've made reservations at the hotel."

Fiona was confused. "But the hotel isn't open yet."

He smiled. "I know." He dangled a set of keys in his hand. "Roger gave me these."

"I'll come."

"At seven."

Chapter Seventy Three

After he left, Fiona stood against the door for some time just breathing. Her interlude was interrupted by the vigorous stomping of feet on the back porch and the opening of the kitchen door.

"Hello?" called Ben. Now that the barn was finished, today was the day they had been planning to get everything set up to repatriate the Goat Formerly Known as Robert. As always, Ben was exactly on time, but in the chaos of past hours, Fiona had completely forgotten that he was coming.

"Ben!" said Fiona, suddenly seeing clearly what must happen next. She went to the kitchen to greet him. "Just the man I wanted to see. I need you to help me with something."

"Sure," said Ben. He had swung back from adolescence to charming boyishness today and was resembling his father more than ever. "What do you need?"

Fiona smiled at him, her eyes sparkling. Despite the fire and the lack of sleep—despite everything—she was buoyed by her own enthusiasm.

Feeling nervous, Fiona needed to get through the anticipation of the next few hours. It helped that she had a lot to do. She spent the morning with Ben, then left him to work on getting the barn ready. Nancy was bringing the goat in her trailer that afternoon, but Fiona had a few quick things she needed to do at the office.

She was sitting at her desk when she heard Oliver's steps in the hallway. She could always tell it was him by the speed of his walk. He came in and acknowledged her with a cool nod. Effusive greetings were not in his repertoire.

Fiona watched as he carefully hung his jacket, poured himself a cup of coffee, and meticulously wiped the counter around the coffee pot. Saturdays were, apparently, burgundy days, and Oliver was wearing a new sweater made with heathered yarn. Its heavy stitching and complicated cables looked homemade. Fiona wondered who might have done it.

He was still straightening out the coffee closet when Fiona spoke.

"You know, Oliver, we had originally said we would review your situation here each month for six months. It's nearly six months now, and we haven't even discussed it." She gazed at him frankly. "What would you like to do?"

Oliver tipped his head to one side as he considered, reminding Fiona of Rocco's head tilts when he was concentrating on understanding Fiona's words.

"Do you like it here?"

This snapped Oliver out of his reverie. "Like would be the wrong word," he said, with the air of having been insulted. "But it is tolerable."

He paused, still considering, and Fiona had to restrain herself from rolling her eyes. "Yes," he said, finally. "I will stay." He cleared his throat. "In the valley where there is no tiger the hare is master."

Fiona was surprised by the sense of relief she felt. She hadn't quite realized how much she liked Oliver Robert.

He looked Fiona in the eye. "But I will require a raise."

Nancy began watching the clock at about the time the four o'clock ferry was docking. This, she knew, was Pali's last run today, and he had promised to stop by on his way home. She waited, fidgeting around the house, feeling uncharacteristically nervous. Within less than an hour, she heard Pali's deliberate steps on the wooden porch, and a knock.

"Thanks for coming," she said, opening the door for him to enter. He ducked slightly to avoid hitting his head and stood courteously just inside, acknowledging the puppy's effusive greeting.

"It's soft weather, so I thought we'd sit on the porch. But, I have some business to discuss, and we need a drink for that. Beer? Or whiskey?"

"I'll have a beer, thanks," said Pali.

His curiosity had been piqued, but he asked no questions.

He played gently with the puppy as she poured his beer. Handing it to him, Nancy motioned toward the screened porch. Pali led the way, and she followed, stopping to pour a neat whisky for herself. Nancy gestured for him to sit and seated herself across from him. The puppy, clearly well-exercised, curled up on his soft bed nearby and went to sleep.

Pali sat, took a drink, and looked at Nancy with his steady Scandinavian patience.

"Well," began Nancy with her customary briskness. "I don't want to be too mysterious about this, but I did feel we needed to have a proper conversation. I've been doing some thinking about the future. I'm not getting any younger—who is?—and I want to make sure the farm is properly taken care of. This place has been in my family for five generations, and I'm the last of the line."

Pali nodded slowly, still unable to imagine what this conversation was about.

Nancy continued. "I hate to admit it—and maybe I'm just getting sentimental in my old age—but I don't like to think about the place falling into the wrong hands."

Nancy pressed her lips together, and Pali realized with surprise that she was emotional. He recalled Nika saying to him once that the coolest, toughest women often had the softest hearts, and he wondered suddenly whether he had misunderstood Nancy all these years.

"I want to know that it will go on. I suppose we all like to think that we've made a little difference somewhere, and this farm has been my work my whole life. I want someone to care for it who will love it as much as I do, and by pure, dumb, luck, I have found just the person."

Pali was still looking at her uncomprehending.

"I'd like to leave the farm to Ben."

It took Pali a moment to absorb.

"We don't have to tell him right away," she continued. "In fact, I'd rather we didn't for a while. "And," she added with a sparkle, "I don't intend it to be for a long time to come. But I'm hoping he will go off and finish his schooling somewhere knowing he can come back home and make a good life here. He's an Island boy, Pali, and he deserves an Island legacy." She paused a moment in the silence. "I want your permission, first, of course."

Pali stared at her. "I think I'd better switch to whiskey."

Nancy disappeared into the house to get it, and returning with the bottle, handed his glass to him. Having made her case, she was eager to settle the question. "So, what do you think? Do I have your permission?"

Pali nodded his head slowly and solemnly. "You have my permission."

Nancy raised her glass to him. "In that case, Skal, Ver Palsson!"

He rose, and they stood facing one another. "Skal!" said Pali.

They looked into one another's eyes as they drank, and Pali smiled his slow, warm smile.

Nancy refilled their glasses.

"Maybe it isn't all just dumb luck," said Pali. "Maybe some things are meant to be."

Nancy shrugged, as if she were indifferent, but her face

had changed. "Maybe so," she said.

"To you, Nancy," said Pali, raising his glass again. "And to many years ahead."

"To Ben," said Nancy. She took a drink and quickly brushed her face with the back of her hand.

Fiona arrived at the hotel at precisely seven o'clock. All was silent, but there was light in the windows. Walking up the path, she was more nervous than she had ever been. She turned the handle of the heavy old door and walked into the hall. There were candles in hurricanes lit on one set table, but there was no one in sight. Her footsteps sounded hollowly on the wood floors.

"Hello?"

There were quick steps overhead, and Pete appeared on the stairs. He was freshly showered, and his hair was still a bit damp. He came down smiling, still buttoning one cuff.

"Sorry. I was hauling wood for the fireplace, and it got later than I thought."

She eyed him, smiling, but suddenly shy.

He did not sweep her into his arms as she had rather hoped.

"I would have thought you'd had enough of fires for a while. You're staying here?"

"Yes. Elisabeth suggested that it would be convenient. It's certainly quiet. I don't think I've ever had an entire hotel to myself. Want a drink?"

"Yes, please." Fiona followed him into the bar where a fire was roaring against the chill of the autumn night. She would need to have a chat with Elisabeth about all her plotting.

He held up a bottle of wine. "This okay? Or would you like something stronger?"

"It's perfect."

He poured them each a glass and came back around the bar to hand one to her. Silently, they clinked their glasses and drank.

Fiona looked up to see Pete's eyes studying her, a quizzical smile on his face.

"It's good?" he asked.

She smiled. "It's good."

Oliver Robert was sitting at Nelsen's, basking in the flush of his recent successes. The post-rehearsal custom of coming here for a drink had begun a new habit, as was his new-found taste for cocktails. It had been pleasant, this past week, to have strangers come up to him to offer their congratulations on both his theatrical and his professional endeavors. He had to admit, it was a new feeling for him: the feeling that he was beginning to belong somewhere.

His life on the Island felt sweet. He did not miss the feeling of being on a treadmill, every day the same, joyless, dutiful, and without meaning. He was no longer an anonymous drone serving a corporate hive. Not that he was ever going to get rich on his earnings here, but money, he was learning, wasn't everything. "An inch of gold," he thought to himself, "cannot buy an inch of time." He raised his nearly empty glass toward Eddie to indicate his desire for a refill of his brandy old fashioned—sweet—his mind on his next musical endeavors. Now that he knew what kind of talent he had to work with, it would be easier to select the right vehicle.

It was All-You-Can-Eat Spaghetti Night, and Eddie was busy, but he acknowledged with a quick nod that he had seen.

Oliver was beginning to daydream a bit, imagining his growing fame in Door County as his productions were acclaimed and well-attended. He was startled when someone approached and spoke to him.

It was Emily Martin. Behind her, Oliver could see the waitress seating the Martin family at a table. He hoped that would mean a brief conversation.

"I've been thinking about your show," she said, getting immediately to her point, as usual. "It was really quite good. Quite good." She paused for a moment, reflecting. "I am sure if I had been directing I might have done a few teeny little things differently, but overall, it wasn't bad. Not bad at all."

Oliver continued to listen with a growing sense of resentment. Emily did not appear to notice.

"So, I have been thinking about your next show. It should be a play, this time. Not a musical. Something to really flex your creative muscle. Of course," she hastened to add, "I would make myself available to you. To help with the directing. In Winnetka, I was part of a very good theater group. Very good. They were practically professionals. I am sure I could offer you some very good advice. Some very good advice."

Oliver looked at her warily. He had no illusions about the general tendencies of Emily's advice. He attempted, without quite managing it, to look polite, succeeding only in looking as if he had heartburn. Silently, Eddie plunked the fresh drink on the bar before him and added it to Oliver's tab before moving on to the next order.

"What did you have in mind?" asked Oliver, after he had tasted his drink. He had the feeling that he was about to need it.

"It's a play I've just heard about. I haven't seen it, but some friends saw it in London and said it was just hilarious. And I thought, with the title, it would be perfect for the Island." Emily looked at him expectantly, and out of the sheer force of habitual good manners, Oliver looked at her and arranged his face in a look of mild curiosity.

"Oh?"

"Yes," said Emily. "And I think, with this playwright, too, that it will have literary value, too, for the school and the children. He's extremely well known. Extremely."

Oliver Robert pondered Emily's habit of repeating almost everything she said, as if no one would believe her the first time she said it.

"What is the play?" he asked, now genuinely curious. He was mentally running through the lists of great plays that might still be in production that would have such universal appeal.

"It's by Edward Albee. It's called, *The Goat, Or Who is Sylvia.*"

Oliver choked a little on his drink and gazed at Emily in

open amazement.

"You can't be serious."

Emily looked affronted. "Of course, I'm serious. I never joke. Although, of course, I do love to laugh." She laughed now, heartily, to prove that this was so. "'Who is Sylvia'— that's a reference to Shakespeare you know, and you can't do better than Shakespeare for universal appeal."

Oliver's eyes were wide. "Have you seen the play yourself?" he asked, incredulously. "Do you know what it's about?"

"Well, no," admitted Emily. "But with a title like that, I'm sure it would be an absolute riot."

Oliver Robert, who, unlike Emily Martin, rarely laughed, looked amused.

"Well, it might cause one, anyway." He took another swallow of his old fashioned. Island life, he was beginning to realize, had its own kinds of entertainment.

Their dinner started out formally, but by the end of it, Fiona and Pete were friends again. Fiona was careful not to ask any questions about his work, and he did not volunteer much except about his travel to Ukraine and a long overdue stay at home in London, where his mother had been ill.

There was a gap in the conversation, and they sat looking at one another.

Fiona was still silent, but she casually began tapping her fingers on the table while watching his face. His expression changed rapidly from confusion to glee. When she finished, he tapped back. She laughed. "I have now exhausted my knowledge so far, but I'm working on it."

"What inspired this?" he asked, plainly delighted.

"I couldn't stop thinking about what you said about how that woman saved her husband's life. And I thought—what if I needed to save you?"

Fiona could not remember a time when she been able to so thoroughly surprise him.

"You can learn anything on the Internet," she added. "And you were right about Ben. He helped me practice."

Walking down the driveway from Nancy's house to his truck, Pali looked up at the stars. He was spinning with his news and filled with gratitude—toward Nancy, yes; but also for the stars; for the blue night; for the last frogs singing; for his wife; for his brave, good-hearted boy; for the ancestors whose courage had brought him to be on to this tiny Island. He looked up, and felt the hum of the universe reverberating within himself.

He was almost to the road when he felt something else—a firm, but gentle pressure on his shoulder.

Pali did not turn around. Instead, he stopped and joyously breathed in the night air, watching the galaxy in its spiral overhead.

"Thank you," he whispered into the still night. "Thank you for this."

There was no answer, only the singing frogs. But Pali knew he had been heard.

Chapter Seventy-Four

Pete and Fiona walked along the pier, watching the sunset. The air was clear and very cool, and Fiona wrapped her thick sweater more closely around herself.

"While you were away…" she stopped, and Pete stopped, too, listening gravely.

"While you were away, I was haunted by memories."

"I have been remembering my childhood since you were gone, and everything I saw in Chicago, trying to understand the horror and ugliness of the world. I know now that's why I came here: not to escape, not exactly. But to try to understand…to understand why people suffer."

She turned to look into his face. "I couldn't have done that if you had been here. Somehow, I think I needed my own suffering. I needed my grief for you."

Pete frowned a little, but he was silent, listening.

"Everything seemed entwined into a knot of loss and grief. I kept mixing it all together—the shootings, the deaths I'd witnessed as a reporter, and my childhood, also lost, in a way; also dead. It was all mixed into strange dreams and my earliest memories." She frowned, and shook her head. "It's odd, you know, but my earliest memories—my most powerful childhood memories—are of fire."

Together, they faced the western sky as she spoke. Pete listened and nodded with understanding. When she was tired of talking, they stood together watching the sun go down over the water.

The sky glowed with the deep blue of early evening as they walked back up the hill to the hotel.

"We've had a lot of wine," said Pete, after a while. "Let's walk."

"It's kind of a long way to my house."

He shrugged. "Three miles."

Fiona looked down at her Italian sandals and sighed. "It's not often I can say this to you, but you are not taking local conditions into account."

He looked at her feet and grinned. "We could stay here. Okay," he added quickly, before she could respond, "we'll drive. And if necessary, we'll sleep by the side of the road."

When they got to Fiona's house, they got out of the car and stood together in the driveway. Fiona was looking up at the slowly revolving evening sky. "Nowhere on earth," she thought, "can the motions of the planets be more plainly evident to human beings."

She spoke. "It's another beautiful night on Washington Island."

"It is," said Pete. He drew a breath.

Fiona sensed what was coming, and she felt suddenly free beneath the spinning stars. Her love was for him but it still belonged to her. She was strengthened by it, fortified. Her soul knew his, and that was all. No detail about his life could change any of it. She felt complete, whole, and without need.

"You don't have to tell me anything," she said. "I only care that you are here, that you are who you are, and that you did what you did." She paused. "Thank you."

Pete's eyes met hers, and the old connection between them flashed. "What does this mean?" he asked, slowly.

"It means I trust you. I know you. I don't know everything about you, but I know you. I know myself. And it's enough."

He smiled, a slow, weary smile.

She put out her hand and he grasped it. "And I am proud of you," she said. "I am incredibly proud of you."

"You know," he said, "for a woman living on a remote Island with no crime, you certainly need a lot of saving."

"Let's have a deal," she said. "How about next time, I get to save you?"

Pete smiled again, his familiar, quick, brilliant smile, and held her hand with both of his. "Maybe you already have."

Down the road, the ferries lay at their moorings after their last trips home, silent and gently swaying with the waves. The crews had checked that the lines were tight, the cabins secure, and the decks cleared of the day's debris, ready for tomorrow's journeys. Overhead, the stars were still revealing themselves in the night sky, and clustered to the north were the beginnings of the shimmering green curtains of Northern Lights. Somewhere in the distance, waves thumped against the prow of a fishing boat. A fox called, and an owl.

All at once, from the barn, as if turned on by a switch, another voice was added to the sounds of the evening.

"BAWWB!!!!" it said. "BAWWWWWWWB!!!!!"

And then the screaming started, sounding like a horror film, or a particularly bloody massacre.

It was a cool night. But, amidst the noise, Pete and Fiona stood together outside the new barn, surrounded by the autumn scents and crisp breezes of an Island evening. They stayed there together, beneath the misty cloud of stars, for a very long time.

Coming soon

A Small Earnest Question
Book Four in the *North of the Tension Line* Series

Excerpt from *A Small Earnest Question*

Prologue

*P*ete and Fiona were strolling among the rocks at School House Beach. The summer night was prolonging the sunshine, and the pastel colors of sunset were just beginning to gather.

Pete was collecting rocks to skip, a skill he had developed to fine art. He had a mind that needed always to be doing something, and his perfection of small things like this were a part of his character and of his well-being.

They were due soon at the Washington Hotel, where they would be dining with Roger and Elisabeth, and, of course, Rocco.

Fiona's head was full of dreams. Her term as town chairman was coming to a close, and she was eager to relinquish the steady stream of meetings and obligations that holding office entailed. She wanted to write a book, to travel, and she was ready to leave the Island. Not forever. She was bonded irrevocably to the place. But she needed to be in the world for a while, if only to be able to appreciate the mystery of what was now home.

Pete was suddenly behind her, his hands on her arms as he turned her around to face him. She stumbled on the rocks and fell against him laughing. He kissed her.

"I have," he said, "a small, earnest question."

Fiona, smiling, was unprepared for what came next.